FINDING LOVE IN THE SNOW

C.S. Kjar

THE LAVENDER PEN

Editor: Becca Martin

Available in eBook and Print

Print ISBN 979-8-9853553-0-7

E-Book ISBN 979-8-9853553-3-8

Registered with the Library of Congress

This book is dedicated to all those who love to curl up with a good book on a snowy or rainy day. May it warm you like a cup of hot chocolate.

CHAPTER 1

S ome days aren't worth the effort of putting on makeup. This was one of those days for Marissa Williams.

She stood in the doorway of her boyfriend's apartment, not believing her eyes. But there he was, Tyler Smith, her boyfriend since middle school, embracing another woman.

Still not certain, she checked the number on the door. It was the right apartment, but how could this be Tyler, the only man she'd ever dated? The one she'd given up a scholarship to the college of her choice so she could go to the college of his choice. The man she thought was going to propose to her on Christmas Eve.

His face was the same as the old Tyler. The apartment furnishings were the same. He was wearing the Ralph Lauren shirt she'd given him as a birthday gift.

This had to be her Tyler.

But who was that strange, blonde, female snake coiled around him on his sofa?

"Who are you?" the snake hissed as she uncoiled slightly.

The scene sucked everything out of her, leaving her an empty shell standing in the rubble of her hopes and dreams. She had no wand to zap the intruder kissing her Tyler or broomstick to flee on after she did.

Tyler didn't try to untangle himself from this girl, his only reaction was a crooked smile on his lipstick-smudged face as he sat there still embracing his companion. "Hey, Marissa. What are you doing here? I thought you were coming tomorrow. It's not Christmas Eve already, is it?"

He didn't rise to greet her or try to explain what he was doing with this other woman. He simply stared at Marissa like she was trespassing. The man she had loved for practically all her thirty years had no shame or guilt showing in his eyes.

"Babe, can you come back later, and we'll talk?" the two-timing buzzard said as the snake coiled around him again. "I'm a little tied up right now."

An invisible sledgehammer hit her gut and almost knocked her down. Her legs wobbled slightly but moved enough to carry her away from the awful scene. Her mind could take no more. She left Tyler to his snake.

Not waiting for the elevator, she rushed down four flights of stairs to the lobby and burst outside into the gray afternoon of Denver, Colorado. Standing in front of the apartment building, tears threatened to fall from the blackness inside her.

Her brain was too stunned to remember where she'd parked. In her haste to surprise the love of her life, she'd forgotten what her rental car looked like. It was red. Maybe that and the key fob in her pocket would be enough to help her find it.

Walking down a row of parked cars, she saw a red Toyota Camry nearby that looked promising. Walking to it, she heard the door locks click as its fob neared. Success on one level was better than none.

The interior of the car made a nice cocoon where she could isolate herself from the world. No tears came even though they wanted to. No screams of anguish arose because the energy needed for them was gone.

Her mother would say she was in shock. She needed to rest. But where? It was far too early to check in at her hotel. She couldn't sit in her car in the parking lot for hours. She had to get away. As far away from Tyler as she could.

Without looking back, she left the parking lot and drove nowhere specific. She just drove. The many streets gave her innumerable options limited only by her gas tank.

As she went by a shopping center, she spied a coffee kiosk.

Caffeine might kickstart her brain.

As she waited in the drive-through line, she felt the need to talk to someone. Someone who would provide a calm voice of reason. Who?

Not her mother. She would freak out when she heard of Tyler's betrayal and be on the next plane to Denver. The scene between her and Tyler would be too ugly for Marissa to witness. After that, her mother's analysis of Marissa's mistaken beliefs about him—she wasn't ready for that.

Her mother could wait.

The young woman in the kiosk seemed cheerful as she handed Marissa the steaming cup of peppermint bark latte. It was good but not right. The aroma was too festive. She should have ordered black coffee to match her mood.

She sipped her beverage as she wandered around the streets of Lakewood in her car, not caring about where she was as long as it was moving away from Tyler. It was too early to check into her hotel, leaving her adrift in an ocean of strangers, concrete, and self-pity.

Her phone rang, pulling her attention back from the brink of crying. Without her consent, the Bluetooth function answered.

Hello? Marissa? Are you there?"

The voice of her best friend from college brought welcome relief. "Abby! How did you know I needed a friend right now?"

Marissa pulled into the parking lot of a Food-N-More store and stopped. She told Abby of the horrible sight that had turned her surprise back on her. She poured out her grief as her friend listened without interrupting. Abby had always been a good listener which was what Marissa needed more than anything. Maybe she could expunge it all from her soul and move on like it never happened.

When the story was told, Marissa finally took a breath. "How am I ever going to get over this?" she asked, begging for an easy answer.

"First off, take a deep cleansing breath. You need it."

Although Abby's calm tone eased Marissa's anxiety, talking to her only magnified all she'd lost. Abby was happily married with one child and another on the way and still had time to do her daily meditations and yoga. She had everything Marissa wanted, but it was now further out of her reach.

The call wasn't helping. The only way to end it was to do what was requested. Marissa took a deep breath.

"Good," Abby crooned. "Don't forget to breathe. Oxygen will make you feel better. As far as Tyler goes, all I can say is you should be glad you found out what kind of man he is now instead of wasting more time on him."

That all the advice she had? Marissa had hoped for something more profound. "But how can I be glad when I've wasted my life on that bum?"

"Your life isn't over yet. There's lots ahead of you, and you want to go through it with a man who respects you and treats you royally. Tyler is not the one for you. Let him go and look ahead for someone else."

So easy to say. So hard to do. "But, Abby, I loved him. I can't toss that aside like an old coat or wash it away like dirt."

"Agreed. It will take you a while to move on, but you can and will.

Frankly, I warned you about him in college. Remember?"

A bad feeling stirred inside Marissa's hollow chest. This was no time for I-told-you-so. She'd have called her mother if she wanted that.

Abby went on. "Walk away from him. Don't waste any more time on a loser."

The truth hurts, especially when you don't want it to be true, but Abby was right. She'd given Tyler all she was going to give him.

Abby must have put her hand over the microphone because muffled sounds came through. When she finally came back, she said, "I have to go, Marissa. Little Miss Someone didn't make it to the potty in time, but I do have an idea for you. Before Zach and I had kids and we had the time and money to go on skiing vacations, we stayed at a place in the mountains outside of Denver called Spruce Canyon Lodge. Lovely rustic place owned by really nice people. They have one room with a fireplace and a hot tub. Call them and book that room. Go relax and think about how lucky you are not to be marrying that jerk. Count your blessings and you'll feel better in no time." More muffled talk came through. "Gotta run now. Love ya, girl!"

The call ended. Abby might have a stinky, dirty mess to clean up but with a little water and air freshener, it would be gone. If only Marissa's stinky, dirty mess was that easy to clean up. Hers would take a whole lot more work and time.

She searched the web for the phone number of the Spruce Canyon Lodge. Ski season and Christmas break were in full swing so rooms might be scarce.

Good fortune smiled on her when she got through. The room with the hot tub was available for the night so she booked it. It would take two or three hours to drive there but it didn't matter. She had nothing but time and needed to get as far away from Tyler as she could

Chapter 2

Would this nightmare ever end? Every muscle in Marissa's body was tense, her knuckles white as the snow outside the car window. Her car slipped and fishtailed on the icy road like it had a mind of its own and wanted to go back to the dry roads in Denver. She should have never listened to Abby.

What was she doing here? That unfaithful Tyler had driven her to it.

The few cars passing her didn't seem to have a problem driving on ice, but this girl from Dallas had no business on a snowy Colorado mountain road in an unfamiliar rental car.

The road got worse as she made her way higher up the mountain. They said the snowstorm had left the area as forecasted, but if that were true, what was that stuff falling out of the sky? Looked like snow to her.

The white road blended in with the white surroundings. How did people drive in this stuff?

The car slipped again, taking her breath away. Maybe if she gripped the wheel tight enough, the wheels might grip the snow and go straight. Or she might bend the steering wheel into a pretzel.

Maybe she should turn around. But Tyler and his snake were that way. Maybe she could keep going. Her GPS said it wasn't much farther. She'd come this far without dying, maybe she could make it the rest of the way.

Deep regret didn't help with the traction. With every slip and slide she released her pent-up emotions into the car's cocoon. She hated snow. She hated driving. She hated Tyler for making her risk her life driving in snow. She'd wasted the best years of her life with a man who had an empty heart. And head. He'd be the biggest loser in this deal when she cut off all his season tickets and trips. Let that bimbo buy all that stuff for him.

The tires slipped again, and a scream escaped her lips as she tried to maintain control. Going slower didn't seem to be working. Maybe she'd get there faster if she got out and walked. In Dallas, she could do the nine miles easily, but uphill in at these elevations, the thin air wouldn't fill her lungs as full as they were used to being.

Resigning herself to the slow pace, she kept pushing on.

Mother Nature had decorated the mountains for Christmas. Snow-laden trees marked the slope on one side of the road. On the other, icy water bounced and foamed around snow-covered rocks and ice in the river below.

Going around a curve, the car slid again. The road edge seemed nearer than ever so she steered back toward the middle. The road wasn't wide enough for her liking, especially on her side where it dropped straight down to the river. There were no visions of sugarplums in her head, only visions of being upside down in her car in the river. Driving on the wrong side of the road became more appealing.

The headlights of a line of vehicles trailed her. Even though she might be impeding local traffic, she was going as fast as she dared. For self-preservation, she kept up her snail's pace. They would have to be patient with her.

Most of the line behind her turned off when she passed a sign about a ski area. When they reached the first straight section of road, the vehicle behind her roared around, throwing up so much snow in its wake, she drove blind for a few seconds. The driver couldn't hear her complaints, but she threw them out anyway. A jerk! That's what he was, endangering others on the road.

Fire swelled in her. This was all the fault of that black-hearted, good-for-nothing buzzard named Tyler. If he'd been faithful to her, she'd be snug and warm in Denver. Instead, she was risking her life to get to a place Abby said was relaxing. It better be, or Abby would hear about it.

She should stop thinking about Tyler or Abby or the river so far down she couldn't see it anymore or the mountain that disappeared into the cloud or the snow falling on her windshield. Concentrating on driving was more important now. Keeping her eyes on the road, she crawled along the windy road. A blinking yellow light gave hope that some sort of civilization lay ahead.

Her car decided to do its own steering, eliciting a shriek from its driver. The car spun so far around she was sideways in the road, facing the cliff edge. Her heart felt like a kettle drum mimicking the sound of cannons in the 1812 Overture.

She leaned her head against the steering wheel, eyes closed as she took deep breaths to calm her nerves, heart, liver, kidneys, and all the other organs that felt her terror. Her eyes burned and blurred as a tear hit her wrist. She teetered on the threshold between maintaining control and losing it. Like the snow piling up on her car, she felt buried, unable to get out of her predicament.

But no one was coming to help. It was all up to her.

Conjuring a few bits of courage, she backed away from the edge and swung her car up the road. According to her GPS, she was only five miles from the lodge. Her focus had to stay on the hot tub. It was getting closer with each turn of the wheel.

A couple of trees appeared on her right. A comforting sight, they were like a guard rail between her and the river.

She glanced at the GPS again. Only four and a half more miles to the hot tub and relief from the stress. The water would feel good on her cold feet. She could almost—

A violent jerk spun her car, making everything white go black.

CHAPTER 3

P atience had never been one of Jared Sullivan's virtues, and what little he had was stretched to the limit. On his way to make a grocery delivery to the Spruce Canyon Lodge, a red car creeping along the road blocked him and the many skiers on the way up the hill. The snow squall and the twisting road prevented any of them from passing the snail-paced car, wasting his precious time away from his Sullivan's Food Mart in Milo Creek.

The snowplow operator going downhill waved at him as he made his way along the winding road. The large blade threw snow away from the highway like a rooster's tail. He had probably been working all night to keep the road to the ski area clear.

Once Jared got to the only place to pass, he sped around the fishtailing car and went his way without any more problems.

His heart and his car sped up as he passed a ravine that went uphill out of sight. Bearkiller Slide area. The ravine was the site of many avalanches, so many that a blinking light flashed a warning. The area was blocked by a slide at least once a year, making drivers familiar with the route hurry past.

Three white crosses on the side of the road marked where the snowslide killed a family fifteen years ago. He'd never forget it. The girl had been in his class at school.

The few trees growing out of the top of the cliff above the river amazed him with their tenacity. Somehow, they'd taken root in almost solid rock and thrived there despite being buffeted by the edges of the avalanches.

While nature could be beautiful, it could also be deadly. A moment of carelessness might be your last. It triggered both appreciation of its beauty and high regard for its hazards.

Not one to waste time, he arrived at the lodge, unloaded the groceries while declining to stay for lunch, and quickly headed down the hill. Being shorthanded at the store during the holidays meant long hours at work. The sooner he got back, the better.

A list of things to do scrolled through his head like an epic movie's credits. Managing his crazy-busy grocery store during Christmas week was always a challenge. Bookwork, inventory management, and ordering were constant. Stocking shelves, cleaning, getting rid of the last of the Christmas trees, deciding what goes in the clearance bin. It was the busiest time of year.

He came around a corner just as a snowy cloud enveloped his SUV like a dense fog, blinding him from seeing what was happening outside.

But he knew. Bearkiller was running!

His heart pounded as his nightmare came to life. He threw his SUV into reverse and gunned it. Unable to see the road edge, he didn't go far before he slammed on the brakes. Was he far enough away to avoid being caught?

The reverberation and snowy cloud continued for several minutes before it eventually thinned, and trees and mountainsides reappeared. A few large snowballs rolled down the clumpy mass of snow and over the cliff edge to the river far below. The road was completely blocked beneath tens of feet of snow.

He'd told Chad Morgan, his assistant manager, he'd be back as soon as possible. Possible just became hours long.

Something caught his eye as he stared. He blinked several times, still not believing what he saw. Parking his SUV, he ran toward something red shining like blood against the snow. As he got closer, he recognized it as a red car fender sticking out of the edge of the slide beside a tree.

His heart stopped cold. Would there be four crosses now? He wanted to run away but something stopped him. He was no coward but feared what he might find. He didn't have the stomach for death, but he'd never forgive himself if he didn't try to help.

Clawing at the hard snow with his bare hands, he yelled out asking if someone was there. This would never work. He ran back to his vehicle and got gloves before starting to dig again. Occasionally stopping to shout, he listened for any hint of a response. Hearing none, he resumed digging.

Sweat started to soak his inner clothes, and his fingers were getting numb. He stood up and leaned back to take a large breath. Checking his watch, five minutes had passed since the avalanche had run. If he didn't get the car door cleared soon, his efforts would change from a rescue mission into a recovery effort. Not wanting that, he let out another yell asking if anyone was there.

Just as he bent to dig again, he heard a muffled sound from the car. "Where am—?" A female voice let out a moan.

"Hang on!" He yelled with all the hope inside him. "I'm coming for you!"

The snow flew like a snowblower as he clawed it away.

The voice inside the car came again, only this time in a scream. "Help!" The southern drawl broke the word into two syllables.

A shrill shriek followed, giving Jared something to aim for. The snow soared past him until his hand brushed against the car window. He pushed the rest away to reveal a face misshapen with terror. Snow filled most of the car. The back window must have busted out, leaving only a space where her head, one shoulder, and one arm were clear. She struggled to dig her other arm out.

A jolt of adrenaline gave him renewed strength to push the last of the snow away from the car door. He pulled on the door handle with all his might. It didn't move.

"Push on it as I pull," he shouted before trying the door handle again.

The door groaned against the effort, opening only a crack before stopping again. No amount of pushing or pulling moved it.

The woman inside began to beat on the window. "Get me out!" Both her hands were red, and her fingertips had a blue hue.

"I'll get something to break the window," he shouted as he began to back away.

"Don't leave me!" she screamed.

Assuring her he'd be right back, he ran to his SUV and dug through his center console until he found an orange tool. Running back, he held it against the window. "Cover your face with your hand." After she followed his instructions, he shattered the glass.

Brushing the shards away, the woman grabbed onto his coat. He used the razor on the tool to cut her shoulder strap away. "Can you help me get the snow out of the way?" he asked as he reached inside.

Her feeble attempts did little as he clawed the snow around her. As he leaned inside her car, he made a mental note to carry a shovel during the winter. They'd be out of here if he'd had one.

Glancing upslope, he knew if a secondary slide came, they were both goners. With renewed energy, he scooped out snow until her other arm was uncovered. Before he could free the rest of her, the lap belt had to be cut to get her out. Lying on his stomach, he reached in and raked more snow away from her body. When he thought he was close enough, he pushed his hand through the snow toward her hip. He felt the strap that held her and cut through it with his tool. She was free.

She wrapped both arms around his neck as he leaned back and pulled. Her body moved slightly.

Her hand latched onto his wrist with a vise-like grip as her other hand searched for its own handhold. Jared put his arms around her torso and pulled. Slowly, her body moved. With a final tug, he slid her out of the car window. They lay side-by-side, panting on the snow. A small snowball bounced past them.

"We have to get out of here," Jared said as he got to his knees to help her. His arms around her, he pulled her up. She tried to walk but her legs wouldn't hold her. He lifted the slim woman and walked toward his SUV.

On the way, she began to wriggle, almost causing them to fall. "My bag. I've got to get my bag."

Jared put her down and steadied her. "There's too much danger. We'll get it later."

Her glassy eyes held disbelief and sarcasm, making him wonder if her mind was stuck in neutral. White powder from the air bag covered her face, shoulders, and long, dark hair. Her nose and several areas on her face were red.

Jaw set, she pushed her hair behind one ear. "I don't go anywhere without my bag."

She pushed away from him and walked a drunkard's path back to the car. Once there, she dove in headfirst.

This was ridiculous. She'd narrowly escaped death but was worried about her purse. Whatever she had in her bag must be very important. Looking down at his feet that grew colder by the minute, he waited until he couldn't stand still any longer.

As he went back to the car, he looked up the ravine piled high with snow. "We have to get out of the danger zone. Now!" he shouted but not too loudly so he didn't upset her or the loose snow above them.

"Not yet! Not without my bag," her muffled answer came back. Several handfuls of snow came shooting out, hitting Jared in the chest and face. A strain and a reach, then she cried out. "Got it. Pull me out." Her feet wagged as if beckoning him to grab them. He accepted the invitation and grabbed the woman by her icy ankles and pulled. Much like birthing a breach calf, he pulled the woman free of the car with a giant handbag coming out after her.

Jared lay back in the snow, panting from his exertions. He looked up at the cloudy sky and wondered why his day had gone so wrong.

CHAPTER 4

Warmth hit Jared's face as soon as the Spruce Canyon Lodge owner, David Larson, opened the large wooden door. Rustic comfort encased him as soon as he walked inside carrying the crazy bag lady. David's wife Ashley appeared from around a corner.

"Jared! Why—what—come in!" she exclaimed. Her hand went to cover her baby bump.

"Accident," he panted. "She needs help." The bag she wouldn't go anywhere without slipped off her arm and fell to the floor. Her head went limp against his shoulder, and her soft hair rubbed his neck. It felt good, followed by a twinge of guilt for feeling that way.

Ashley directed Jared to a large doorway and said, "David, go get Linda."

Jared rounded the corner and went to the sofa where he laid the woman in front of the large, stone fireplace. Ashley arranged the pillows under her head, then brought a woolen throw to put over her before she turned to Jared. "She looks frozen. And so do you. I'll stoke the fire."

Ashley added three more logs to the fire. The flames began to crackle and grow with the additional fuel.

The heat felt good on Jared's face. His fingers began to thaw, bringing pain along with it. He wished he could take his damp shoes off to warm his feet, but he couldn't remember whether his socks had holes in them or not.

Linda rushed in and knelt beside the sofa. A wave of smelling salts brought the woman around. Her eyes seemed more focused than they had been before. Her words were starting to make sense.

"Where am I? What happened to me? Where's my bag?" She tried to get up, but Linda pushed her back down.

The woman held her red hands in front of her face. "My hands. They hurt!"

"I'm Linda Schultz. I'm an EMT. You've been in an accident. You're at the Spruce Canyon Lodge."

The woman let out a sigh. "Oh good. I finally made it here. Where's the hot tub?" Her body went limp as her eyes closed.

Linda looked at Jared. He shrugged.

Turning back to her charge, Linda waved the salts under her nose again.

The woman woke again.

Linda looked closely into her eyes. "Relax. We'll take care of you."

The woman shivered slightly. Linda got another throw to put over her. She went to Jared and turned him away from the sofa.

Ashley joined them in the huddle. "I checked our registration. A woman named Marissa Williams from Dallas was supposed to arrive this afternoon. I wonder if that's her?"

"Judging from her cry for help, I'd say that's right," Jared said.

The three of them turned to look at the woman who was staring into the fire.

Reforming their huddle, Linda said, "No matter who she is, what happened? Was anyone else hurt?"

A chill ran through Jared like a north wind. After he dug this woman out, he didn't look to see if anyone else was in the car. What if there was? So much snow filled the car he didn't know for sure. A blizzard swirled on his insides. "I don't know. I...I really didn't look for anyone else. She's the only one I saw."

"Where was her car?"

"She got caught in Bearkiller. Her car is hanging on the side of the cliff."

Both women let out gasps.

Jared rubbed his aching hands. "Bearkiller was running when I got to it. She must have almost been through it when it hit. Her car was caught on a tree before it went over the edge. Her guardian angel must be a good one."

David came around the corner. "Linda. Brett needs to know what you want out of the ambulance." They stared at the woman who seemed oblivious to them talking about her.

"Just the bag. I think she's fine other than slight shock and hypothermia."

"Did you figure out who she is?"

Ashley said, "We think she's the guest due here this afternoon. Marissa Williams. She was caught in Bearkiller, David. She's lucky to be alive."

"That means the road's blocked," David said as he looked at Jared. "I should go call the DOT so they can clear it before the skiers start back."

Ashley added, "I should make her some hot tea."

"Not too hot," Linda told her before she and David left.

Linda knelt beside the sofa and stared in the woman's eyes. "Was she unconscious when you found her, Jared?" She brushed Marissa's hair aside.

"I'm not sure. I called out and got no response. After I dug a lot of the snow away, she yelled for help. That's how I knew she was alive."

The woman lay still, watching them with her brown eyes.

Linda knelt again. "How do you feel? Do you know who you are?"

The questions seemed to tickle the woman's funny bone, and she broke out in laughter which quickly morphed into a short crying jag.

Jared spun around and faced the fire. He'd never understand women. He'd rather walk through the fire than figure out this strange female. Let Linda deal with her.

Checking the time made him more anxious. He needed to get back to the store, but he was trapped.

A cold sweat broke out on his forehead. Did the truck bring the extra snow shovels he needed? He'd had numerous requests for them. Were the live Christmas trees sold out, or would he have a bunch left to dispose of? Who would make sure teenaged Jason wouldn't flirt with girls instead of stocking shelves? He ran his hand through his hair. The store would fall apart without him there to oversee it all.

Maybe dealing with a distraught woman was better than dealing with his crazy thoughts.

Brett came in with a medical bag, pulling Jared away from his worrying. He and Linda exchanged a muted conversation before she pulled a light out of the bag.

Flashing the light in the woman's eyes, she shared, "Her pupils are responsive and equal." She leaned over the woman and asked again, "Do you know your name?"

The woman stared at Linda without making a sound or a move. Then her eyes shifted between her and Brett. "My name is…" She seemed unsure as she turned her head and tried to remember. "My name is Marissa." Her eyebrows moved closer together as she thought. "Marissa Williams."

A smile spread across Linda's and David's faces. Even Jared felt the corners of his mouth move as his shoulders relaxed. Progress, at last.

"Nice to meet you, Marissa," Linda said as she took Marissa's pulse. "You might have a slight concussion. Do you remember what happened to you?"

The firelight flickered in her brown eyes, drawing Jared's attention to them. Her dark hair fell around her face in a soft caress. Her nice clothes and manicured hands suggested she shopped someplace other than Walmart. Even with smeared mascara and a bruised face, she was pretty.

She seemed to sort through her thoughts, then said, "I was trying to drive to a lodge with a hot tub, but..." she paused as her eyebrows came together, "...something hit me."

Linda pulled the blanket over Marissa's arm. "You were caught in an avalanche."

Marissa's eyes flew open as she let out a soft shriek. Her trembling hand emerged from the blanket and covered her eyes.

She tried to rise, but Linda held her down. "Relax. You're safe now. Jared here pulled you out and brought you here."

He felt heat rise in his cheeks, and it wasn't from the fire.

A nod of Linda's head prodded him into taking the floor. He adjusted his stance and cleared his throat. "I'm glad I was there to help you." The words seemed inadequate, but they were the best he could muster.

Linda leaned over her and patted her shoulder. "We're glad he was there too. Was anyone else in the car with you?"

Without uncovering her eyes, she squeaked, "No. Just stupid me."

A broad smile spread across Brett's face as his stomach jiggled with silent laughter. He slapped Jared on the shoulder. "She's going to be fine," he whispered as he left.

Marissa uncovered her eyes to stare at Jared. "Did you get my luggage? I had an expensive gown in the trunk." She pushed the blanket back. "Did you get it?"

Linda stood. "You don't need me for this." Giving Jared a wink, she followed Brett's path of escape.

Feeling slightly panicked, Jared didn't want to be left alone with Marissa, a woman worried about her bag, her luggage, a gown when she could have been swept over a cliff with only a white cross on the side of the road to remember she was there.

Telling her she could have died wasn't his job. It might make her hysterical, and he wouldn't know what to do.

He stared at her while she struggled to sit up. Partway, she grabbed her head and muttered something about a bad idea and lay back on the pillows.

His customer service mindset kicked in as he gathered more pillows to help her lay more upright.

"You should probably keep your feet elevated," he said as he stuffed a pillow under her knees. It was the only thing that came to mind. Who knew if it would help.

She stared at him while he helped her.

He tucked the throw around her feet. She still trembled slightly so he found another throw and lay it over her. Surveying his nursing job, he felt satisfied she was comfortable. Not knowing what else to do, he turned to find more firewood.

Her soft voice sounded behind him. "Who are you?"

Sparks flew up the chimney and out toward his feet when he threw another log on the fire. He stepped off the rock hearth and turned toward her. Seeing the fire dancing and flickering in her eyes drew him in like a bear to honey. He couldn't look away. She seemed familiar, yet she was a stranger. The feeling was a new one, and he didn't know what to think about it.

Sitting on the arm of the sofa by her feet, he steadied himself. "I'm Jared Sullivan. I own the grocery store in Milo Creek, a little town down the valley. You're at the Larson's lodge. I made a delivery here earlier and was on my way back when I saw Bearkiller slide had run." He couldn't go on when the image flashed in his mind, bringing back the terror with it. He rubbed his forehead, trying to wipe away the scene. "When the snow cloud finally settled, I saw the fender of your car sticking out of the snow. A tree kept your car from going over the cliff."

Her face froze in horror.

He sucked in a breath. TMI. He could have slapped himself as he stared back at her wide eyes. Now what should he do?

Her jaw moved as her eyes filled with tears. "I..." she gestured wildly with her hands. "I...could have...died!" A loud sob followed, then another.

He'd brought this on. He had to repair his mistake. He rose to give her a comforting pat on her back, but she flung herself into his arms and held on tight. His shirt wrinkled inside her fists as she clung to him. Her body shook as she cried

Without being aware, his arms went around her and pulled her close. It didn't feel uncomfortable like he'd imagined it would. It felt good, like she belonged there.

Apprehension filled him. The feeling was crazy! There was no reason he should feel this way. After Kayla left him, he'd decided to live a bachelor's life, but holding this woman was fraying the edges of his resolution.

After several minutes, Marissa's body quit shaking as she released her two-fisted grip on his shirt. Wiping her eyes, she took a deep breath, then rubbed her hands over her face like he did during a shower.

She tilted her head to look up at him. Her red-rimmed eyes glistened in the firelight. "You saved my life. You're my hero."

A hero? He wanted to be one as a boy but digging someone out of an avalanche wasn't what he had in mind. No capes or masks or flying abilities were involved.

He looked to see if her irises were the same size. "I think you hit your head harder than you think." He reached out a hand toward a red spot on Marissa's head, but she brushed it away.

The side of her mouth went up. "Momma always told me I'd feel better after a good cry." She lay back against the pillows, fanned her face with her hands, and let out a soft hoot. "She was wrong. I still feel scared to death."

"I bet she's never been in an avalanche and survived. You have every right to be scared." He covered her with the throws.

Marissa smiled, brightening the room. "My mom's from Houston. Hurricanes, tornadoes, floods, hail, and other natural destruction she's seen and survived. She's even seen snow there, but there're no hills for it to slide down."

He let out an appropriately loud snicker.

Ashley came in carrying a tray with a pot and cups on it. Setting it on the coffee table, she poured a cup of hot water, then dipped a tea bag in it.

Another woman would understand her better. His brain and emotions needed a quick break to reset. He went into the quiet lobby and leaned against the wall. Why did he feel this way? It didn't make sense.

Why was she so obsessed about knowing where her bag was? Was there something illicit in there? Was he aiding and abetting criminal activity?

"Hi, Mr. Jared."

The soft voice of the Larsons' daughter slowed his runaway train of thoughts. He turned and saw the child there with her dog that appeared to be a mixed breed with some German Shepard in it. A drug dog breed. Maybe if the dog sniffed Marissa's purse....

"Why do you look funny?"

Jared blinked himself back to reality. "What? Oh, hello, Molly. I've had a wild day so I probably have a wild look in my eyes." Hoping a smile would stop the questions, he gave her his best.

The child's eyes narrowed. "I heard you were in a snowslide. You were traumatized by it. You might need to see a psychiatrist to get over it."

His eyebrows rose. "Goodness, Molly, your vocabulary has expanded."

"I watch PBS. I learn a lot from it. Did you know your brain weighs about three pounds?"

Her scrutiny and challenges were too much for him, causing an ache in the three-pound organ between his ears. He mumbled something about watching too much TV and went outside for fresh air.

CHAPTER 5

Warm liquid slid down Marissa's throat and heated her like an electric blanket. Hot tea had never appealed to her, but its calming effect took hold as she took more sips. Her body thawed from the inside out.

Linda poured herself and the pregnant woman their own cups of tea. They shared a smile before Linda spoke. "As I told you, I'm Linda Schultz, EMT, cook, sometimes maid here at the lodge, and this..." she pointed to the pregnant woman, "...is Ashley Larson, one of the owners and my good friend. My husband is Brett, and David is Ashley's husband, the CEO and chief bottle washer of this establishment. And this is their daughter Molly with her dog Sebastian."

Molly stared at Marissa while she took a sugar cube. It disappeared into her mouth as she led her dog to the other side of the room. Just then, her rescuer came around the corner.

"And of course, you know Jared Sullivan," Linda said as he walked back into the room.

She'd never forget Jared. He saved her. Her hero forever.

He accepted a cup of tea and put his fingers around it. There was a serene aura around him that spoke of loyalty and commitment.

The things Tyler lacked. No ring circled a finger on his left hand. Interesting....

Ashley refilled Marissa's cup. "David called the DOT, and snowplows were already on the way. Skiers had called them. In an hour or so, the road will be clear. Our guests will be able to get back here, and Jared can be on his way back to his grocery store." She gave him a wink.

Jared set his teacup down. "My store! They'll be wondering what happened to me." He reached in his pocket and pulled out his cell phone as he hurried away.

A knot in Marissa's throat choked her. She took another sip of tea so she could speak. "Did you say his name was Sullivan? Like the one who owns the Sullivan Food Mart in Milo Creek?"

Linda and Ashley traded glances. Ashley poured more hot water into her cup. "You've heard of it?"

As she stared at her cup of tea, Marissa's insides twisted into every kind of knot. Of course, she'd heard of the store. It was one of the reasons she had to come to Colorado. Next week, she was signing papers to buy land in Milo Creek so her employer could build a large Food-N-More store that would put Sullivan's Food Mart out of business. Her mission was top secret to keep land speculators at bay. Whatever stealth she hoped to maintain was in peril. But worse, it would undercut the man who pulled her away from death's door.

Marissa rubbed her forehead. "Yes, I've heard of Sullivan's. Heard it's a very nice place, but I've never been there."

"So, my store has a good reputation? That's good to know."

The smile on Jared's face melted Marissa's heart as he came back in the room. Her hero was near her again. His eyes warmed her insides like the tea. He was handsome in a down-home kind of way. Someone who could have been a model on a fireman calendar.

She felt a strong tie to her rescuer, yet she was sad for him because he wasn't aware of why she was there on business. Sure, she'd come to see Tyler, but then she had to attend to setting in motion the construction of a new store. That store would hurt her rescuer.

Her heart began to hurt. She looked away. Her brain must not be working right. Maybe the air bags had knocked all sense out of her. This stranger was pushing Tyler out of her thoughts and mending her heartache without doing anything. As good as that was, she couldn't allow it. Eventually, he would hate her. She was here to destroy his livelihood.

David came in announcing the road crew was already working on the slide. Things should be open soon.

Jared bent to pour himself more hot water and dunked a tea bag in it. "Chad said he and Martha would take care of the store until I get back, but I don't know…" A heavy sigh finished his thought. "I hope the highway crews get to work fast so I can be there by closing time."

"That's why you have an assistant manager to fill in when you can't be there," David said as he tugged on Jared's arm. "Quit being a micromanager."

Jared shook his head. "It's such a busy time for us. All hands-on-deck time. And here I am."

Ashley shushed David's rebuttal and gave him a stern look. "He's a business owner. We understand."

Linda waved her teacup at him. "I know how much you work, Jared. If I were a doctor, I'd prescribe something for you. A life. You need a life."

Jared snorted a rejection of the idea.

That didn't stop Linda from continuing. "When was the last time you took a day off? When you had pneumonia? Don't look at me like that. Everyone knows you literally worked until you dropped, and an ambulance had to be called."

Marissa almost spilled her tea. "You passed out at work because you were so ill?"

"I didn't feel that sick." Jared's face reddened as he sipped and held the cup in front of his face. "I was more embarrassed than sick."

Linda raised her eyebrows at him. "You were in the hospital for how many days?"

He answered with a raised hand with the fingers held apart.

Linda shook her head. "Five days. And you didn't feel sick? That store is going to kill you if you don't take some time for yourself. You're more than a store. And don't tell me how you'll never leave Milo Creek for love or money. That's ridiculous. Words like that keep you away from some of the most beautiful things of life."

"Bah humbug." Jared narrowed his eyes before he looked away. "I suppose you'll tell me I'll be visited by ghosts from Christmas past as I sleep tonight."

"You sleep?'"

Checking her watch, Ashley reminded the men how soon the sun would set and how much snow still needed shoveling. The men left, followed by Molly but not before she got another sugar cube.

The exchange had been revealing. They all respected each other because they faced similar problems and difficulties that came with owning small businesses during the holidays. One owner found time to enjoy it. The other saw it as an overwhelming workload.

Jared had exposed his true self along with his biggest weakness. What was it Linda said? He wouldn't leave for love or money? His grocery store was his life and his identity. Taking it away from him, or even harming it a little bit, would take away from his soul. He'd fight to the death to protect his store.

She felt like a louse. Her rescuer may eventually wish he'd left her in the snow. He might even wish he'd pushed her car over the edge. His store might be saved, but not for long. No nothing would stop what was already in motion. Her large corporate employer Food-N- More would send someone else to do what they'd sent her to do.

The town of Milo Creek was very familiar to her. From her research, she knew he owned the building his store was in. When the new store opened, he could easily reorganize his business into something more progressive and unique. He needed to redirect his focus, but from what the others were saying, that was unlikely. Funny how some captains preferred to go down with their ships rather than get a bucket and bail.

She could help him. She owed him that much. But how could she talk to him about what was coming without revealing what she was there to do? Advice coming from a stranger would mean nothing, but she had to try.

She watched him dunk his tea bag many times before tasting it, then wrinkle his nose slightly when he sipped it. Apparently, tea wasn't his cup of coffee.

"Tell me about your store."

He looked up at her. "My store is the best one in the county. Started by my grandfather and passed down to me. I've got good people working for me, and we make a great team." He lifted the cup to his lips, then sat the cup on the table.

Marissa took another sip of tea, then spoke. "Your customers are probably loyal to you."

"I have a captive audience for now. It's a half-hour drive to the next grocery store. Being the only one around helps business. But Milo Creek is growing faster than my store is able to keep up with."

Jared sighed. His eyes glazed over as he mentally traveled somewhere. "Rumors are swirling about some big grocery store looking at the big lot close to the truck stop. When they built the truck stop, it pulled interstate business away from downtown. Putting a big grocery store out there will ruin me."

"If that happens, do you have a Plan B?"

The question prodded him to start pacing. He stopped to face her, but the ringing of his phone washed his answer away. Two quick steps and he was gone, leaving her alone.

A surge of pity went through her. His answer became evident when his lips had formed the word "No".

Curious, she sat upright and turned to look behind her. Her foot hit something on the floor. Her bag. She picked it up and held it against her in a hug. She might have lost all her other stuff, but her bag held the most important items.

She ran her fingers through her hair, then reached into the bag to find her small mirror. Seeing herself in it made her cringe and almost scream in horror. One of her fake eyelashes was missing, her mascara was smeared, and her hair was a tangled mess. But that was nothing compared to the purple bruises around both eyes and her slightly swollen nose.

A soft groan emanated from her. No one should ever see her like this. These strangers must think she was an old hag. No matter. They'd seen her at her worse so she might as well go all the way.

First, she removed the remaining eyelash. Second, a brush detangled her long dark locks, and a scrunchie tamed them into one tress. A smearing of color on her lips and a quick glance in the mirror confirmed she at least looked less ruffled.

The fire crackled, drawing her attention away from her appearance. She looked around and was left breathless by the scene in the large windows on the other side of the room. The snow had stopped and the clouds were moving apart to reveal a panorama of rugged, snow-covered mountains across the valley. The snow-laden trees and undisturbed carpet of white reminded her of a Christmas card. She took her phone out of her bag and went to the windows to take a photo. No one at home would believe her crazy story without proof.

In the corner by the large windows was a huge Christmas tree, abundantly decorated with woodsy ornaments, strings of popcorn, strands of red and gold ribbon, and white lights. A longing for childhood and home washed over her as she looked at the multicolored gift boxes under the tree. No one knew where she was or how close she'd come to not being here. The generosity of strangers, taking her in and helping her, illustrated the spirit of Christmas. She was thankful they had room for her at this inn.

Jared came up beside her and asked how she was feeling. She mumbled a response because she didn't want to spoil the aura of the place. He took the hint and left her with her thoughts.

The fact that she was here showed he was a compassionate man. He could have left her entombed in her car, but he'd dug her out of the snow and brought her to safety. She owed him a debt of gratitude. She had to repay it before he learned she was the enemy.

CHAPTER 6

J ared threw another log on the fire, then rubbed his furrowed brow. The call had been from Chad Morgan asking what would be on the delivery truck later that afternoon. The grocery store was full of customers asking for marshmallows to top yams and canned fried onions for green bean casseroles. Both were running low. Nothing Chad couldn't handle, but it was his job was to stave off the complaints and assure people they'd be on the next truck. Not Chad's.

The store was his life, but he knew he was probably fighting a losing battle. The population of Milo Creek was booming. With that came the demand for more inventory, and he had no room to expand. Most troublesome were the rumors flying around about a big grocery chain coming in. If that happened, the family business would fade away like the silver mines had decades ago.

Realtors had offered him a lot of money for his building on Main Street, but he would never give up or walk away. He couldn't. Not after the vow his father made to his grandfather and his own vow to his father. Promise you'll never sell or lose the store, he'd said on his deathbed. If you do, you'll dishonor me and your grandfather.

That's why he had to hang on. He couldn't leave Milo Creek. Not for love or money. No matter how much. They were the same words spoken by his father. Maybe those words would doom him like Linda said. Maybe they already had.

. His chest felt tight. His anxiety didn't allow him to stand still too long. Pacing seemed the only way to release it.

How much longer before the highway was cleared? The hour-long drive back would put him back in the late afternoon.

His phone buzzed with a text message. The number of voice mails were building up. Before listening to them, he asked Ashley if he could borrow a pencil and paper. She pushed both to him and left him to his business.

Finishing the notes about his messages, he stuffed them in his shirt pocket. Most of them were simple things that should be intuitive. A few lights were burned out on the store's Christmas trees, should they be replaced? Two households were delinquent on their food bills, should they cut them off right before Christmas? Should they put more salt on the ice by the front door? The answers were obvious to him, but not assuming anything, he answered them quickly. Yes. No. Why ask? Do it if it needs done.

He checked his watch. Almost three o'clock. and no word from the highway department. Ashley was in the large room where she was listening to Marissa gush about the scenery and the tree. Both turned to watch him as he walked in.

"And here's my hero!" Marissa chimed out.

He felt his face flush. That H-word was the last thing he deserved. It was a situation he'd been thrown into without being asked. What else could he have done? Leave her there? Yeah, right. His parents often accused him of being far too soft-hearted. Maybe he was, but seeing a car sticking out of tons of snow was nothing he could ever walk away from. If he was a hero, he preferred to remain unsung.

Tired of dealing with business, he slipped his phone into his pocket. Marissa's arms were crossed in front of her as in a self-hug. She looked different with her hair pulled back. She'd fixed herself up while no one was looking. Typical woman. Wanted to look good despite what she'd been through. He'd found that trait annoying at times, but not now. She was even more beautiful and with what little he'd seen of her personality, so was her heart.

His stomach did a flip as she walked up to him and took his hand.

Little streaks of heart-stirring electricity went up his arm.

Her eyes moistened as she said, "I owe you my life."

The coolness of the large windows did little to chill the warmth flaring up in his chest. The feeling was uncomfortable. Unexpected. Unavoidable.

This woman was a stranger from Texas. Even if they developed feelings for each other, nothing could come of it. Just like his old girlfriend, Kayla, who'd left him to go to the big city, Marissa would go home and leave him behind. He wouldn't fall for that again.

With an invisible hand, he brushed his feelings for Marissa away like dust from a tabletop. Clean surfaces had few distractions.

Ashley came in and asked if they'd seen Molly.

Turning his back to the window and Marissa, he remarked, "No, we haven't. What a nice Christmas tree you have this year, Ashley, but it's so big. How did you manage to get it in here?"

"We had a hard time. Even had to cut a foot of it off before we stood it up." She laughed at their gasps as they looked at the top that was at least ten feet over their heads. "I have work to do so I'll leave you two admiring it."

As her footsteps faded, Jared's heartbeat picked up its pace. The feelings were back. This woman had some sort of magnetism that kept drawing him back in. He needed out but his feet wouldn't obey his mind.

Marissa bounced past him like a child. "This is just like something you see on TV. A beautiful Christmas tree, snow on the ground, a fire in the fireplace." Her smile lit up the room more than the lights on the tree as she spun around to face him. "I feel like I'm in a winter wonderland."

Jared laughed as she started to do a fancy step around the decorated tree. He considered himself too mature to make such a display but her joy brought the Christmas spirit into the room.

Humming a Christmas carol, she spun a tight circle. She suddenly stopped and grabbed her head.

"I shouldn't have done that." She teetered.

With a swift move, he caught her before she tipped over. An arm around her waist, he helped her to the sofa. "Maybe you should listen to good advice and rest." He helped her lie down and pulled the throws over her. His cell phone vibrated in his pocket, bidding his attention return to Milo Creek.

She pulled up her knees and indicated that he should sit on that end of the sofa. Sinking into the soft leather, he answered a text message and was starting to answer another when she said, "You should loosen up a little. It's Christmas. Time to feel like a kid again."

He let out a sharp breath. "Some of us are still working. I should be back at the store instead of here."

"David said you had an assistant manager."

Her volley of his words left him wondering how to return it. "We're short-handed. Several people took time off for the holidays— which I think they should—but more customers come in right before the holiday so it's hard to balance personal time with business demands."

"All businesses have that problem." Her eyes studied him, making him feel transparent and vulnerable. She put her hands behind her head. "Tell me more about your store."

She did it again. There'd be no small talk with her. Unable to stop the natural response, he smiled. "My grandfather started the store with just a few shelves of canned goods. The more customers he got, the more goods he could buy and sell. He eventually expanded to include a butcher shop. My dad took over from him and passed it on to me. It's not a big store like they have in Dallas or Denver, but Milo Creek is a small town, and it serves our people well. We've become known around the area for our good beef and pork. My butcher buys it on the hoof and processes it. Since it comes direct from the farmers, it's all organic and tender. He also does custom butchering for ranches in the valley and out on the plains. It's become our biggest department."

"Wow! That's quite the draw. Do you market your brand much?"

He felt his chest swell a little but remembering his last conversation with his meat department manager, Benny Truvo, took it down again. Benny had recently hinted about getting out and starting his own meat market. Without him, the Sullivan Foot Mart would struggle to stay on the profitable side of the column. Somehow, he had to convince him to stay.

He heard her take a slow breath in. He glanced at her from the side of his eyes and saw the quizzical look on her face. His mind had drifted, and she'd noticed. He set his phone on his leg. "Enough of me. What do you do for a living?"

A flash of worry streaked across her face before it left behind a pleasant smile. "Nothing interesting. I'm one of many moving cogs in a large corporation in Dallas. This was supposed to be a business trip, but as you know, it's turned into anything but that."

"A business trip over the holidays? Who do you work for? Ebenezer Scrooge?"

Her soft giggle tinkled like bells on a Christmas tree. "It was my idea. You see—" She sucked in a breath as her eyes went back to the fireplace. Her face must have followed her mind into a very dark place as something unpleasant stopped her words.

Was it worry or despair he was seeing? Maybe her job was in jeopardy. "They won't fire you over what happened, will they? The avalanche was an act of God, and you being in that spot was fate.

I mean forcing you to work over the holiday is bad enough, but to fire you for something completely out of your control would be criminal."

Curiosity nudged him to ask for more, but social manners told him not to pry. The time to ask wasn't now.

Her expression softened as she shook her head. "No, I won't get fired. Not for that anyway." A one-sided smile came at him, then she shrugged slightly. "You see, I timed my trip so that—"

A Highway Patrolman came into the room, breaking the mood. He took a quick glance around before walking over to the sofa. He stood with his hands on his utility belt. "My name's Trooper Mike Olson. You two the ones who were in the avalanche?"

Jared stood and pointed at Marissa. "She was. I dug her out."

The trooper nodded. "You were one lucky lady. We have freed your car. It's being loaded to haul off to the junk yard. You—"

"No!" Marissa lunged off the sofa, but a throw tangled across her legs and almost tripped her.

Olson jumped back and put his hand on his gun for a second.

Jared threw himself between them as he reached down to help her back to the sofa.

Her hand went to her head. "I did it again, didn't I."

"Yes, you did," Jared said as he lifted her legs and moved them to the sofa. "You have to take things slow, like getting up and spinning around and all those other things you apparently love to do."

"But my car! All my stuff is in it." With wide eyes, she looked at Jared. "My clothes. My work computer. I will get fired if I lose my work computer." She turned back to the trooper. "Sir, please, can I get my things out of my car before it's hauled off? PLEASE!"

The trooper shifted his weight. "I'm pretty sure it's already loaded."

She let out a cry of desperation. "I've got to have my computer!" She stopped and stared. "You have that thingy—that—that—" She pointed at his shoulder with the mic on it. "Can't you call them and tell them to stop?"

The trooper looked at Jared who shrugged. He didn't have the power to do anything, much less control Marissa's outburst.

Trooper Olson turned as he used the mic to call home base and tell them to halt the wrecker with the car. He arranged to have the contents from the wrecked car emptied into someone else's vehicle. He'd return to the scene after he got information for his report.

Digging through her bag, Marissa pulled out her driver's license, proof of insurance, and the rental agreement for the car.

"From Dallas, huh," Olson remarked. "What were you doing on snow packed roads?"

"Being an idiot," she replied.

The officer neither agreed nor contradicted her statement but wrote it down in his notebook. The pair told their stories of what had happened while the officer made notes. Satisfied, he folded up his notebook and returned it to the proper compartment on his belt.

"You can follow me down the hill if you'd like. Your luggage will be at the accident site."

Marissa thanked him profusely as he nodded and left. The voices from his shoulder mic faded as he went around the corner. The lobby door squeaked as it was opened and shut.

As Marissa returned everything to her bag, she mumbled about her computer. She turned to Jared with wide eyes. "They'll fire me for sure if I lose that computer."

"Why? It can be replaced. Aren't your files backed up on the cloud somewhere?"

She wrung her hands. "You don't understand. There are documents loaded on there that they don't want on the system. It's like top-secret stuff."

"What are you? A spy?"

She paused and tossed him a worried look. "Nothing that glamorous."

Suddenly, she grabbed his hand. "Please. Let's take your truck and go after the officer. We'll be that much closer to your store."

Her puppy-dog eyes made his resolve fluctuate. She needed his help, but what other demands might she make? He was being sucked into this Texas-sized pit of quicksand with no bottom. How deep would it go? "You have a reservation here. Look, I can go get your computer and bring it back here."

"No! I have to go with you. I have other things too, like my luggage, my evening gown..." Her hand went in front of her mouth like she'd let too much slip out.

Jared stared at the pleading eyes. An evening gown? He didn't want to know the story behind that one. Too many obligations pulled him in different directions, but how could he refuse her request? The route would lead him back to his store. Maybe Officer Olson would bring her back here.

His phone buzzed in his pocket as he looked into the beautiful imploring eyes. Her hand squeezed his, gluing him in his spot. All he could do was surrender to the overwhelming force. "Okay, let's go."

Her hands clasped together, she replied, "Thanks so much. I'll find some way to repay you for this." Letting go of his hand, she cried out, "Follow that trooper!"

David rushed in. "Jared, what did Mike say about getting the road cleared?"

He pulled David into the lobby area as Marissa gathered her bag and untangled from the throw. He spoke in a low voice while looking for eavesdropping ears. "He didn't say and I forgot to ask. Marissa went berserk about getting her computer out of the car before it's hauled to the junkyard."

David smiled. "I heard that part. You couldn't resist telling her yes, could you?" He winked.

"She's a good beggar."

Marissa came around the corner and sauntered to the reception desk. She gave Ashley and Linda an ultra-white smile and said, "I'm going with Jared. Cancel my reservation. No refund requested. I'm past the cancellation time, and you deserve it and more for taking care of me."

Pulling a light out of her pocket, Linda leaned in close and flicked it across Marissa's eyes. "You're okay to leave. Just remember to take it easy, and I mean easy. No strenuous workouts. Don't even walk around town tonight. Stay in bed or a comfortable chair and read a book or watch movies. Understand?"

"Yes, ma'am." She leaned over and picked up her large bag. She wobbled a little as she threw it over her shoulder.

"Jared," Linda said, "maybe you should carry her purse."

Marissa's grip on her bag was tighter than a miser's hold on his wallet. Giving up, Jared opened the door, hoping it would speed things along.

"Thank you for your hospitality and medical care," Marissa said as she moved toward the door straightening her coat. "I hope there's a hotel in Milo Creek where I can stay tonight? Or maybe I can find a strong, handsome guy to take me to Denver?" She fluttered her eyes at Jared.

He looked away. Those eyes had already caused enough trouble, making him do things he didn't want to, and stirring up feelings he didn't want. At the moment, they were wasting his time with all the drama of leaving.

Ashley walked around the desk. "Jared doesn't mind taking you. Do you, Jared."

Jared looked to David for help but all he got was a silent expression of why-fight- it. Having no ally or defense, he compromised. "Edith runs the Milo Creek Motel. It's clean and well- kept but don't expect the same elegance as this place. You can probably find someone in town who'll take you to Denver."

Her brilliant smile faded a bit. "That's good," Marissa said. She turned to the four people standing around the reception desk.

"Thanks so much for taking me in, for the tea, for everything! I'll never forget this place."

Ashley walked up and put her arm around her. "Come back sometime when you can stay longer. Say, in summer when there are no snowslides to avoid."

Agreeing and giving Ashley a hug, Marissa finally stepped out into the cold.

Jared stood, looking at the people who'd forced this stranger on him. "I'll get you for this."

"You two are perfect for each other," Ashley whispered loudly. "Don't let her get away."

He let out a huff and left the snickering people behind.

CHAPTER 7

Marissa stared out the window as Jared steered his SUV out of the parking lot of the lodge. The scenery was much prettier when she wasn't driving.

The pit of her stomach felt like lead. Her "helpless woman" ruse had little effect on Jared. He was too smart for that. He'd done his job, rescued her from her car, and he wanted nothing more to do with her impositions on is routine.

Little did he know, she was the bad penny he couldn't get rid of.

An imposition and a bad penny. Neither were things she wanted to be.

All her bad luck went back to Tyler. When the offer of a large salary to work for the Food-N-More Corporation came along, Tyler pushed her into taking it. She became part of the big-corporation machine that built large Food-N-More stores and ran small businesses out. Her work transformed her into the Godzilla of small towns, wreaking havoc wherever she went. As the company's bottom line got bigger, her esteem got smaller.

The job allowed her to live in high style but it led to the misery of others. A heartless drudge needed this job, not her. Tyler benefited from it, but she hadn't. The sixty-hour work weeks left her with no time of her own.

She'd worked hard through college so she could open a law office to help people with estate planning and real estate issues in honor of her grandfather. That's what her heart wanted. Maybe it was time to follow that dream.

Her life would change, not because someone forced it but because she wanted it to. Liberated from Tyler, she could do anything she wanted. The first thing would be to free herself from bondage at Food-N-More. When she got back, she'd turn in her resignation.

Decision made.

She leaned against the car door to look at Jared. His brown hair needed a cut, and his face was clean shaven. His green eyes had a sense of determination. His loyalty to the town and his family's business was unquestionable. Everyone at the lodge spoke highly of him. But the walls he'd built around himself were impenetrable. As much as she found herself attracted to him, she'd need a battering ram to break them down.

The wrinkles between his brows told her his thoughts were serious. Thinking of his store no doubt.

He must have felt her gaze because he glanced at her. "Are you in pain?"

"No, just thinking and wondering how I'm going to get back to Denver."

"I'm sure you'll be able to find a way. Is there someone who can come get you?" His eyes were pleading with her not to ask him. "Is there a coworker who could come? Or are you the boss that no one likes?" He shot her a look of amusement.

A sense of humor. She loved that.

"All my minions fear me," she emoted. "Sadly, they are in Dallas."

The sides of his mouth rose. She could tell he was fighting back a laugh.

She wrinkled her forehead like his. "I'll think of a way."

The New Age music coming softly from the radio was something she liked. Calm and relaxing. Exactly what she needed. Christmas music would be more appropriate, but this was a nice alternative.

Soft humming drifted across with his wonderful cologne. She could be wonderfully comfortable with him.

The humming stopped as Jared stared at the scene they were approaching. Black smoke rose from the pipe of a grader as it pushed snow over the edge of the cliff. The snow mirrored the red and blue lights of Officer Olson's patrol car.

Her rental car sat behind a wrecker. The car was almost bent in half like it had hugged the tree that kept her from going over the cliff. She couldn't remember the details of what happened, but the sight told the story. That evergreen tree was all that had kept her from dying. She reached a trembling hand up to stop her quivering chin from moving.

Jared reached over and put his hand on her arm. "You don't have to get out. I can get your things out of the car for you."

"No. I'm going."

Marissa watched as Officer Olson, the road crew, and the wrecker driver gathered around her car. A few scratched their heads and others had their hands on their hips as they stood there discussing— what? The miracle that she had survived?

She opened her door and said, "I need pictures to prove this crazy story. I'm having trouble believing it myself."

She eased out of the car and hung onto the door until she was sure her footing would stay under her. Jared was soon by her side as she sidled her way toward her rental car.

"You okay?" His voice was soft and kind.

Nodding, she kept moving as the men pounded and pried the trunk of the car.

The snow was slick, and her feet slid in different directions. Her body twisted and pulled until her knee almost buckled with pain shooting through it. Strong hands caught her before she fell.

"Let me help you."

Goosebumps spread along her arms. She'd long fantasized about hearing those words from a strong superhero who rescued her from some imaginary crisis. Now it was real, and it made her dizzy.

Her veins filled with ice as they shuffled toward her red, crumpled car. Beyond it, a bulldozer pushed a large pile of snow over the cliff edge, opening the route to the flatter lowlands. The sooner she got off this crazy hill, the sooner she could relax in a hot tub. And the sooner she could decide it had all been a bad dream. But first, she had to get her stuff out of the car.

"Yoo hoo!" she called out.

The men turned and gawked at her slipping across the snow, with only Jared holding her upright when her feet went astray.

Officer Olson spoke a word to the other men. The bearded, overall-clad brusque men turned into gentlemen and gathered around her, voicing their amazement at her survival. She was one fortunate lady. The oldest man talked about a family who were swept over the edge and killed in the snow and rocks. Anyone as lucky as she should go buy some lottery tickets.

They meant well, but it sent tendrils of fear moving through her. Adjusting her coat to hide a shudder exploding, she pressed her lips together as she looked at their thick boots. Their tales of near misses were draining her self-control.

Taking a deep breath, she replied, "I appreciate your help in getting the car out. I'm not feeling particularly well so I wonder if you could get the trunk open so I can get my things out. Please. The keys are probably still in the ignition. Just hit the trunk button...never mind. I don't think it's working."

With a few soft chuckles, the men assured her they'd get the trunk open, then went back to work.

Pulling away from Jared's grip on her, she took pictures with her phone. She couldn't keep her body still. The trembling was more from her nerves than the cold. Realizing the photos might be blurry, she asked Jared to take some for her.

Her heart pulsated as she got closer to the crumpled metal form. The men strained to open the trunk, but it wouldn't budge. A husky man took a turn with a prybar. With a strained groan from the man, the trunk let out loud squeaks as it inched up.

The man pulled out her computer bag and dangled it by the strap. The red-and-blue Food-N-More ID tag was visible for only a second, but in that second, her heart nearly stopped beating. If Jared noticed it, his generosity would end.

She made a dash for the bag and grabbed it, saying she wanted to check it. She made a great show at unzipping and peeking in without opening it too wide. With a quick motion, she removed the ID tag with her company's name on it and slid it inside her coat pocket. Her heart started beating again after her identity was concealed.

"All is well." Her voice crackled like a prepubescent boy's. Having something in her arms to hug like a teddy bear helped her knees stop wobbling.

Her other luggage and the garment bag were freed from the mangled wreck and handed to Officer Olson and one of the men. She thanked them all for their assistance as Jared pried her fingers away from the computer case and took it from her stiff arms.

Her bare hands went into her pockets where her fingers found the tag that could ruin everything. She had to keep her rescuer from becoming an adversary any sooner than necessary. If he knew the truth, he'd leave her here in the snow. Or push her over the cliff.

With her things loaded in the back, Jared helped her into the passenger seat. The warm leather felt good against her legs and backside. He spoke briefly with Officer Olson and shook hands with him before he got in and started his vehicle.

Another shudder shook her as she took one last look at the mangled remains of her car. Only by the Grace of God was the car not her tomb. She would always say prayers of thanks in the coming years of her life.

The grader made one last run through the cut in the snowslide. The operator waved at them to follow as he turned around. Slowly, Jared moved his vehicle behind the grader.

The snow towered over the SUV as they moved through the plowed lane. Every nerve in Marissa's body stood on end as claustrophobia seeped in.

A clump of snow fell out of the sky in front of them. Jared gasped.

Her throat clenched, trapping the scream inside. Although the grader kept them creeping along, her foot wanted to sneak over and push the accelerator to the floor.

They rounded a slight curve and could see the other end. As they emerged from the icy crevasse, the grader stopped alongside the bulldozer. The dozer operator waved at Jared as they passed. Behind him, a line of cars was parked, with snowsuit-clad people standing around them, staring at the one vehicle privileged enough to go through.

Their stares made her uncomfortable. It wasn't her fault the avalanche delayed their trips. They'd only lost some time. She'd lost her car, her dignity, her sense of security, her confidence, and Tyler.

Her mind paused. Good riddance to that last one.

Her eyes started to burn so she pushed everything out of her mind and concentrated on the music floating in the cab. The quiet tune helped relax her muscles so she could sink farther into the warm leather seat. The mountains seemed less threatening when she was with someone who knew how to drive on ice.

The last of her panic began to subside. She was on her way down the mountain. Back to the plains where snow didn't try to push you over a cliff.

"You've had a hard day," Jared commented without looking at her. "I hope you'll like Edith's hotel. She works hard to keep it clean and up to date on the inside. She has internet, cable, and a good-sized TV in every room. You could stay there until you figure out how to get to Denver."

"Any hot tubs?"

He shot her a glance. "No, but one of the rooms has a big claw-foot bathtub. I hear it's pretty nice for reading books." His cheeks reddened as he cleared his throat and squirmed in his seat.

Marissa looked out the side window at the snow-covered trees to hide her smile. Few men would blush at telling a woman about a bath experience. This unusual gentleman—there was no other word for him—was a rarity. It made him intriguing.

The clouds parted and sunshine flooded the canyon and the enormous expanse of tree-covered slopes wrapped in fresh snow. Beside the road, piles of snow formed a channel that separated them from the fresh, unmarred white blanket. The beauty took her breath away.

The Christmas spirit edged its way into her and forced out the soft humming of a Christmas carol.

Jared switched channels to one that played Christmas music. He joined in her humming until his rich baritone voice began to softly sing along with the words.

Her family told her she had a beautiful voice, and she wasn't afraid to use it. She joined in, singing slightly louder than he did. When the next carol came on, he sang a little louder than her. Thus, their competition began. The farther they went down the road, the louder their caroling became. By the time they reached the merge ramp onto the interstate, they were singing at the top of their lungs.

CHAPTER 8

The town of Milo Creek lined a small river as it meandered along the valley floor. The sun had already set behind the high mountains. Marissa could feel the temperature drop as they drove into the shadows.

The high speeds and noise of the interstate stayed behind as they went down the road leading into town. The older buildings exuded the feeling of nostalgia. Time, progress, and the interstate had passed by without leaving much of a mark.

Jared pulled in front of a motel that looked like something out of a 1950s Look magazine. A painted wooden sign announced there were vacancies at the Milo Creek Motel. The office was the front parlor of a house that was attached to a long line of doors with numbers on them. The exterior paint was in good condition, and the empty parking lot was neatly plowed.

"Skiers aren't back yet," Jared remarked as he got out.

It wasn't as fancy as her hotel suite in Denver, but it held a certain charm. She was so tired any room would look good.

A bell over the door rang out their arrival as the pair went inside. The sound of a TV game show came through a door behind the desk.

Jared hit a doorbell button on the reception counter that sounded in the back. Several minutes later, a short older woman came out, wiping her mouth with a napkin.

"Hello, Jared," she said cheerfully. What brings you here?" Even as she said the words, her eyes were on Marissa.

"My friend needs a room for the night. Marissa Williams, meet Edith Campbell, Milo Creek's hostess, city council member, and one of many who have lived here their whole life."

With a chuckle, she reached out her hand toward Marissa. "I wear many hats, but I love it. Nice to have you in town."

Taking her hand, Marissa returned the greeting. The gray hair and twinkle in the elder woman's eyes reminded her of her grandmother. She immediately liked the woman.

"How long will you be staying with me?" Edith inquired as she set to filling out a paper form.

That was the million-dollar question. She had no car. Jared wouldn't take her to Denver. Offered enough money, someone somewhere would take her, but she was too tired to think more of it. "I'm not sure. Maybe two or three nights. Can we leave it open ended?"

"Of course." The older woman pulled out a key and turned the sheet of paper around and put a pen on top for signatures. "We're not full. Stay as long as you like."

Jared leaned on the counter. "Give her the good room."

Edith's eyes narrowed. "The good room, huh." She leaned toward him but looked at Marissa. "It costs more."

"This woman survived the Bearkiller slide this morning. She deserves it."

Patting her heart, Edith gasped and put her other hand over her mouth. Her eyes bounced between Jared and Marissa.

"Thanks to Jared, I survived," Marissa answered, hoping it would take the focus off her and put it onto him. "He's the one who pulled me out of my car as it hung on the side of the cliff..." Her voice trailed off as visions of how close her car had been to going over returned.

For an instant, she felt light-headed and must have wobbled because Jared reached out to steady her. His touch sent energy through her, warming her as it spread.

"She needs to relax after her unusual day," Jared said.

With a shake of her head, she told Marissa, "You poor dear. I heard it had run, but I had no idea someone got caught in it. How terrifying it must have been!" She pulled the key back and got another one. "You need the best room. No extra charge."

Marissa's face felt hot under Edith's intense gaze. "I don't mind paying extra—"

"Oh, honey." The woman's eyes turned as tender as her grandmother's used to when she talked to six-year-old Marissa. "Don't you worry about that. Nothing but the best for you at the Milo Creek Motel. We know how to take good care of our visitors."

Edith reached below the counter and pulled out a lavender bath bomb. "It's my best room because it has the biggest tub and the biggest TV. Take a long warm bath. Read a book. It'll relax you and do you a whole lot of good." She pushed the key across the counter.

With one burden lifted off her shoulders, Marissa murmured a sincere thanks as she offered her credit card. She filled out the paperwork while Jared moved his SUV down to what was probably her room.

She had a place to stay and the space to be alone. People had surrounded her constantly since her lonely trip toward the lodge was abruptly interrupted. If she had to hold herself together one more time as someone told her how lucky she was, her mental state would collapse for sure. She needed solitude as much as she needed to sleep.

"I serve a continental breakfast in the morning," Edith told her before she left. "Nothing fancy. Pastries, coffee, and fruit. I set it out by six-thirty and will leave it out until everyone has eaten. If you're not coming, please let me know." Her grandma eyes returned. "Dear, if you need anything—and I mean anything—you call me. You may think you're friendless, but you're not as long as I'm around." She extended her hand across the counter.

A crying jag threatened to explode like a shaken can of soda. Marissa looked away as she clasped the offered hand. The day might have been one of her worst, but she'd never forget the friendship offered by strangers. Her grandmother had once told her kindness from strangers is the most precious because it's freely given with no obligation. How true. God had provided help when she needed it the most.

Marissa blinked away the moisture in her eyes that blurred her vision. "Thank you. That means a lot." She hurried out the door before control escaped her grasp.

Although the walk wasn't icy, she took tiny steps on her way to Room Twelve. Falling was not an option. Enough had happened today without adding sprained ankles or broken bones.

Jared opened the rear hatch on his vehicle, then came to offer his elbow for support.

Accepting the help, they made their way to the red door. She unlocked it and let it swing wide. The smell of disinfectant drifted up her nose. The room was small, with a king-sized bed taking up most of the space. A large flat-screen TV hung on the wall opposite the bed. Beyond the TV was a clothing rack next to a table. Going in farther, she could see into the turquoise tiled bathroom. As promised, a large clawfoot tub sat beneath a faucet and showerhead. The tub curved up in the back, providing a comfortable head rest.

Her body ached to slip beneath warm water.

"Nothing fancy," Jared remarked as he put her luggage on the foldout luggage rack. "Probably nothing like you're used to, but it's clean and from what I hear, comfortable."

"It's perfect." Marissa said as she sat on the bed. Jared put her computer bag beside her before he went to get the rest of her luggage.

With her luggage set on the table and her garment bag hanging up, Jared's eyes darted around as his hands searched for somewhere to be. He looked like a bellboy waiting for a tip.

Fatigue robbed her mind of anything profound to ease the feeling. She settled for the obvious. "I can't thank you enough for bringing me here. I needed off that mountain."

The words seemed to free Jared from staying longer. He went to the door and stood. "I'm glad you're safe. That snowslide has killed before. Your guardian angel did a whale of a job in saving you."

He paused as his eyes grew misty. He wiped his face and cleared his throat. Reaching inside his jacket, he pulled out a business card. His hand quivered as he held it out. "Here. Call me if you need anything."

"I know of two things I need."

"Name it."

"Food and bubble bath."

A mental lightbulb lit his face. "I bet you're starving. I know I am. We have the best deli around. I'll get a delivery guy to bring you something from there, along with a bottle of Mr. Bubble." Giving a half smile, he added, "It's all we stock in terms of bubble bath."

"Perfect. Between that and this ..." she pitched the bath bomb into the air and caught it, "...I'll have all I need."

They shared a smile before he left. When the door closed behind him, she hugged herself. "Alone at last!"

CHAPTER 9

J ared's office in the back of the store was a welcome sight. No
doubt several crises stacked up during the day, ready for him
to solve or bury for another time. He slipped on his Sullivan Food
Mart apron before going out front. "You finally got back."

Martha Baker continued checking out her customer as she called
out to her boss. She'd done the job for so long she could have
done it blindfolded and asleep, and no one would have doubted the
total. She knew everyone and knew what was happening to them.
She was the town bulletin board with discretion. Her projected
retirement date was coming too quickly, and Jared wasn't sure
what the store would ever do without her.

He waved his hand at her as he walked by and called out a
greeting to the line of people waiting to check out. He found Jason
the stocker and asked him to go help Martha. Continuing on his
way, he passed a bare end cap that should have held chips of all
kinds. Gaping holes on the shelves seemed like caverns. It must
have been a very busy day at the store.

Running his hand through his hair, he mentally kicked himself.
Hard. He should have never gone on that grocery delivery. Why

hadn't he sent Chad? Then he remembered. All the other day's events had buried the memory he wanted to forget.

His ex-girlfriend had walked into his office that morning, looking better than he remembered. Kayla had returned home from Washington D.C. for the holiday to introduce her new beau to her family. The only woman he'd ever loved, the one he wouldn't leave his store for, was happier than he'd ever seen her. The big city and her new man suited her in a way he and Milo Creek never could.

Kayla hadn't come to gloat, but merely to see how he was. When she left, her perfume stayed behind, resurrecting old feelings and old memories he thought were buried and gone.

Sitting behind his desk, he leaned his head on his hands. He'd always said he wouldn't leave here for love or money, but the results of his mantra were hitting him hard.

A sense of failure permeated him. Everything he tried to make her happy seemed to backfire and made her more miserable. He'd changed how much time he spent at the store. He'd drawn up plans to remodel his family's home. Nothing. When that job in D.C. came open, she accepted it even after he begged her to stay.

His heart felt empty the day she left. It was better that way. If he didn't look for love, he wouldn't get hurt again. His store became his girlfriend and focus in life. Happiness and purpose were found inside its walls, and he was content with that.

Until today.

Until he'd pulled Marissa from the wreck. Seeing her helpless had stirred something in him. Something he didn't want to deal with. He had to keep her at arm's length to protect his heart, but something about her drew him like iron to a magnet. Like fish to a lure. Like gravy to biscuits.

Driving back down the mountain, he felt comfortable with her. Like there was nothing to fear. Like they had a lot in common just waiting to be explored and discovered. He didn't understand it. Logic told him it wasn't going to—

A knock at the door sounded before Benny stuck his head in. "Hey boss, you okay? We heard you had a rough trip."

Jared waved his friend to come in. "You wouldn't believe what happened to me. I'm not sure I do. Bearkiller ran after I passed it. Not only that, but a car got hit by the slide but didn't go over. I had to dig her out..."

Benny's mouth fell open. "Wait." He slid into the chair in front of the desk. "Say that again. You saved someone from the slide? A 'her'?"

Stubbornness in the Truvo family was legendary around town. Benny continued the tradition. Jared had said too much to back out. Benny would insist on knowing what happened, but there was too much work to do to have his staff speculating and retelling the tale. "It's a long story. They need help out front."

Jared stood to go.

Benny waved him to sit down again. "It can wait a few minutes. I want to know what happened." A look of determination filled his eyes. Jared could either tell Benny or answer questions while he trailed him around the store. More productivity and privacy would be gained if he resigned himself to relating the event now.

Releasing a sigh in surrender, he returned to his chair and reported the events of the day like a 30-second news item, ending with, "And that's the story." He rose to go again.

Benny didn't move except to cock his head. "Was she good looking?"

A vision of Marissa filled his mind. Warmth moved into his chest and wormed its way up to his face. He didn't want that feeling. He tried to push it down but it was like putting Styrofoam peanuts back into the bag. His heart was supposed to be as unfeeling as a Star Trek Vulcan so what was this strange stirring? He hated being at the mercy of something uncontrollable. No one could predict what a woman would do.

A howl of laughter broke him out of his momentary trance. "You're in love!" Benny yelled.

"Quiet!" Jared rushed to the door to make sure it was firmly shut. "I am not. You asked if she was good looking, and I was thinking, yes, very much."

"That's not what I saw. You got a silly look on your face." Benny joined Jared at the door and smirked. "You're smitten whether you know it or not."

"I am not. Now get back to work." Benny chuckled as he left the office.

Jared pressed his lips together as he watched Benny sauntering past the dairy aisle on the way to his meat department. Without Benny's promise to keep the news secret, everyone would soon know about it. His employees and customers would give him a good ribbing about it. Teasing was always hard for him to take, but he'd do it. The hubbub would eventually pass, and everyone would forget about it. All he had to do was endure it while it lasted.

He shut the door and returned to his desk, not ready to face anyone. He needed to check his emails to see if any deliveries were delayed and look over the inventory list to see what was selling and what was not. Sixty-four unopened emails glared at him. He sat back in his chair and ran his hands through his hair. This was exactly why he hated being gone on vacation or getting sick. Just his few hours being away had brought on a mountain of business to handle before closing time.

His stomach rumbled softly, triggering the reminder he was supposed to send food to Marissa. He'd put it together, but he'd send Jason to deliver it. The less time he was around her the better. Those eyes would find their way back into his mind if he was around her too much.

Locking his computer, he left his electronic business behind to see what his real business was doing.

CHAPTER 10

Marissa called her office while she waited for sustenance. Most people in the office were gone for the holidays. The ones unlucky enough to have drawn the short straw included her secretary who was relegated to manning the switchboard for everyone.

He answered in a voice dripping with the disappointment of a child finding no gifts under the Christmas tree. She gave a quick account of had happened to her. Her story must have made him sit up straight in his chair because his usual business voice resumed.

"I'm glad you're okay," he said. "What can I do to help you?"

Other than deflecting any business matters that might come her way, there was nothing he could do for her. She'd handle the car rental agency since she wasn't sure they'd believe him. They might not believe her either, but she had pictures and the police report to back her up.

With business out of the way, she unpacked a few things and hung them on the metal hangers. She unzipped the garment bag and pulled out the red dress she planned to wear on New Year's Eve when she thought she and Tyler would announce their engagement. She wadded the expensive, altered gown into a tight ball and threw it against the wall as hard as she could. If scissors had been handy, she'd have turned it into red confetti.

True to his word, Jared sent a delivery guy with a large bottle of bubble bath, hot soup, a sandwich, chips, a large piece of cake, several pieces of fruit, a diet pop, and a package of bottled water. But he also sent something more: a bag of Hershey Kisses. His note said he'd heard chocolate has a calming effect after a hard day. His thoughtfulness made her smile.

While she ate, she called the car rental agency. The Christmas music playing while she was on hold added a holiday ambience to the small room.

When an agent finally came on the line, he listened to her tale. He was silent for a moment.

She didn't have to see him to know he was skeptical. "I have pictures and should have a police report in a few days to prove it," she added. "Or call the Highway Patrol and ask for a copy of the report."

He put her on hold again.

Song after song played, entertaining her as she ate. The tomato bisque complemented her ham and cheese sandwich. A few grapes were enough for dessert. The cake would taste better later.

As she ate, she wondered if the agent could find anyone to help her. Likely no one at the agency wanted to touch her case with a two-meter avalanche probe.

Seven swans were swimming when someone came on to grill her about the accident. Was she driving on a highway that was closed? Had she driven around any barriers? Were there any warning signs?

Once the man decided the avalanche was an act of God, the reporting process went faster.

By the time the call ended, the fee she'd paid for the extra insurance became golden. They would work it out, and it wouldn't cost her a dime. A replacement car awaited her in Denver, or she could pay an extra fee and have it delivered to her in Milo Creek. She chose the latter.

Her head ached a little when she hung up. She pushed aside the remnants of her meal and let the bed embrace her. A headache after being hit with an airbag seemed natural. She couldn't remember all the details of the accident, but she didn't really want to. The narration by Jared and the sight of her crumpled car were quite enough.

The warm bath and a book prescribed by Edith were next on her agenda. She didn't have a book. All she had with her was her Kindle. An earlier experience with a soaking tub and her Kindle made her reluctant to try that again. A week in rice hadn't saved it. Reading would wait for drier surfaces.

Her phone's playlist would suffice, or maybe she should call the car rental company back and request to be placed on hold while she soaked.

The roar of water pounding into the large tub called her into the state of bliss. Warm water would soon caress her battered body and ease the aches. A half bottle of bubble bath would hide the bruises.

She situated the bag of chocolate Kisses so she could reach them from the tub. Not waiting, she slipped a candy into her mouth and let the chocolate do its magic. Her clothes were kicked into a pile at the foot of the bed.

Slipping into the warm water was heavenly. The Mr. Bubble scent took her back to her girlhood days when she didn't care about boys. Without opening her eyes, she reached out and got another chocolate and let it melt on her tongue. Edith and Jared were right. Chocolate, warm water, and bubbles. A soothing combination.

An image of her wrecked car flashed in her head. She pushed it away and concentrated on the feel of the water and the sound of softly popping bubbles.

Her phone rang, pulling her out of her meditation. She'd left it on the bed for good reason. Nothing was going to interfere with her bath. Whoever it was could leave a message.

She picked up another chocolate and closed her eyes again. The water lapped at the edges as she kept time with the lively ringtone before it went to voice mail.

Her playlist resumed, including a song she and Tyler had played during their last date. Now sounding like fingernails on a blackboard, the song wrecked her moment of bliss. She shot out of the tub, but immediately felt dizzy. She leaned against the door jamb while her head settled back to one spot.

The song went on, throwing out barbs with it as the memories came back. She stumbled to the bed and stopped the grating noise.

A bang on the door scared her, making her release a short shriek of fright. She grabbed a towel and wrapped it around her. "Who is it!"

Edith's concern came through the door. "Marissa, you okay? Jared tried to call you and said no one answered. He got worried and told me to come check on you."

Putting her hand over her pounding heart, Marissa leaned against the door jamb again. Why didn't everyone just leave her alone! Her mother didn't even dog her steps like these people did.

At the same time, she was thankful they cared.

Trying to hold back the annoyance from her voice, she responded, "I'm fine! I'm relaxing in a warm bath. Tell Jared I'll call him later."

"Okay. Sorry to bother you, dear." Shuffling footsteps faded. Marissa returned to her watery bliss and got another chocolate.

After her bath, cleaning out her playlist was top priority. Then she'd call the endearing worrier Jared.

When thoroughly wrinkled and the warmth of the water gone, her soak in the tub ended. She threw on leggings and a sweatshirt and stretched out on the comfortable bed. The bath had refreshed her, and she felt better than she had since early morning.

She checked the channel options on the laminated list beside her bed. Her favorite old movie channel was listed much to her delight.

Her phone buzzed with a text from her mother asking how things were going. Having to explain Tyler's betrayal and how close she'd come to dying would cause too much anguish and would ruin her mother's holiday with her sister that they'd been planning since July. What she didn't know now wouldn't hurt her and wouldn't make her jump on the next plane headed to Denver.

Marissa sent her a vague text about relaxing and enjoying the scenery and left it at that. It wasn't the whole truth, but it wasn't a lie. It was just enough to satisfy a mother's curiosity.

Pulling a pillow across her lap, she studied the unknown number displayed in her phone messages. Jared's voice came on when she started it.

"Hi, Marissa. This is Jared. How ya doing? I called to make sure you're okay. Um, I wish you would answer. If you're passed out on the floor, you need help." A short silent gap was followed by, "I'll call Edith."

He seemed genuinely concerned about her. His tone held no pretense or demand. His message was simple. He cared about her wellbeing.

That was more than Tyler had shown. He hadn't contacted her at all. After all she have done for him, he hadn't called or texted. It was like she didn't exist to him.

She slammed her fist into the pillow. A total stranger expressed more concern for her than the jerk she'd known all her life and given her heart to for years. She punched the pillow again and again and again. How could she have been so blind? So stupid? She let out a whispered scream, fearing someone might hear her agony as it poured out of her. Only her pounding head made her stop.

It took a while for her to calm down and let her breath return. Tyler wasn't worth the energy. The farther she got away from him, the better and more peaceful her life would be.

Jared, however, attracted her even though she didn't want to feel anything for him. Handsome. Kind. Fiercely loyal. He was the kind of man she'd wanted Tyler to be. How could she not be attracted to him?

A warm spot grew inside her.

She hit the call button. He answered on the first ring. "How are you? I've been worried."

"I have a headache and I'm sore, but otherwise I'm okay. Thanks for checking on me."

"Did you like the meal?"

"Oh yes, it was delicious, especially the Kisses. Thanks for sending everything over. Start a tab for me, and I'll settle up tomorrow."

He laughed. "The first meal's on me. Is there anything else you need? Tylenol or aspirin?"

There seemed to be no limit to his kindness. Marissa felt her face move into a smile. So different than high-maintenance Tyler. "No thanks. I have all I need."

After a few minutes of small talk about the town and what was on TV, he assured her he'd call again later that night to check on her.

After she hung up, the quiet room felt overbearing. Turning on the TV, the local news showed stores full of shoppers and good cheer. More snow wasn't expected until the next week, providing ideal travel weather for those traveling home for Christmas.

Home. She'd never felt so far away. Her holiday expectations had imploded. The more she thought about the last few conversations with Tyler, the clearer it became that he intended to dump her.

Her belief in getting engaged had clouded everything, especially her good sense.

She clicked the off button on the remote with enough pressure to crush an unshelled pecan and got up. A groan escaped her lips as nerve ends cried out in protest. Her formerly relaxed muscles had stiffened, making it hard to walk without pain. There was only one place that would give her peace.

She stripped as she ran bath water again, this time with the bath bomb in it. Her image in the mirror reflected bruised ribs and arm on one side, along with large bruises down both legs and ankles. Her cheekbone was bruised, and she had a slight shiner below her left eye. The sight brought home how close she had come to not being here. The airbags and the red car had given their lives to save hers.

The water cloaked Marissa like a blanket fresh out of the dryer. The bubbles produced by the remaining bubble bath hid her body. Using her toes to rock her body slightly, the water gently caressed her as she lay back against the headrest. The bathroom grew darker until the only light came from the lamp by her bed in the other room.

So where should she go from here? For the first time, Tyler wasn't in the plan. Maybe she could find someone else to love. Having dated only one man her whole life, the thought terrified her.

Reverting to her childhood method of releasing disappointment, she flailed her arms and legs and screamed in a hoarse whisper. Water and bubbles rained all over the small bathroom.

The fit passed. Acting like a child didn't solve anything in her adult life. She had to clean up the mess she made, both on the bathroom floor and in her life.

CHAPTER 11

After a nightmare-filled night, Marissa woke with a start. The strange surroundings left her confused until she remembered she was in Milo Creek, the middle of nowhere. Her phone dinged with a Christmas Eve greeting from her mother, followed by another from her brother. She halfheartedly returned them, doing her best to sound cheerful even though she didn't feel that way.

Her body strongly objected to being moved as she climbed out of bed. Her image in the mirror almost scared her. Her hair went every direction and swelling distorted her face enough that she didn't look like herself. She could do something about her hair, but her face...her makeup bag didn't have enough to hide it.

After changing her clothes and taming her hair, she stepped out of her room into the cold. Christmas Eve had come with a deep blue sky and sunshine so bright she needed sunglasses to find her way to the office.

Somewhere in the distance sleighbells jingled, and the sound of laughter came by on a gentle breeze. The Christmas spirit abounded in this setting and was highly contagious. It cheered her as she walked to get her continental breakfast. She braced herself for the stares that would come her way because her story would inevitably provide conversation fodder wherever she went in this small town.

As she walked into the office, a couple looked up from their newspapers and toasted bagels. Their looks went through a procession of emotions, oscillating between shock and concern, finally landing on pretending not to stare. They both gave a smile and muttered something about a good morning.

Returning their greeting, Marissa fixed a small breakfast for herself and sat near a window where the bright sunlight fell across the table. Its warm beams heated her clothes as she ate, relieving some of the achiness. Her long hair blocked the view of her face as she bent over her meal.

Unbidden, Edith sat down across from her.

Looking up, Marissa watched the woman as her expressions went through the same process as the couple's but settled into a pleasant smile.

"Merry Christmas Eve, hon! How are you feeling today? Is there something I can do to help? All you have to do is tell me what it is, and I'll do it." Reaching out, she touched the back of Marissa's hand.

The concern in the gray-haired woman's eyes crossed the table and entered Marissa, making her eyes suddenly feel damp. The woman again reminded her of what her grandmother would have said to her when she was feeling blue. Pulling her hand away, Marissa looked down and wiped her mouth with her napkin, hoping it would keep her eyes from spilling over.

"Thank you, Edith," she replied when she could do so without her voice breaking. "The only thing I need is a room for a couple more nights. The rental company will either bring me a new car or send a driver to take me there but not until after Christmas. I don't feel comfortable asking for a ride to Denver on Christmas Eve because it would interrupt people's plans, and I don't want to do that. So, I'm stranded here at least until the day after Christmas."

"You can stay as long as you need to although there's no maid service or breakfast tomorrow. I'll put an extra towel in your room. Be sure to pick up food at the grocery store to get you through because everything will be closed tomorrow, including my kitchen."

"Thanks. I'll do that."

Marissa finished her breakfast while Edith chatted with another couple who seemed in no hurry to leave. She rose to go, but her hip seemed to lose strength and she stumbled slightly as she took a step. Catching her balance before Edith got to her, she stood until she took inventory and found all the parts working again. With a mumbled apology, gritted teeth, and a herculean effort to conceal how much it hurt to walk, she went out the door without help. The farther she went, the more her muscles loosened, and her gait got better. She made a mental note to be more graceful about it next time.

Back in her room, Marissa opened her computer case. As long as she was here, she might as well get some work done. Her mission was to scout the town, estimate projected effects the new store would have on the local economy, and sign the offer for the land.

It didn't take an economist to see that the impact would be huge. A map of the town took up a small portion of the bed. Her fingers traced the two-block-long downtown. The Sullivan Food Mart was on a corner across from the bank. Next to the grocery store was a real estate office with a hardware store beyond that. A closed, deteriorating gas station took up half of the next block. A cafe, a bar, an antique store, the town library, a medical clinic, and City Hall completed the downtown inventory. The Milo Creek Motel was on the southern edge of downtown.

Residents of Denver had discovered the quaint small-town feel of Milo Creek, trading a shorter drive to work for a better place to raise their children. Developers, having learned from ambulance chasers, were taking advantage of the population shift and buying land in large chunks to build subdivisions and line their pockets. The influx of new people to the small town brought its own problems with overtaxed utilities, crowded schools, increased maintenance, and rising property taxes.

Milo Creek was in transition. The growing population would demand more services. Her research showed the businesses downtown had done well but recently had plateaued. Locals had little choice but to patronize what was available unless they wanted to drive some distance to a larger town. More and more people were willing to do that.

The large, new truck stop that sat beside Milo Creek's exit from the interstate, was recently incorporated into the city limits. While it drew in more business, it killed the gas station downtown. A new store selling everything for a dollar, built beside the truck stop, pulled money from the Food Mart. A large hotel chain had bought the commercial property across from the truck stop with construction scheduled to begin in the spring. The grandmotherly woman who cared about her would probably go out of business.

The large commercial property Food-N-More was buying for its store was on the other side of the interstate from the truck stop. The new store would include a pharmacy, hardware, clothing, some furniture, gas, and groceries, providing a one-stop shopping option. The designers left room for a drive-through coffee shop and fast-food location for whoever wanted to develop those sites. Those new amenities would attract people from Milo Creek, the interstate, and the surrounding areas. The investment in the new store would pay off in dividends.

The resulting shifts in commerce would end the need for many of the town's older businesses. Edith's neat, clean motel and the Sullivan Food Mart would likely be the next abandoned properties, crumbling along with the gas station downtown.

The furrows in Jared's brow would grow deeper all because of what she was there to do.

With a sigh, Marissa put away the plat and lay down. Her head throbbed again, not from the accident but from knowing what her assignment would do to Jared.

She'd helped acquire property for other stores in other states, but this time it was different. The man who had rescued her from an icy death would lose his life's passion because of her.

She slammed her computer shut. She hated her high-paying, high- finance job. Oh sure, she lived in a luxurious apartment, drove a paid-off 8 Series BMW, had a large nest egg invested and growing, and all the fine jewelry, clothes, and shoes her heart desired. It all came from finding those spots where her company would make good money. Only this time, the blood money would come from people she knew, who valued their small businesses, their town, and its friendliness. The same people who'd taken her in when she had no one to help her.

Guilt washed over her like an ocean wave.

Her plan after law school was estate planning. Her grandparents lost everything to a scammer. Their lifetime of hard work didn't go to their children, but to someone who didn't deserve it. That scam cemented Marissa's aspirations to help people find their way through the maze of laws, regulations, red tape, and misinformation about how to organize their financial futures so it wouldn't be taken away from them.

Her plans all changed when the Food-N-More corporation offered an insanely large six-figure salary immediately after she passed the bar. Greed lured her away. She told herself after she had a nice nest egg, she'd start her own practice. Eight years later and here she was, ruining people's lives instead of helping them. She'd become what she'd wanted to help people avoid.

Her phone rang, interrupting her mental flogging. Jared's cheerful voice plunged her farther into her pool of remorse.

"Come see my store," he invited in a cheerful voice. In the background she could hear people talking, Christmas music playing, and a child crying. "We have a great deli for lunch. I can send someone to give you a ride. You are probably pretty sore."

Marissa sat up with aches hounding her efforts. "Thanks for the invitation. I'd love to see it. It's not that far so I'll walk. I get stiff if I sit too long. It'll do me good."

Happy for the chance to get away, she gathered her work materials and computer and looked for a place to hide them. If anyone discovered her secret, the word would spread like wildfire, and they'd probably run her out of town. Make her hitchhike back to Denver.

Her ballgown still lay on the floor in a pile about the same size as the money she'd spent to buy it. Heaving a sigh, she picked it up and rehung it in the garment bag. She stuffed her computer and work files in the suitcase and zipped it shut before locking it.

A little preening in the mirror, a few extra items in her purse, her coat and boots bought specially for this trip, and she was ready for her stroll. Her new felt hat had been forgotten in the wrecked car so she wrapped her scarf over her head and wrapped the tails around her neck.

The parking lot and sidewalks were dry which made walking easy. The sunshine warmed her face and her muscles. Vehicles went by loaded with smiling people. Wreathes hung from the downtown light poles and the four-way stop signs at the intersection on Main Street. The joy of Christmas penetrated everything.

All the parking spaces around the grocery store were taken, with one car waiting for someone to leave. As Marissa walked in, everyone froze in place. The checker held something in her hand as she stared. Her customer didn't seem to mind since she was doing the same thing. The lady in line behind him didn't seem to mind. Not a cart moved while everyone looked. Only the Christmas music continued as everyone turned to statues.

Marissa stood paralyzed by their stares. She should have put on more makeup and concealer. The gazes were more intense than she'd imagined they would be. The urge to turn and run almost overpowered her will to stay.

Somewhere a child's voice rang out. "Mom, can we get this?"

As if responding to a green light, the hum of conversations and moving carts began again. People resumed their activities as they looked away.

Relieved not to be the center of attention, Marissa dropped her head so her face was not so visible and quickly moved down a narrow aisle, edging past a full grocery cart. She'd never blend in but maybe she could be less conspicuous.

Going around a corner, she spotted the deli situated in the back corner. People were seated at small tables as they visited over their lunches. A refrigerated case held a variety of sandwiches and salads. A heated case held burritos and chicken tenders for those who wanted something hot. Two soup pots were next to them. The aroma made her stomach voice its desire for something.

The woman behind the deli counter stopped and stared at Marissa. A few followed her gaze and stopped what they were doing to gawk at the stranger in their midst. The deli fell silent.

Knowing she was quite the sight with her battered face, Marissa resigned herself to being a curiosity in the small town. "Yes," she said for all to hear, "I'm the one who got caught in the avalanche yesterday." Opening her arms wide, she welcomed any remarks. Better to face them than have them staring and quietly whispering.

A voice behind her made her turn. "Forgive our rudeness." The checker she'd seen at the front strolled toward her. "We've all heard the story of how our boss saved you. You're the embodiment of his heroism. We can't help but stare." She held out her hand to Marissa. "I'm Martha Baker. I work up front. That's Holly Dingaman behind the deli counter. I hear your name is Marissa."

Holly waved her hand and smiled.

Martha hand signaled a couple sitting at a corner table. They quickly took their last bite, then stood to clear off the table and offer their seats. Martha sat and motioned for Marissa to take the seat across from her. After requesting her usual from Holly, she asked what Marissa wanted.

Ordering a bowl of soup, Marissa sat back and let Martha take the lead.

The large woman with graying hair posed a commanding presence. A leader who seldom acknowledged she was one. Every ear focused on the words she spoke. "Tell us what happened. We're dying to know your story."

A young woman leaned on her grocery cart handle as she gazed intently at the two. "Yeah, tell us what it's like to get hit by a snowslide and live through it."

Marissa didn't mind public speaking, but this was different. Her usual audiences expected numbers and graphs. This audience expected a total recounting of The Event. Butterflies fluttered inside as she glanced at Martha who gave her an encouraging nod.

Why fight it? "Truth be told, it happened so fast I don't remember much." She waved her hand at her face. "I was driving along and have a vague memory of being slammed like...like a giant hammer hit my car. I was trapped inside, almost completely covered in snow. I couldn't get out. Lucky for me, Jared came along and dug me out of my snowy tomb. I'm very thankful he was there to help me."

She stopped, thinking it was adequate and everyone would move along. When no one did, she added, "That's pretty much it. If you want more, you'll have to ask Jared. He knows more about what it was like than I do."

"Did you go over the cliff?"

In a gruff voice, Martha answered for her. "Of course not. She wouldn't be here if she did."

Marissa added, "My car was smashed against a tree. That kept me from—" Her lifelong fear of falling kept her from saying the words. Running her hands along the tabletop, she mimed going over the edge and made the best explosion sound she could manage. "That's all I know."

Disappointment flashed over the woman at the cart, but it was followed by sympathy.

Holly set a tray with their lunches between Marissa and Martha. "Jared is always doing nice things for other people. He's like the town's best friend. You were super lucky he was there to help you."

Several left to resume shopping, talking amongst themselves as they went.

A few individuals approached Marissa, saying they were glad she had survived and wished her the best. A few Merry Christmas greetings also came her way.

Holly left to wait on customers as Martha leaned across the table. "Now, tell me the whole story. Where were you going, and what were you doing when the slide hit?" She dipped a chicken tender in barbeque sauce and took a bite.

Marissa's skin tingled as her interrogation began. She lifted a spoonful of soup and blew on it. She wasn't sure how much she wanted to share with this Martha person. Her life wasn't an open book for those who'd never been in her library. She looked down at the bowl of soup and slice of bread in front of her and crammed an edge of the bread in her mouth.

Martha prodded her again. "I'm not trying to pry. Just curious about how you and Jared met."

Martha's remark sent a streak of guilt through Marissa. Big-city, high-style living had instilled suspiciousness in her. Her mother kept telling her it made her seem too unfriendly. The lecture fast-forwarded through her head. Not everyone in the world was out to deceive her, and she should learn to look for the good in people.

Yeah, Mom, yeah. I know.

"Are you okay?"

The worry in Martha's questions made Marissa blink her eyes like she was refreshing a screen. "Yes, I'm fine. I'm thinking of my mom."

"I understand. I'm not your mom, but I want to be your friend... really." She paused and cocked her head slightly and widened her eyes. "Sometimes a woman needs to talk things out with someone. I'm here for you."

Martha's relaxed face had a slight smile. No sign of deception or meanness was there. Her expression invited friendship and left the impression that Martha was sincerely interested in her welfare.

What would it hurt to reach out? Right now, having someone to lean on meant more than keeping her privacy. She would leave soon and be forgotten, other than being an anecdote in someone's stories.

Tears burned Marissa's eyes as she leaned forward and whispered, "You're right. I need a friend. I'm trapped in a strange town with no one to talk to. I only know Jared, but...well, you know...he's a man. It's not the same as having a girlfriend." She pulled a napkin out of the holder and wiped her nose.

"Girl, I know what you're saying." Martha whispered back. "Everything you tell me is just between us."

While her soup cooled, Marissa emptied her heart's burdens in low tones over the table. Martha frowned at the part about Tyler's betrayal and nodded in understanding at her desire to flee Denver. Her eyes widened at the parts with the avalanche and being dug out by an angel of mercy. A smile moved her face when Jared came to her rescue, and upon hearing how they sang together as they drove back to Milo Creek.

Martha shook her head and picked up a chicken tender to wave as she talked. "You've been through a lot. I know what it's like to have the rug pulled out from under your feet. It happened when my Jerry died and left me with our three teenaged kids." Her eyes glazed over as she peered into her past. "So much uncertainty. So many questions. I didn't know how I was going to handle it, but it all worked out somehow. And if I can make it, you can too."

"You're obviously a strong woman," Marissa replied. Losing a spouse was much worse than what she was experiencing. Her predicament meant good riddance to a bad situation. Losing Tyler was nothing compared to Martha's don't-leave-me time and weightier obstacles to overcome. The perspective on her personal tragic events shifted, and Marissa felt as lucky as everyone had been telling her.

Tension left her shoulders, and she felt more at ease. This new friend had proven her worth.

"I wasn't very strong back then," Martha said, "I just did what I had to do. Now about—"

"Hello, ladies."

Marissa looked up into Jared's eyes looking into hers. The beginnings of crow's feet gathered beside them as he smiled. He looked different with his white apron over his clothes. More like one of the workers rather than the owner. She liked that. He wasn't above getting down in the trenches with his employees.

His eyes never left Marissa. "Sorry I wasn't there when you came in. Our produce truck got here late, and being short-handed, I had to help get it off and put away."

She waved off his explanation. "It's no problem. I've enjoyed the visit with my new friend Martha."

Martha looked at her phone. "Boss, I've got five more minutes in my lunchtime."

Jared laughed. "I'm not here to crack the whip, Martha. I'm here to apologize to Marissa and make sure someone took over my hosting duties. In fact, take an extra three minutes for lunch."

With a facetious gasp, Martha replied, "You're too good to me, boss."

The three laughed together.

Jared pointed to Martha and told Marissa, "She's everyone's friend, and we're glad to have her with us." He shuffled his feet. "It's Christmas Eve and we're closing early. I'd be happy to make supper for you if you don't have other plans."

"I have a better idea," Martha piped up, catching Marissa by surprise. "She and I will have dinner together tonight. You're welcome to join us girls if you'd like. Then tomorrow, you can entertain her when I visit my kids in Dillion?"

His lips pressed together as he brushed something from the edge of his apron. When he looked up, his eyes seemed happy. "I like that plan. What about it, Marissa?"

Not wanting to spend the holiday alone, she quickly agreed. Being with friendly strangers was better than sitting alone in a motel room. Infinitely better.

A man came up behind Jared and whispered in his ear. "Okay, I'll be right there. By the way, this is Chad, my assistant manager."

Chad greeted her and left.

Jared told them, "Marissa, I'll call you later." He pointed at his watch, then at Martha and winked. He left in a hurry.

Turning back to her new friend, Marissa observed, "He doesn't stand still too long, does he."

Her words found no receiver. Something was happening beyond her that made Martha stop listening and her eyes to narrow. Pushing away her tepid soup, Marissa turned to look.

Jared stood at the entry to the deli with a woman who looked like she'd just stepped out of a fashion show for winter clothing. Jared's ears were a little red as he spoke to her and tried to avoid eye contact. Each step he took back, the woman moved forward as she talked. He spoke a little, then pointed in their direction.

Turning around, Marissa felt her face flush. Being the topic of conversation was something she'd never get used to.

"What's she doing here?" Martha growled in a low tone.

"Who is she?"

"That's Kayla, his former girlfriend. She ran off to Washington and broke his heart. She's got family here but what's she doing in his face? I better go rescue him."

Martha gathered the remnants of her lunch, then glanced at Marissa. "How do I get a hold of you?"

Her first impulse was to pull out her business card, but she stopped before she sabotaged her secret. A napkin would have to do. She quickly wrote her phone number on it and handed it to Martha. "Call me."

Martha put the napkin in her pocket. "I'll come by your hotel about five tonight to get you. Don't worry, I'll get you back before Santa makes his rounds." She threw her garbage away. Before leaving, she bent over near Marissa's ear. "We'll talk about Jared tonight."

CHAPTER 12

The store was crazy all afternoon. Jared mostly watched for empty shelves. Requests for more hams, bags of brown sugar, and candy canes came from every direction. Martha ran out of quarters up front and sent him running to his office safe. He was stopped twice on the way by people asking if he had more canned cranberry sauce. He sent out an SOS to Benny and Chad to help up front.

Their early closing pushed frantic shoppers inside for last minute things. Rather than calming the savage beasts, the Christmas music reminded people that Santa would come tonight which only fueled the frenzy. The excitement of Christmas Eve made the children harder to handle, their mothers constantly reminding them that Santa was watching whether they were naughty or nice.

Jared's team came together and kept people rolling through. Benny left his son in charge of helping customers at the meat counter while he went to find the cranberry sauce. Chad restocked the milk and eggs which disappeared almost as soon as he set them out. Holly's deli emptied as the afternoon went on. Martha ran people through the check stand as quickly as she could. Her years of experience made her fast, but not fast enough to keep up.

Bouncing from one crisis to the other, Jared felt like a firefighter putting out fires wherever the strong wind blew the sparks. This year's last-minute rush seemed much worse than usual. It was all the newbies in town. The mayor ought to do something about it. If he were mayor, he'd quit issuing so many building permits. The small- town feel was disappearing.

But he wasn't mayor so he could only do what he could do. Next year, he wouldn't be so generous in granting holiday leave. His employees would have to stay to help handle the increased business. That would turn him into a tyrant in the eyes of those who had been there a long time, but he had no choice. To keep his business alive, he must become a despot.

The harder he worked, the more a secret thought moved to the top of his worry list. His store was too small to serve his community. He should have expanded into the space next door rather than leasing it to a real estate company. The money they offered was too much to turn down, but it was proving to be a short-sighted decision.

The plans for a larger store would have to wait. Just buying the land for it would cost more than he could afford, yet could he afford not to? He was too poor to go big but too successful to stay small.

He slammed cans of cream of mushroom soup on the shelf. One bounced off and flew back at him, nearly hitting him in the mouth. He paused and took a deep breath. His family had faced adversity before and overcome it. He could do it too. He had to. If he didn't have the store, what else would he do? What else could he do? His father had trained him for it all his life, leaving little time to learn any other vocation.

There wasn't time to think of long-term problems. There was too much to do in the now.

He greeted all he could by name as they passed him. This was his town, and he would serve them to the best of his ability. If that wasn't enough to keep their loyalty, then they deserved the cold, impersonal service of a conglomerate.

When the hands on the clock declared it to be four o'clock, Jared locked the entrance door to his store. Anyone needing one more can of green beans would have to wait until the day after Christmas. The last few customers finished shopping and went on their way. Ten minutes later, the exit door was locked and secured.

They'd survived the rush.

Noting the drooped shoulders and sighs of relief from his crew, he watched as they did their end-of-day tasks. They'd worked together smoothly and without complaint. He was proud of them.

Everyone gathered in the deli before going home, comparing stories of the day. A full basket of frozen goods left by the bathrooms that melted after the shopper abandoned it. The child who ate all the grapes before the mom got to the checkout. The fourteen bottles of pancake syrup, twenty packages of turkey wienies and hotdog buns, and countless bags of chips old Mr. Howell bought for his family's visit on Christmas Day.

Ever since his wife died, his diet had deteriorated to junky, easy-to-fix food. Maybe next Christmas Jared should do a buy-one-get-one-free on wienies for Mr. Howell, or instead, he could fix him a box of healthy foods in appreciation for his continued patronage.

In all his years working at the grocery store, he'd seen lots of strange things in customer orders. He never questioned it or share what he'd seen. Everyone had weird habits; some were just more noticeable than others.

Benny began to dance around, making the bells on his Santa hat jingle with each step. He took Martha by the hand and danced with her to the Christmas music coming over the intercom.

Slipping away to his office, Jared got the Christmas bonus checks out of his safe. They weren't as big as he wished they could be. Profits had been slimmer this year, but he didn't have the heart to take it out of the bonuses. His people meant everything to him. They were the family he didn't have close by. He'd tighten his own belt before making them do it.

On top of it all, all his plans might be canceled by some fancy-schmancy box store. That was the rock crushing him in this hard place. If the rumors were true, there might not be a next year.

Raucous laughter came through the office door. He was missing the fun. Pushing away the blues, he locked the safe and went to join the party.

Everyone was gathered around Benny as he read a humorous Christmas poem he'd written. Although his literary skills weren't the caliber of his butchering skills, it wasn't half bad. When it was over, he bowed to the applauding audience.

Benny glanced at Jared and took off his Santa hat. "And now may I introduce the star of the show...straight from the North Pole...it's who we've all been waiting for...ladies, gents, and germs...make welcome—"

A voice came from the back of the room. "Get on with it, will ya!"

Benny put his hat on Jared. "—the big guy himself...Santa Claus!"

The praises and shouts washed tension out of Jared. He let out his merriest and loudest ho-ho-ho as he went to the middle of the room. "My good elves, thank you for a good year and all the toy-making hours you've put in, especially during this holiday season." He let out a loud whew! "The past couple of days have really been crazy, haven't they?"

He received tired nods in return.

"I said, haven't they?" he asked louder.

Whoops and hollers rose from the gathering as he clapped with them.

He waved his hands in the air to get everyone's attention. When quiet came, he turned serious. "I can't thank you all enough for your good work ethic and customer service skills. Without you, there would be no Sullivan's Food Mart. I'm in your debt." A lump in his throat caused him to pause until he could continue. He waved the checks in the air. "I wish I could give you all a million dollars, but I can't. This will have to do."

Calling out individual names, he asked each person if they'd been naughty or nice before handing them their bonus check.

Hugs and sincere thanks followed along with more cheers. The spirit of love and friendship swirled through the room like wind-swept confetti.

Time flew by without anyone noticing until Martha checked her watch and exclaimed she had to leave. Her statement doused the flame of good times, and everyone said their goodbyes. Families awaited them at home to start their Christmas Eve celebrations and trips to the churches. The good feeling confetti settled to the floor leaving only Jared, Benny, and Chad to clean up.

The three men didn't say much as they moved tables and chairs back to their places. Jared carried the trash out to the bins. Back inside, he noticed his two friends passing signals. "What's going on?"

The two men shuffled and pointed at each other like they dreaded being the first one to say.

It had to be bad news to make these two do this ridiculous dance. Jared grew tired of it. "Chad, you're assistant manager. Spill it."

Benny's shoulders lifted and he continued to move chairs and fuss with how the napkin holders and condiments were lined up.

Motioning both men to follow, Jared went to his office and sat behind his desk. The other two men sat in the chairs in front of it. For several minutes, they just stared at each other.

Tired of the game, Jared said, "You going to tell me or not?"

Chad began. "Julia Siefert, the realtor, came in today. You were busy so she pulled me aside. She's got a meeting next week with representatives from the Food-N-More company about buying that commercial land out by the interstate. She's excited about it because it would be a huge commission for her realty company, but she's afraid of what it would do to downtown."

Sitting back, Jared crossed his arms. The rumors had changed from possible to probable. He rubbed his eyes to hide the emotions welling in them. It was the beginning of the end unless he could persuade the mayor and the landowner to reject what would likely be an amazing deal for the town. The jobs and taxes it would bring in would be huge. Milo Creek would benefit from it. Only he stood to lose.

Benny cleared his throat. "Those bonuses you just passed out. You were very generous with them. Tell me, did you get one?"

Jared pressed his lips together as he gazed at the invoices on his desk. He'd hoped his actions wouldn't come under scrutiny. Some things were better left unknown. "It doesn't matter. You all deserved it. It's my chance to tell you how much I value your work."

Chad leaned forward. "That's all well and good, but it's no way to run a business. I know we're not doing that well. You haven't passed on food price increases as much as you should have. I see the invoices. It's costing more for us to keep the shelves full, but you're not changing the codes in the computer."

Jared didn't want to answer, but he had to. "It's been so busy lately, with the holidays and all. I forgot, but I'll get that done after Christmas." He reached for a piece of paper and made a note.

"That's a job for an office manager. You didn't replace Debbie after she retired. Why? Because you couldn't afford it?"

The grilling was wrenching his insides. Despite doing his best to hide it, Chad and Benny knew the truth. They were smart. Too smart to work for what Jared paid them. If Food-N-More came in, they could go there for bigger salaries. And who could blame them? Chad's family was growing, and Benny had a kid in college. Both needed the money.

But rising prices weren't something Jared wanted to pass on to his customers. So many lived on fixed incomes, although the new influx brought a more affluent crowd into his store. If he could charge one price to his old customers and another price for the newbies, he would. He liked the idea, but it was illegal and would never work.

A faint memory darkened Jared's mind. His father caught him adjusting the total for a customer who didn't have enough money to pay. After closing that night, his father had raged against him, how his heart was too soft to be a good businessman. How he'd run the family business into the ground if he didn't get tough. It was the worse day of his young life and haunted him more and more often. His father's prediction was coming true. The business was doomed. Along with his work family.

He needed help. "What do you suggest I do?" Benny and Chad exchanged glances.

Leaning forward, Chad replied, "You can't keep doing Debbie's job, stock shelves, check customers out, and oversee the store. You need to either hire someone to do the office work or turn more duties over to me. Let me run the store for you while you work in the office. I can stock shelves, watch for shoplifters, and help at the checkout just as good as you." He leaned back. "Trust me enough to do it."

"Trust me to help too," Benny added. "You have to pass those cost rises along and manage the inventory. Otherwise, you'll have to lay people off because you're starting to give away more than you make."

Rubbing his aching forehead, Jared responded, "Some people can barely afford groceries now. If I raise prices too much, they'll be worse off. How can I do that to them?"

Chad stood to lean on the desk. "Quit trying to save the world. Business is business, and you gotta do what you gotta do. If you go bankrupt, it'll cost everyone way more to drive to Dillion or down to Denver. Paying a little more for groceries won't be anything compared to that. Not to mention me, Martha, and the others losing their jobs."

Jared stared at his hands. There was no denying Chad and Benny were right, but he had no regrets. At least not today. The regrets would hit when the town he loved and the people he valued would be without Sullivan's Food Mart.

"You two mutinous dogs," he said with a facetious chuckle. "You're ganging up on me." He swiveled in his chair and made sure the safe was locked. With everything stowed for the night, he stood. "Looks like the new year will bring all kinds of changes. Go home! Your families will wonder where you are. We'll discuss this another day."

As they started turning out lights, Chad asked what plans Jared had for Christmas day. Jared slapped his forehead. He'd forgotten about getting food for the meal he'd promised to cook for his guest.

"I'm having Marissa over for lunch," he told them. "I'll grab some frozen dinners—"

Chad cried out, "To serve to a beautiful woman? No way!"

Benny took him by the arm and led him to the meat case. He wrapped two T-bone steaks and shoved them toward Jared. "At least show a little class."

Chad led him to the frozen food section and picked out a vegetable blend before showing him frozen twice-baked potatoes. "These are my wife's go-to things when the in-laws unexpectedly pop in." His friends topped off the meal with a frozen apple pie and a tub of ice cream. They continued to give him instructions as they walked out the back door and locked it.

On the way home, the troubles of the day were pushed aside by the excitement of having Marissa over. Thoughts of her made him feel warm inside and made his troubles seem lighter. He hardly knew her yet was so drawn to her. He couldn't understand it, but he wasn't sure he wanted to.

Chapter 13

Marissa was mesmerized by the scenery in the window of her hotel room. The sky was pink in the evening's sunset glow turning the snow-covered mountains surrounding town the same color. Never had she seen nature so breathtakingly beautiful. The town seemed serene, like a Hallmark movie about going home to the farm. The few cars going by broke the quiet as their tires crunched through the icy slush on the road. In some ways, she missed the hustle and bustle and bumper-to-bumper traffic of last-minute shoppers and people rushing home. At the same time, she loved the calm and bright setting. The sacredness of the holiday seemed closer.

A call home left her feeling blue and isolated. Panic stirred inside her, feeding on the realization that she was truly stuck here away from home and the people she loved. The man who was supposed to be her family had deserted her, leaving her surrounded by strangers upon whose mercy she must depend.

Her other piece of unfinished business were her tickets to the New Year's Eve Ball in Denver. The swanky affair raised money for a battered women's home, a cause near and dear to her. When her boss found out she was going, he asked her to meet an investor in the Milo Creek store at the ball. Let him know how much they appreciated his support.

She'd spent weeks finding the right ballgown to wear. She chose a fitted red, sequined gown that flared at the bottom with matching shoes to grab Tyler's attention. The tickets to the ball, the tuxedo rental, and a room at the hotel where it was being held were her intended Christmas gifts to him.

The tickets had cost a bundle and were too much to just toss. She could go alone. The crowd would be so large maybe no one would notice she was there without an escort. If anyone asked, she could say he was getting her something or was talking to someone. Before midnight, she'd sneak away. That way, her stag-ness would be concealed.

She was still paying for her unused reservation at the Denver hotel. Once she got a new rental car, she'd leave this charming little town and go to her much plusher room. Room service and old movies would keep her company as the new year came in.

Next year, she'd write the shelter a big, fat check and forget the ball.

Her phone dinged, reminding her of her promise to spend Christmas Eve with Martha. Stashing her computer and notes, she got ready for whatever would come next. She applied a little lipstick and ran a comb through her hair.

Her hands shook slightly. She was stepping into the unknown. While Martha seemed friendly, she didn't really know her. The past couple of days had pushed her into uncharted territory, and this additional venture outside her comfort zone added more stress. It wasn't that she minded it, but it was getting to be too much.

A honk from outside her door announced her ride had arrived. A deep breath followed by a long exhale steeled her nerves as she grabbed her purse and opened the door. Smile, wave, she told herself. That would set the evening off in the right direction on her part. She left her motel room and her sense of security behind.

Christmas carols poured out of the sedan that had seen better days. Martha greeted her warmly and related how excited she was to have someone to share Christmas Eve with. Singing along with the carols on the radio, Martha backed out and bounced down the street.

Marissa joined in with the singing while taking note of the route they were taking. Down Main Street to the second right, then down a dark street. She was relieved when Martha pulled into a driveway before the end of the first block. It would be easy to find her way back to the hotel if need be.

Snowflakes started falling when they walked out of the detached garage. Martha let out a whoop as happiness filled her face. "Snow on Christmas Eve! That means good luck for the coming year!" She looked at Marissa, then paused. "That's what I've always been told. Don't you believe?"

The idea seemed preposterous to Marissa at first, but more and more flakes fell, gently floating between heaven and earth. One landed on the dark fabric of her coat. Its intricate, lacy, six-sided form became visible in the streetlight. Fragile, unique, and beautiful. Made by nature just to sit on her arm for a brief time. The magic of the season was tangible in the ice crystals.

The revelation washed away her apprehension. She let out a whoop. "Yes, I believe!" With arms spread wide, she lifted her face to the sky and turned a circle. "I believe!"

Martha let out a laugh. "Come inside before you believe too much and fall on the ice."

They entered the small house through the kitchen. As Martha set her sacks of groceries on the countertop, she explained how she usually spent Christmas Eve alone, but this year was extra special. She had a guest.

Marissa took her coat and snow boots off and pulled slippers out of her bag. The house reflected its age but was clean and neat. The kitchen had an eating bar for one that opened into the living room. End tables hugged a recliner in front of a large flatscreen TV while a worn sofa sat by the wall. A doorway at the far end of the room must have led to the bedrooms and bath.

A black feline face peeked around the end of the sofa before ducking away when Marissa looked at it.

"My castle ain't much, but it's mine and it's paid for," Martha remarked as she put groceries away. "Make yourself at home. I hope you don't mind frozen pizza, popcorn, and a movie. I always watch *It's a Wonderful Life* on Christmas Eve." She pushed a diet Coke toward Marissa. "Hope you like this kind."

"I do." Marissa popped the top and took a sip. Her shoulders relaxed as the bubbly fluid went down her throat. "I appreciate being invited to your home. I mean, you don't know me yet you invited me here. I'll never forget your kindness."

Martha set the oven and turned it on. She sniffed before speaking. "I couldn't stand to let you spend Christmas Eve alone in a hotel room. It would've ruined my celebration, such as it is." She got her own soda.

Something touched Marissa's leg. She looked down to see the black cat rubbing her before going over to do the same to Martha's.

"There you are, Marvin! I wondered where you were." She picked up the cat and held it close. "He's my boyfriend. Keeps me company." The purring started as soon as she stroked his fur. "I tell him all my complaints and gripes. He's a good listener."

Unable to resist, Marissa ran her hand down the cat's back. "I had a cat when I was living at home. My mom cried when I said I would take her when I moved out. I left her there since she meant so much to Mom."

"I'd never left home if I had to give up my cat." Martha filled a bowl with cat food and the two ladies watched as Marvin chowed down.

After washing her hands, Martha ripped the pizza box open with the strength of a wrestler. "I got pepperoni. I hope you like it," she said as she slid the pizza out of the box and onto a cookie sheet. She sprinkled the top with a little more cheese before popping it in the oven. "It's really hard trying to decide what to cook for company, but I figured I'll fix for me and hope you like it too. It was a crazy day, and I'm too tired to cook anything else."

Marissa would have been happy with a baloney sandwich but appreciated what had been done. "I'm glad you're not going to any trouble. Pizza is my favorite food so it's perfect for me."

A broad smile came across Martha's face as she set the timer. "I knew I liked you for a reason. Now that that's done, let's relax and talk about men."

Martha settled into her recliner while Marissa sat on the sofa. It was worn in the right places which made it the perfect place for relaxing with a new friend. All the tension crept out of her shoulders, this time to stay.

Putting the footrest up, Martha said, "Tell me about this bum who stood you up."

Marissa took a drink of soda and leaned her elbow on the sofa's arm. "His name is Tyler. We met in elementary school, and I decided he was the one I was going to marry. He's the only guy I've ever dated. I even refused a scholarship so I could attend the college where he went. That was my first mistake."

A snort and a roll of the eyes came from Martha, but she never interrupted.

Marvin jumped in her lap and curled up.

Continuing her story, Marissa said, "While in college, we talked about the future. Where our careers would take us, what it would be like to be married. I thought it was all sewed up. All I was waiting on was for him to propose. We found jobs, me in Dallas and him in Denver, and worked it out. We talked every day, and we met at least once a month. I thought we had a good system. But when he came to Dallas at Thanksgiving, he seemed uneasy. Sort of jumpy."

Another swig of soda helped Marissa go on. "I thought he was nervous about popping the question. Most men are."

She paused for a sign of consensus, but Martha didn't say anything.

Disappointed in not getting agreement for that statement, she went on. "I convinced myself that was it. I was sure that at Christmas, he'd give me a diamond ring. I mean, what a perfect Christmas gift! I was already looking at my calendar and picking out wedding dates."

She cast a sideways glance at Martha who seemed genuinely interested. Why wouldn't she say something?

The lull in conversation wasn't being filled so Marissa kept going.

"I had a business trip planned up here for next week. I thought it would be fun if I came a few days early to surprise him for the holidays. Then...he was..." Her throat got tight like Tyler's invisible hand was reaching out to choke her. She tried to rub it away.

"Hon, you all right?" Martha leaned over her armrest. Her eyes were soft with compassion. "You need something stronger than diet Coke?"

"No, thank you," Marissa whimpered. She buried her face in her hands. This was ridiculous. Tears stung her eyes, but she gritted her teeth to keep them inside. Crying was not polite in social situations. Especially on Christmas Eve. She must be jolly. Save the tears for the end of the movie. She always cried when George Bailey found out he had lots of friends. At least then, her crying wouldn't be embarrassing.

The sofa moved next to her and an arm went around her shoulders. Martha's voice came close to her ear. "Go ahead, hon, cry it out."

The words and the hug broke the dam that had held back her emotions. She buried her head in the soft shoulder and let the wave gush through the breach.

Marissa let the tears flow. The warm embrace felt good, much like her mother would have done had she been there. A few of the tears were dedicated to missing her mother.

A shrill buzzer went off. With her outburst, she'd missed smelling the pizza as it finished cooking. Martha stayed beside her, but Marissa sat upright and looked for tissues. She saw makeup staining Martha's shirt. "I've ruined your blouse!"

Martha looked down quickly and laughed. "If you feel better, it's worth it. Besides, this old thing is washable. It'll come out so don't worry about it." She reached over and got a box of tissues and gave them to Marissa before hurrying to the kitchen to turn off the timer alarm.

The smell of pizza flooded the room as she opened the oven door.

Feeling emotionally lighter, Marissa wiped her eyes and nose, then joined Martha in the kitchen.

The pizza was quickly divided in half, then fourths. A quick grace was said and the women returned to the living room to eat. In between bites, Marissa told the rest of the story of catching Tyler with that younger woman. This time, Martha interjected comments along the way.

With the second quarter of pizza, Martha gave a summary of her years with Jim, her husband killed in a work accident fourteen years before. Her three kids were teenagers, and she had to find a way to support them. She had no work experience, but Jared's father gave her a job when no one else would. His generosity brought her loyalty. With her kids grown and living far away, she volunteered for church and community activities.

Both stories and the pizza ended at the same time.

Marissa leaned against the sofa back. Her stomach was full, and her heart was emptied of its turmoil. It hadn't been the Christmas Eve she'd planned for, but it provided the healing she needed.

Martha gathered the plates and took them to the kitchen. "Your face is relaxed. See? I told you a good cry would help you out."

"I'm embarrassed about my ugly crying. I usually have much more control over my emotions."

Martha stopped and pointed at her. "If you keep your emotions inside, they will fester and spread like a cancer." She rinsed the plates off and put them in the dishwasher. "My momma always told me bad feelings will eat your insides so it's better to get them out of there." The noise from the kitchen paused. "We used to talk about everything. She's the only person who could get me to spill my guts. I could never keep a secret from her."

Marvin let out a meow.

"Except for you, Marvin dear. You know all my secrets."

"I'm very close to my mom," Marissa said. "She's one of my best friends. I don't know what I'll do after..." her voice stuck. Only a hard swallow let her go on, "...after she's gone."

The cat trotted over to stare at Marissa. Its yellow-eyed gaze was unnerving. A little too mystical for her liking. The cat finally went into the hallway out of sight, much to her relief.

Finishing her chores, Martha washed her hands and dug something out of her cloth grocery bags. Tossing a bag of M&Ms to Marissa as she passed, she went to the TV and put a DVD in the player. "My momma is gone, and I still miss her after all these years. A girl never gets over losing her momma, but I hope to see her again someday." She sniffed and got a different remote. "But enough sad stuff. Let's watch a movie that will make us cry happy tears."

The familiar music started as Marissa curled up on the sofa with her bag of candy. Tonight, calories didn't count. That was part of the magic of Christmas.

After the movie started, Marissa wished they'd watched another one, like White Christmas or The Santa Clause. Watching this movie hit too close to her heart because she and George Bailey had a lot in common. His unfulfilled dreams matched her shattered expectations of a life with Tyler, especially on the night she thought he'd propose. The cry had done her good, but it hadn't taken away the feelings of failure.

By the end of the movie, both women were sniffing and passing the tissue box back and forth.

Martha threw a handful of M&Ms in her mouth.

Her own bag of candy unopened, Marissa put it aside. The movie had done nothing to cheer her or make her crave the sweetness of her favorite candy. Now what? Maybe it was time to go back to the motel.

"Friends and family," sniffled Martha as she struggled to get out of her recliner. "It doesn't get any better than that. Except for chocolate. Want some hot cocoa and popcorn before we start Elf?"

The mention of the funny movie perked Marissa up. She needed to laugh. Her mother told her that was the way to push out the blues. Laughter solved a lot of troubles, she'd said. She had plenty of troubles. Bring on the laughter.

"No popcorn for me, but feel free to have it yourself. Can I help?" Marissa didn't want to feel like a burden. She took her empty soda can to the kitchen, leaving the M&Ms behind. They were beginning to appeal to her.

Martha gave her a bag of popcorn to put in the microwave, then poured a quart of chocolate milk into a pan. "My kids loved when I heated up chocolate milk. I can't remember how it got started but it's the only way I make hot cocoa now. It's the best!"

A few minutes later, armed with a large mug of hot cocoa, Marissa settled down in her seat again. "This is fun! I'm so glad you invited me over. Thanks for letting me crash your Christmas Eve."

Martha sat quietly for a few seconds. She sniffed. "Girl, you needed someone to talk to, and I needed company tonight. It's hard listening to my coworkers talk about their plans with their families knowing I'll be alone. I needed a friend, and so did you. God put us together tonight because we needed each other. Let's enjoy the blessing and have a good time. Eat, drink, and be merry, as Solomon said."

Wrapping both her hands around the warm mug, Marissa lifted it to her lips to get a small sip. The cocoa and the words warmed her body and soul.

Marissa had seen Elf before but seeing it with Martha was like seeing it for the first time. Their whoops and catcalls and laughter rang the rafters of the little house. By the time it was over, both complained about how their belly muscles hurt. Marissa's M&M bag was almost empty.

Martha hit the stop button for the DVD player and sat silently with a huge smile on her face.

Her smile no less small, Marissa joined in the silence, glad she'd come. The journey outside her comfort zone became a night to fondly remember.

"We haven't talked about Jared yet," Martha remarked without moving.

The words popped her happy balloon. It was time to get serious. "Tell me about him."

Martha spent half an hour talking about a hard-driving father and the mild-mannered son who took over the store when his father died. It was no secret that Jared wasn't the businessman his father was, and the store was struggling financially. The biggest problem, the one nobody talked about, was Benny was leaving. She wasn't even sure Jared knew about it. Benny wanted to start his own business, a customized butchering and meat shop that specialized in working with nearby ranchers and farmers. Sullivan's would continue to have a meat department by purchasing meat from Benny's company.

Jared rarely dated but he'd fallen head over heels in love with Kayla who was a bookkeeper at City Hall. He had been crazy about her, but no one thought they were a good fit. Kayla had ambitions that couldn't be contained in Milo Creek. When she was offered a job with some big accounting firm in Washington D.C., she grabbed it. Jared did his best to persuade her to stay, but the big city and its never-ending opportunities drew her away. He was heartbroken and never seemed to quite get over her. He rarely dated now but would occasionally bring a date to a city festival.

No woman could compete with his dedication to the store. His mantra of never leaving for love or money seemed to wall him off from any woman who took a liking to him. He was the lonely guardian of his fortress, afraid to lower the drawbridge lest another enemy creep inside.

"He's a wonderful person, but a sad man," Martha observed. "Kayla being here isn't helping. Word is she brought her new love interest home to meet her parents. That can't be easy for him to see."

Marissa tossed another M&M in her mouth. She felt sorry for him, yet she understood him. She'd gone all in on one person only to be rejected. They had heartache in common.

Martha kept talking. "She seems to be living the life in D.C. and that man she brought home...girl, he's one fine-looking man! That has to jab Jared straight in the heart."

Marissa sighed. "Poor guy."

Martha turned in her recliner to look straight at Marissa. "But that's changed a little. Ever since he brought you down the mountain, he's...he's got a little twinkle in his eye. And don't forget, he pointed to you when he was talking with Kayla."

Shaking her head, Marissa countered, "He was just showing her the ragamuffin he pulled out of a snowbank. I'm like a lost puppy that followed him home." Inside, she hoped that wasn't true. He was her knight in down-filled armor who saved her from an icy fate.

Martha's eyes narrowed. "I know him. Know him well. He sees something special in you." She sat back in her recliner and sighed. "I can tell you're a very nice young woman who's been hurt as badly as he has. Have you thought that maybe God is bringing you together when you need each other the most? Just like he did you and me?" She cocked her head and peered at Marissa.

The thought had never entered her mind. She was here to do a job, a job that would hurt Jared more than Kayla had.

The more she got to know Jared, Martha, Edith, and the others, the worst her job got. But it was like an avalanche coming down the mountain; there was no stopping it. Maybe she could warn people what was coming, and they could make plans to act rather than react after the news broke. Every disaster brought new opportunities to rebuild. If only she could get him to rebuild. There were so many things Jared could do in that location.

Words and ideas jumbled around in her head like pieces in a shaken jigsaw puzzle box. She had to fit them together right to make the plan work. She had enough clout in her company to pull a few strings. Benny could have his meat store. Martha could have a great job at Food-N-More and so could the others.

But what about Jared? He needed to listen to her, but he was too busy. She needed to get him alone. Her extra ticket to the ball might provide the opportunity, but would he go? She needed at least one ally to persuade him.

"Can I ask you something, Martha? "Of course."

"I have tickets to the New Year's Eve Ball in Denver—"

Eyes wide and eyebrows raised as high as they would go, Martha gasped as she leaned over the arm of her recliner. "You mean that hoity-toity affair that only rich people go to? That one?"

The outburst caught Marissa by surprise. Her voice caught in her throat and only managed a squeaky yeah. A sip of hot chocolate cleared the way for her to explain how she'd bought the tickets to support a cause she strongly supported and as a gift for Tyler. Tyler was out, but it was such a waste to let the tickets go unused. She needed a date.

"Do you think Jared would go with me? Showing up alone would give a bad impression. With those affairs, looks are everything."

Martha sat back. Her brows shifted up and down as her internal debate went through the rounds. They shot up right before she said, "I don't know. He's a plain sort of guy so a shindig like that might scare him. He's not one for stepping into unusual situations."

Boy, that was the truth. The man was stuck in his ways. Like a boot caught in the mud that wouldn't come out.

"Still…" Martha looked off into space. "We've been trying to get him to take a few days off and get away from the store. He could use the break. If we all worked on him, he might go for it. He could stay with his sister while he's there."

Interrupting, Marissa said, "I'd pay for his hotel room on New Year's Eve. His tux rental, food, everything. All he has to do is show up and look good."

The frown returned to Martha's face. "A tux?" She shook her head. "The only times I see him in a suit is at funerals. And it's always the same suit."

Marissa shook her head. "It's a black-tie affair. Tux is minimal, with tails optional. He'd be turned away at the door in a suit. Even a new one."

Martha sat back and stroked her chin. Her cat jumped into her lap and began to purr. Stroking her pet, she let out a hardy laugh. "You're right, Marvin. He should go. Marissa, you do the asking. I'll do the manipulating."

With that, Project Cinderguy began.

CHAPTER 14

The sky was still dark when Jared woke. Christmas morning always felt odd to him. His usual routine was disrupted with no place to go and no one to see. No emails to send or deliveries expected. No rowdy kids to knock over a display, and no complaints about how much a can of pinto beans had gone up. No one needed him. He was useless every Christmas Day.

As happened every other year, his sister's family was visiting her in-laws in Phoenix. In the years they were home for the holiday, he'd drive to Denver to be with them. He was especially fond of watching his niece and nephews open their gifts. Their excitement put the joy in Christmas. The food was as abundant as the noise. When he got tired of listening to his sister's arguments on why he should sell the store, he'd retire to the den to shoot pool with his brother-in-law. The trip was usually his only foray out of Milo Creek. This year, there would be none. He didn't mind, but his friends thought it was all wrong.

When his parents were alive, he always had family around, but with them gone and his siblings scattered to the four winds, he was alone most of the time. He'd become a hermit of sorts. Instead of holing up in a cave on the side of the mountain, he holed up in the store. Some days he resented it, but he wouldn't break his word to his father. He'd keep the store running for as long as he lived.

As he lay in bed contemplating his lonely fate, he remembered this Christmas Day was an unusual one. Marissa was coming.

His heart beat faster, rousing him to get out of bed. He needed time to get his home neatened and ready for such an auspicious visitor.

Without her knowing it and without his consent, his heart fluttered when she was around. He didn't like it, but he couldn't help it. The feeling was as baffling as trying to figure out why people would leave Milo Creek when everything was so perfect.

The big question was, how did she feel about him? She seemed grateful for his help, but was that all she felt? Why should he care? Her company would be good on an otherwise dreary holiday. As soon as she found a ride to Denver, she'd be gone forever, and his hermit lifestyle would resume.

While he dressed, he went through what he needed to do to prepare dinner. Firing up the grill to cook Benny's generous gift would take about ten minutes. The frozen vegetables needed five minutes of boiling. The brown-and-serve rolls would need more time. The precooked baked potatoes, he didn't know, but the instructions would say. The alarm on his cell phone could help remind him when to do what. What had he done before that electronic gadget?

He surveyed the living room and picked up his discarded newspaper from last night to put in the recycle bin. The house looked pretty good. He'd changed nothing from when his parents lived here because he liked it that way. Besides, he only slept here. Most of his waking hours were at the store so why waste money on redecorating? His cleaning lady kept everything neat and clean. It was his one indulgence. He could clean it himself, but he liked it better when someone else cleaned it. Plus. he had the satisfaction of giving work to a single mother trying to support her children.

The smell of coffee soon permeated the house, setting off his caffeine craving. Pouring himself a cup, he grabbed a bagel before going to his home office to review his email accounts. The usual greetings from his siblings were there, and he quickly sent out responses asking for pictures of their celebrations. Even a hermit needed human contact once in a while.

His family duties were soon completed. Before tackling his store emails, he got another cup of coffee. The accountant had sent a preliminary report and asked for the latest numbers as soon as possible. His heart sank when he saw the downward trend. All his sales, special services, and personal contact with customers hadn't stopped the decline but maybe slowed it. What more could he do to make the curve turn up again?

It didn't take an analyst to know where some of his business was going. On his way back from the delivery to the Spruce Canyon Lodge, he'd noticed the full parking lot of the Dollar Store. The other day, he'd seen a plastic Food-N-More sack caught in a tree, its red and blue logo flashing like a cop's light. People were driving that far to get groceries rather than supporting his store.

The only thing keeping him alive was Benny's department, and he knew Benny wanted to start his own meat market. But if he left, it would be the Jenga block that would topple his business.

Jared slammed the laptop shut and got up. Following the same path his father had taken, he began pacing along the worn line on the carpet.

The Sullivan family was thankful for their grandfather's foresight in hiring Benny's grandfather to work at the store. It was a decades-long relationship that benefited both families.

Benny was one of his best friends. Jared gave him a free hand to manage the meat department any way he wanted. He even gave him a percentage of the take on it. Wasn't that enough? Maybe not. With his own store, Benny could expand his butcher shop, offer more selections of meat, and oversee everything. He'd be his own boss and who could blame him for wanting that.

He knew the problem with his store. The aisles of Sullivan's were barely wide enough for two carts to pass. Their selections were small because of limited shelf space. Everything seemed dependent on space. There just wasn't enough room in the building.

That wasn't the only problem. All the rumors were showing signs of coming true. A big grocery chain was coming in soon. If that happened, his livelihood would be lost. Then what? He had no other skills than running a grocery store.

The grandfather clock chimed the time, reminding him he still had a lot to do. Embarrassed for Marissa to see the pacing track, he moved rugs around until it didn't show. Maybe it was time for hardwood floors. Martha told him those were in vogue. He remembered the hardwood floors his grandmother had when she lived in the house. His mother put carpet over them when she became mistress of the house.

The sun peeked through his kitchen window, drawing his attention away from his problems. A blanket of snow lay on the sidewalk and driveway, waiting to be moved. Only about six inches had fallen during the night so it wouldn't take long for his practiced hand to dig out. He finished his coffee and bagel.

Shoveling snow gave him a way to burn off his nervous energy. The snow was slightly wet, making it easy to clump together. The perfect mix for making snowballs. Down the block, his neighbor was hard at work running his snowblower. It might be too early for the noise on a regular weekend day, but it was Christmas morning and kids would have their parents up by now.

He ran his shovel along the sidewalk as his mind went to a different place. Marissa tantalized him. His insides felt funny. He couldn't deny it. Nothing had quite been the same since he'd pulled her from the snow. Seeing her at the store made him very self-conscious. What did she think of his enterprise? Dare he hope she'd help him with the business one day?

He stopped shoveling and shook his head. His heart kept forgetting she lived in Dallas and would go home as soon as she could. If nothing else, the snow and cold would drive her back to warmer climes. He'd return to his rut and occasionally think back on the day he was a hero to someone.

Throwing the last shovel full of snow onto the snowbank, he yelled out a holiday greeting to a neighbor shoveling his driveway and let loose an off-target snowball. After tossing out a seasonal greeting, the neighbor lobbed a snowball that made Jared move to avoid getting hit.

He surveyed his work. The forecasted sunshine should take care of the little patches of ice.

The phone vibrated in his pocket. Taking his gloves off, Jared's phone displayed his sister's number. They talked about the Arizona warmth and how she wished he'd take some time off to go somewhere warm as well. Wishing her a merry Christmas, he hung up, never having mentioned his guest coming for dinner. He wasn't ready to tell anyone yet. Later, when the time was right, he'd use the news to give his sister a shock. He loved catching her off-guard, leaving her stammering. Those opportunities were few, and he wouldn't let this one pass by.

Back in the garage, he looked through boxes on the shelves. He'd brought home the last unsold Christmas tree. It would take a lot of decorations and lights to make the pitiful-looking shrub look merry.

Somewhere amid the mess were two full boxes of his mother's Christmas decorations, but where? He hadn't decorated for Christmas since...he couldn't remember the last time. He moved boxes and shook a few, but his search was fruitless and time was passing.

Which box had the most dust and looked unused? His eyes immediately went to the corner where cobwebs were the thickest.

Getting a step ladder, he went to the top shelf and shook a box. The muffled sound of jingle bells was faintly heard. Success!

Getting the box down was tricky because it was heavier than he thought, and the snow on his boots didn't help. Slowly, rung by rung, he made his way down. After brushing off the thick dust, he found the tree stand in it. Soon the sad-looking tree stood in the front window inside his house.

Untangling the lights took more time than he'd allotted for it. At one point, he nearly threw them out along with the tree but kept at it. He wanted things perfect for Marissa. Finally achieving success, he wound them around the tree, then quickly hung some of the ornaments, trying not to think about the memories packed inside each one. He'd let the family Christmas remembrances flow when he took everything down. As a final touch, Jared slid a package under the tree. Nothing special was inside. Just a couple of things from the clearance bin.

Stepping back, he surveyed his work that sat where so many other Christmas trees had been. The lights flickered and blinked. The ornaments reflected and glittered with the lights. It wasn't the prettiest tree that had ever stood there, but it wasn't bad. He could almost smell the hot cocoa and cinnamon rolls his mother used to make on Christmas morning. He missed her.

Everything was set out in the kitchen, ready for use. The dining table was set with his mother's holiday tablecloth, cloth napkins, good china, and sterling silverware. Two red candles flanked a potted poinsettia left over from the store's stock. Several other flowers were strategically placed around the house so she'd think he'd decorated for the holidays when all he'd really done was save them from the dumpster.

He checked his watch. Just enough time to shower and shave before he had to leave to go get her. The plan was coming together. His heart raced faster as time grew shorter.

He dressed in what he usually wore to work. Slacks and a long-sleeved shirt. It was all he had other than his black suit for funerals. Digging deep in his closet, he found his one and only item of Christmas apparel. A red tie with little Santas on it. It would look good against his dark green shirt and would set the mood for the day. He gave his house one last look before he left for Edith's motel.

His heart almost stopped when Marissa opened her hotel door and waved, looking as beautiful as any woman he'd ever seen. Her black, form-fitting clothes were topped with a long red Christmas jacket that had Santa, Christmas trees, and gifts all around it.

His mouth suddenly went dry when he got out of his vehicle. He smiled instead of talking.

"Hi," she said. She held her arms out. "Too gaudy?"

He squeaked a no as emotion filled his chest and throat.

She let out a laugh. "Let me get my coat, and I'm ready."

He nodded as she went to get it. He mentally flogged himself for being such a dolt. Sucking in a long breath calmed his nerves enough for him to tell her she looked nice when she stepped out.

"I'm happy you're joining me for Christmas." The words sounded lame to him. He hoped it didn't to her.

She gave him a smile that lit up the whole day. "Thank you for the invitation. I'm glad I don't have to spend Christmas alone. I'm looking forward to getting to know you better."

What did she mean by that? He mused over the statement as he held the SUV door for her. She probably wouldn't be going with him if she had any other choice. It was only happenstance that she was coming at all. He was out of his league, but he'd be a good host and do the best he could to show her a good time.

This might be the longest Christmas day of his life. Or the best one. Time would tell which.

CHAPTER 15

Marissa hoped Jared wasn't getting sick. His hands shook slightly as he turned the steering wheel, and he kept clearing his throat like he was getting a cold. Those tickets to the New Year's Eve ball would go to waste if he was ill.

A short drive later, they pulled in front of a home with gingerbread trim along the large front porch and the two-story peaked roof. Piles of snow lay along the driveway and sidewalks. Bare deciduous trees and snow-laden evergreens would provide lots of shade from the summer sun. A tall blue spruce stood far above the roof in the backyard. The mountains outside of town pushed the horizon high into the sky.

Quaint. Homey. The words popped into Marissa's head. It fit the image she had of Jared.

"Here we are!" he said in a crackling voice. He cleared his throat again. "It's not much, but it's home." He got out and ran to her side of the SUV to open the door. She put her hand in his as she put her bag strap on her shoulder.

As he stood there looking like a teenager on his first date, Marissa finally got it. She thought they were friends spending the holiday together, but it was more to him. It was a date. Martha told her he rarely did this. No wonder he was nervous.

Knowing it was a date changed the mood of the day. As much as she was attracted to him, she didn't mind. Her intent was to ask him on a first date to the New Year's Eve ball. He beat her to the punch, that's all. If they had a good day, her invitation might be accepted, and Martha wouldn't have to orchestrate a way to get him to go.

Going inside the house was like entering a time capsule. Everything looked decades old, but like Edith's motel, it was neat and clean. Heavy drapes narrowed the windows, and sheer curtains hung over miniblinds that were open just enough to tell the sun was shining.

A wall in the living room was covered with family pictures. Some were old black-and-white photos, but others were more recent. The women and children looked pleasant, some of them smiling. In the center were two large photos of men, both with the same brown hair, similar facial features, and stern looks. Jared had the same appearance, minus the frown.

The tree, tablecloth, and poinsettias brightened the room and made the otherwise dull house look festive.

"I'm surprised you're not spending the holiday with your family." She turned to face him.

He shrugged. "My brother lives in Pennsylvania which is too far to travel. One sister lives in California, and the other is in Denver, but she's with her in-laws in Arizona this year."

"So you're alone too." She looked away, not wanting to see if he looked sad or happy.

Her heart froze when she saw one wrapped present under the tree. Surely it wasn't for her. She'd brought an envelope for Jared outlining her proposal about the ball. The mystery of how to give it to him became clear.

"Benny sent some really nice steaks for us to eat. It's not really traditional Christmas food, but they'll be good."

Marissa put on her best smile. "This is a nontraditional Christmas so steak is perfect. From what I've heard, it's the best steak around."

He let out a big breath. "I was afraid you might be a vegetarian. I had a plan B if you were."

She laughed. "I'm from Texas. I eat beef."

He fumbled around a little as if not knowing what to do with himself. His eyes darted around as if searching for a place to land. The silence was filled with uneasy energy.

She stared at him, trying to read what was going on inside him. She might as well be frank. "Do I make you nervous? I can go back to the motel if I make you uncomfortable. I don't want to ruin your day off."

His mouth sagged as his eyebrows went up. "Nervous? No, I'm happy to have company today." He looked down at his hands. "I...I just wanted to make a good impression."

Taking his hands in hers brought his eyes to her face as she said, "You saved my life. You can't make a better impression than that."

She studied his reddened face. This man was truly humble. How refreshing! Too often the men she worked with and met outside of work were overconfident which turned her off. Here was a man who wore his emotions on his sleeve and was honest about how he felt and lived. The antithesis of Tyler and all the others. He was someone she'd like to know better.

"Look," she let out a breath, "can we just be two friends spending a day together? Let's relax and get better acquainted."

Emotions swirled through his eyes until the lines on his face faded and a smile moved his mouth. "You're right. We should get to know each other better." He gestured toward the sofa. They each sat on an end and faced each other. "Where do we start?"

Marissa waved her hand at the wall with all the photos. "Tell me about this house and your family."

For the next hour, Jared regaled her with stories of how his grandfather was a traveling salesman who wanted to be at home with his family. He'd seen an advertisement for a general goods store for sale in a little mining town in Colorado. Taking the risk, he sent money to buy it sight unseen and moved his family to Milo Creek. He got to stay home to work, plus the store gave his children a place to learn and develop a good work ethic. He recruited a man from a local butcher shop to set up the meat market for which the store became so famous. When he retired, Jared's father took over the store. For thirty years, he ran the store, getting rid of the dried goods to focus more on groceries and expanding the meat department. When Jared's father retired, he was the only one of his siblings interested in the family business.

Pride in his heritage was evident with every word Jared spoke, but each word was like a needle pushed into her. She was there to end the legacy.

She did her best to keep a pleasant and interested look on her face, but inside, she was a mess. Her stomach was in a knot, and her chest was tightening. Few mom-and-pop stores survived once a Food-N- More came to town.

Her superiors kept reminding her it was business, not personal. But Jared's tale made it personal.

Like gasoline in a car, the money and profits were the driving force of business. The Food-N-More corporation pushed and prodded her to find them places to build and take over. It secured her position and large salary but ate away at her soul. Looking at herself in the mirror had become more difficult with each small business owner's dream she shattered. She didn't like how she earned money.

Her own family had toiled night and day to find a way out of poverty so she knew how much work it had taken for the Sullivan family to make a success out of their grocery store. There had to be a way to protect it. Somehow, she had to convince him that changing his business plan would allow it to continue under a different banner. Transitioning would save him from bankruptcy.

As he went on, he switched to talking about the pressures he felt to succeed. The space limitations. The rising prices he knew his older customers couldn't afford. The increasing demands for more selection. The emptying of his heart piled up between them. The lines on his brow returned as he talked more to himself than to her. He probably talked to himself a lot. Being alone did that to people.

Maybe she'd become that way too.

"I must be boring you," he said suddenly.

Marissa quickly looked up at him. "No. I'm a believer in talking things out when there's a problem. I don't mind listening."

He adjusted in his seat on the end of the sofa. "I've said enough. Tell me about you. What do you do for a living?"

Looking at her hands in her lap, Marissa pressed her lips together. The question felt like she'd been pushed out on a tightrope and told to walk. She had to maintain her balance to keep peace in this new friendship.

"I'm a lawyer. Currently, I work for a large corporation with nationwide holdings. I travel a lot, but I'd rather be home. And speaking of home—"

"What corporation?"

There was that question she dreaded most, but she had a rehearsed response. "I handle a lot of sensitive material so I cannot say." Looking at her hands again, her mind scrambled for something else. "And speaking of home, I grew up with four brothers."

Glancing at him, his eyes held questions before he looked away. "The only girl, huh. Bet you were spoiled."

Relief at avoiding a taboo topic came out in the form of a silly laugh. "Maybe just a little. Boys were afraid to call me for a date."

His worry lines were gone, replaced by a smile. "I bet. Are you close to your brothers?"

Marissa sat back in her seat. He'd taken the bait to lure him away from her job. She appreciated his willingness to move on. Maybe the worst was behind.

"I'm close to most of them," she replied. "One's a nurse in Houston. One owns his own construction business in Fort Worth. One's in the Air Force stationed in Japan. The other, we have no idea where he is. He got into drugs and other bad things. He took off after Mom and Dad kicked him out of the house, and we haven't heard from him since." A lump cut off any more words. No one knew if he was alive or dead. The family clung to hope and prayers that he'd recover someday and come home.

"Family dynamics are very tricky sometimes," Jared said softly. "My dad expected my oldest brother to take over the business, but he'd have nothing to do with it. To spite my dad, he joined the Army. When he got out, he went to college and is a teacher and coach." Jared smiled. "It fits him. He's much happier doing that than he would have been tending the store. My sisters flat refused to work there after they graduated high school. One married a guy who works for the railroad. My other sister is an accountant who works out of her home in California. She does the books for the store so she's involved in a way."

"Sounds like the business was thrust upon you rather than you choosing it. If given the choice, would you have been happier doing something else?"

His eyes got a faraway look in them as he leaned back and crossed his arms. "I had big plans until my brother enlisted in the Army. When I was a teenager, I read a book about Frank Lloyd

Wright and was amazed. I wanted to be an architect and design buildings like his. Creative. Beautiful. Unusual." He stared into the what-might-have-been and a sad look came over his face. He blinked away the dreams and murmured. "As it turned out, I was the only child left. I had to take the store."

"Your dad could have sold it."

A fire flared in his eyes when he looked at her. "He would never do that. It's our family inheritance, he told me. Grandpa set it up for us, and how dare any of his sons allow that dream to die." The fire died down. "My oldest brother told me he hid behind a chair when my dad asked Grandfather if he could go to college. It became an ugly scene between the two that ended with my dad working at the store for the rest of his life." He closed his eyes and winced like the memory had slapped him.

His shoulders slumped. "I had no choice, just like he didn't have a choice. On his deathbed, I gave Dad my word I would keep the store going. He left the business to me in his will. Just me."

A lump swelled in Marissa's throat. His father's dream was his prison. An unwanted burden that had morphed into a possession not to be forsaken. Devotion to a heritage was an honorable thing, but it could blind a person to what other opportunities might lie beyond.

"That's tough," she remarked as softly as the lump would allow. "Seems unfair. Your siblings got to follow their dreams, but you didn't."

Jared uncrossed his arms and rubbed his forehead, then smiled. "It's fine. I like the store, and the employees are my family. I wouldn't have that if I were an architect in a big city somewhere."

She stared at him. He was so entangled in his family roots there was no escape for him. He'd buried his own ambitions to live up to what his father wanted him to do. He was clinging to a sinking boat.

Her eyes stung a little, making her look at her hands to hide them. "Have you always wanted to be a lawyer at a big corporation?"

His question pierced its way inside her. She took a deep breath before looking at him. "My grandfather had a profound influence on me as well."

She recounted how her grandfather had worked hard to build a construction business based on old-fashioned verbal and handshake agreements. All of it was undone by unscrupulous businessmen with their legal documents and courts. Everything he'd worked for and hoped to pass on to his children was taken away with a bang of the judge's gavel. After that, his eyes lost their glint, and his hair quickly turned gray. She'd watched the transformation as a teenager. Determination to help people like him avoid the same pitfalls pushed her to be at the top of her class in law school. After she reached that goal, the lure of making big dollars pushed her off course.

"I wanted to be the kind of lawyer that helped people like Grandfather in setting up small businesses, estate planning, setting up trusts, doing wills, and other things that make life easier if you have them. It wouldn't pay as well as what I make now, but money isn't everything. I've had my fill of board rooms, CEOs, CFOs, and people who drive expensive cars."

"Why don't you quit and open your own office?"

The question was one she'd asked herself many times. Her private conversations with her logical side told her it was folly to walk away from her large salary. But her gut feelings knew there was something better out there if she had the courage to make the jump. A stalemate had developed between the two sides, leaving her stranded in the land of Do Nothing.

"I don't know. The money I guess." Rather than recounting her internal debate, she lobbed the question back to him. "I could say the same to you. Why don't you sell the store and chase your dreams?"

The look Jared gave her said she'd hit a nerve. His jaw muscles worked vigorously as he took in a deep breath. "I made a promise. It's not an option," he growled as he looked at his phone. "It's time for me to start lunch." Abruptly, he rose and went to the kitchen without offering an invitation for her to join him.

Something tightened around her lungs, and she wished she hadn't asked the question. He was mad at her, maybe to the point of ruining any future friendship. She'd sunk her hope for the New Year's Eve Ball with a torpedo straight to the engine room. Even Martha wouldn't be able to repair that damage.

Spending the rest of the day at the motel alone was looking better and better.

"How do you like your steak?"

His voice sounded more pleasant than the last look he'd shot her way. She straightened her blouse when she stood. "Medium, please."

CHAPTER 16

The meat sizzled when Jared threw it on the grill. His self-talk sizzled as well. He was furious with himself. She'd pushed the one button that always made him growl, and he'd reacted badly. At least he'd held back the harsh words he usually threw at his siblings when they mentioned selling the store. They didn't understand the promise he'd made. Neither did Marissa. Nobody did.

He'd given up everything for that store. He'd struggled and sweated over it until it was part of him.

Where would his employees go without it? He had an obligation to keep them employed. Few choices were left to them if the store closed. They didn't deserve that after they'd been so loyal to him. The weight of their welfare almost crushed him.

He shut the lid to the grill and went back in the house. Marissa was leaning against the counter with her arms crossed. Her eyes were slightly red. Knowing he'd made her tear up sent a stab of regret through him. His experience with women was limited, and he didn't know how to fix it.

His throat suddenly dry, he pulled out a glass and filled it with water. The action reminded him how bad of a host he'd become.

"You want something to drink?"

"Yes, please."

He handed her the glass of water and got another for himself. His kitchen seemed abnormally cold, even with vegetables cooking and potatoes baking. The ice dam forming between him and Marissa was starting to get too big to remove unless he acted. He didn't want to lose her, even if only as a friend.

"I'm sorry about earlier." He felt heat rising in his neck. "Selling the store is a point of contention between my family and me. It causes a lot of conflict."

"I'm sorry I brought it up." Her face was flushed as she gazed at the water in the glass. She shuffled her feet. "I hope you take this the way it's meant, with all due respect and with only curiosity on my part, have you ever thought of reorganizing it into something different? You still have a family business, but in a new category."

His skin tingled like it was getting goosebumps. "You mean not be a grocery store?" His mind couldn't fathom it.

He stared at her. No hostility or malice showed in her eyes. Rather she looked slightly scared.

He turned away from her to look at the rattling lid on top of the boiling vegetables. Turning off the heat under the pot and under his skin, he turned back to her. With effort, he managed a civil tone. "No. Have anything particular in mind?"

The calmness with which she answered stunned him. "May I speak frankly without getting hostility in return?"

He couldn't promise anything, but he nodded and hoped that was sufficient.

"In my job, I specialize in community planning, labor market studies, and business development. Milo Creek's population is growing fast. Property prices are rising which means the old-time residents are living in homes they would have had a hard time selling a decade ago but are now worth a lot of money. That means the temptation to sell is rising. As older people sell out, there will be a change in the population to younger, more mobile people. Is Milo Creek ready for that?"

He felt like the blood drained out of his body and left him standing like a zombie. He heard these same arguments when he attended Town Council meetings. Most of the council members were the old- timers, but their days were numbered and they knew it. Signs pointed to the whole council being replaced by newcomers in next year's election. There was nothing he could do to stop the changes coming to Milo Creek.

Marissa's hand went over her mouth as she took in a breath. "I'm sorry, I must have been too abrupt."

He ran his hand over his hair and down the back of his neck. "No," he said softly. He faced her, watching for deceit in her eyes. "How do you know all this? Have you been here before?"

Her eyes widened before she looked at her feet. "I've done some reading online."

He had to get away from her to think. "I need to go check the steaks."

The cold air on his patio restored the blood flow, and his brain jerked to life again. As he lifted the grill lid, the smoke and tantalizing smell of cooking beef wiped away some of his worries.

The woman had only been here two days and already knew the spirit and goals of his town. Was it that plain to see?

This observant woman was probably reading him like a book. If he was smart, he'd listen to her ideas. Free advice from a lawyer. He'd take that as a Christmas gift.

CHAPTER 17

The taste of the very tender steak lingered in her mouth after the last bite. Marissa had grown up around a beef ranch. This piece of steak reminded her of a meal long ago, making her homesick yet happy she'd tasted the old tradition once again.

She lifted her napkin from her lap and touched it to the corners of her mouth. "That was the best meal I've had in a long time. It rivals any of the best steakhouses in Texas. My compliments to the butcher and the cook."

Jared laughed as he rose and took their plates to the sink. "Now you know why people drive from all over to visit our meat department."

"A standalone meat market would do well in this town."

The words popped out before she'd had a chance to think them over. She wished she could snatch them back, but they floated above the table like smoke from the grill. She put her hand over her lips. "Oops, I did it again. Sorry."

His shoulders rose a little as he stood with his back to her. Over his shoulder, he asked, "Dessert?"

Her heart pounded. She'd crossed the line of being a good guest. Time to retreat. "Can we have it later?" If you let me stick around that long, she thought as she carried what was left of their meal to the counter beside the sink, then backed away. "My stomach is quite happy to digest for a while."

Putting the dishes in the sink, he asked, "A Christmas tradition of the Sullivan family is a mug of hot cider. Want some?"

"Sounds wonderful."

She left him to his chores and went to the living room to get out of his hair. She'd done all the harm she dared to do. She bit her tongue in rebuke for saying too much.

The lights on the tree blinked and twinkled as she sat on the sofa. Her attention went back to the solitary gift sitting under the tree. A little square box wrapped in red paper with smiling Santa faces on it. In most other houses, gifts under the tree were unwrapped and put away or were played with and possibly broken by noon. Whoever this one was for would be happy when it showed up. It meant Christmas would go on a little longer.

Opening her bag, she pulled out the envelope with her proposition and perched it on a tree limb. After their hot exchanges, she wasn't sure he'd even consider going with her. But nothing ventured, nothing gained and only the high cost of tickets and her tailored, non-returnable ball gown and its accoutrements to lose. Maybe she could send the bill to Tyler. He was the one who put her in this predicament.

She resituated the envelope in the tree so he wouldn't miss it. Butterflies tickled her stomach. He might reject her offer. Knowing what she knew about him, he probably would, but she wouldn't accept it as his final answer. Once Martha and the crew at the store worked on him, he might change his mind. Martha was a formidable influence that he may not be able to ignore. She would make him say yes even if she had to drag him to Denver herself.

Marissa settled back into her spot on the sofa. Her eyes couldn't help returning to the lonely gift under the tree. It reminded her of when her grandmother brought her a box weeks after Christmas was over. She'd forgotten where she hid it and didn't put it with the other Christmas gifts. She told Marissa that sometimes the Christmas spirit of peace needs to extend beyond the formal holiday. She couldn't exactly remember what the gift from her grandmother was—a coloring book or socks or a book probably—but she remembered celebrating Christmas with her grandmother on a dreary February day. It was a happy memory that still brought her joy.

Jared leaned across her field of vision and set a mug on the end table beside her, breaking her link to the past. The hot cider sent up a faint rill of steam and a river of aroma. A stick of cinnamon leaned against the side, adding to the full fragrance of warmth. He set his own mug down before walking to the Christmas tree. He paused when he saw the envelope. He took it, then bent to get the lonely gift.

"I see we both had the same idea," he said as he handed the small box to her. He shook the envelope near his ear. "I'm always happy when I get something other than socks."

Marissa laughed. "You'll be really happy because that's not what it is." She turned her package over, delighted to be the one it was meant for. "You really didn't need to do this."

A shy grin and a shoulder twitch were his only reactions.

She ripped into her gift, sending paper pieces flying. Christmas always made her feel like a kid. The surprise had to be unwrapped and discovered before the magic was gone.

Jared's quizzical look before he started collecting the scraps of paper told her she'd gone a bit too far. Again. And he was right. This was someone else's house so it was best to retain some sense of decorum. She slowed her pace as she slipped the last of the wrapping paper from the box.

Jared took the last large piece of paper and neatly folded it. "It's not much but it's something I thought you might need if you stay in Colorado for a few more days."

With a little tug, she broke the tape holding the box lid together. She lifted out a green stocking hat with MCHS Miners and a little bearded man with a pickax embroidered on it. Below the hat were red waterproof gloves. "They're perfect! Just what I needed!"

Letting out a squeal of delight, she put the hat on her head and slid her hands into the gloves. Striking a model's pose, she asked. "How do I look?"

"Very seasonal."

He seemed pleased at her reaction. There was almost a look in his eye of—dare she think it? —strong affection. Even after all her missteps? Goosebumps broke out across her body. Thankful for thick winter clothes to hide her unelicited reaction, she hoped it also muffled her loudly pounding heart.

"Now open mine to you," she said pointing to the envelope.

She bit her lip as he neatly pulled the envelope flap free and pulled out the card. His eyes moved as he read the words. His face twitched a little as it grew redder. He pinched his lips together.

"Wow, that's quite an offer." He slowly slid the card back into the envelope and picked up his half-empty mug of cider. "I don't know what to say." He ran his hand through his hair.

"Please say yes," Marissa whispered. "Help me save face. I'll be humiliated if I show up by myself." Seeing his continued discomfort, she added, "Martha said you could use a few days off from the store."

His eyebrows shot up. "You've been conspiring with my friends? They know about this?"

She'd done it again. Waded into the swamp of his dissension. "Only Martha."

He looked everywhere but at her while his jaw muscles worked at a frenzied pace. "If she knows, everyone knows by now. They'll all be after me to do this."

This was not going as easy as she'd envisioned. He was supposed to be flattered. "I'm sorry if I've caused you undue stress. I only asked Martha if she thought you might go. I wasn't going to ask if she said there was no way."

He didn't seem comforted but sat there with his elbow propped on the back of the sofa and his hand covering his mouth while jaw muscles worked.

Irked at his unresponsiveness, she added, "There's no conspiracy here. It's nothing more than an all-expense-paid vacation to Denver for a night. You get your own luxurious hotel room and tux rental. Escorting me to the New Year's Eve ball is all I ask in return. No personal ties. No commitments. Minimal time away from work. Please just think about it."

His eyes finally found hers. At first, they were harsh but they softened as he let out a breath. "I'm sorry. This caught me by surprise. I was expecting maybe a gift card to the cafe, but this..." He waved the envelope in the air. "...this is much more than that. It's way too expensive. I've heard what they charge for tickets. Knowing you can afford two of them makes me feel very small. I appreciate the thought, but I'm sorry. I can't accept it." He held the card out to her.

Marissa stared at the paper that held her request and decided to refuse his refusal. Martha would tell her when to quit. "At least think about it."

He waved it at her again. "I wouldn't fit in."

This man was stubborn, but so was she. Jared loved honesty so she'd give it to him.

"I don't fit in either, but I have to go. I bought the tickets for me and my former boyfriend who is a messed up, lowdown, good-for-nothing jackdonkey. I won't ask him to go with me for love or money." She shot him a glance to see how he liked his own words being thrown back at him.

His face remained stony.

Marissa explained more. "My boss wants me to make an appearance and shake hands with a few people. He thinks they'll be more open to suggestions if they're in a party mood if you know what I mean." She wiggled her eyebrows at him.

A crooked grin was his only response so she continued. "I need an escort to the gala. Cinderella went to the ball alone, but I don't have that luxury. Appearances are everything in that kind of crowd. Once we make our entrance, you can find a corner and people watch. Or you can eat. I hear the food is great. We can dance a time or two, just enough to show I'm not there alone. Once I make my contacts, you're free to leave. Shouldn't take more than three or four hours."

He stared at her as if frozen by Medusa.

She looked down at her gloved hands. His gift was simple but needed. Hers was extravagant and meant only to save her from embarrassment. She almost felt ashamed for asking him for the favor.

"Will your ex-boyfriend be there?"

His easy question pushed out a big sigh. "I doubt it because there's no way he can afford it. Look, I know I'm using you for my own purposes. You saved my life once. Now I'm asking you to save my business reputation. I don't deserve it, but I'm asking you anyway."

Jared stared at the Christmas tree, a faraway look glazing his eyes. He leaned forward putting his elbows on his knees as he rubbed his forehead.

Marissa waited, unwilling to interrupt his internal dialogue obviously warring inside him. She could almost see a little devil on one shoulder whispering in one ear, while an angel whispered in the other. When he finally sat up, he had a slight smile on his face. "I don't know that I've ever done anything so...so crazy, but it might be fun. Okay, I'll go."

Her gloved hands clutched at her heart, Marissa let out a cry of joy and thanked him. "I will never be able to repay you!"

"I'm keeping a close count on how much you owe me. If I ever need a lawyer, I might be calling you."

Marissa took off her hat and gloves, then took a big drink of her still-warm cider. "I can't tell you how relieved I am. I was really stressing over going alone. It will be fun with you there. I may join you in the corner to watch the parade of sequins, money, and extravagance." She took another sip of cider, then said, "I have only one other request."

"Another one? I'm not sure I'm up for doing any more favors."

"You'll like this one." Feeling playful, she paused to let him worry a little. "Can we make a snowman? I've never lived in a place that got enough snow to make one. I've always wanted to."

A sigh of relief and a hearty laugh escaped Jared. "That's one favor I am happy to do. The snow is perfect for it."

Leaving the mugs on the table, they quickly got coats on and went outside.

The undisturbed snow was like a giant carpet stretched across the yard. It came up to the top of her boots so there was plenty to use. The new hat and gloves kept her ears and hands warm and dry.

Because the snow packed together so well, they didn't stop at making just one snowman. Her creations took on interesting shapes with her artistic eye.

Snowballs began to fill the air between them, initiating the construction of snow forts. Their laughter carried through the air. They occasionally noticed the curtains moving in the neighboring houses and people walking out on their front porches to see what was going on.

The sound of jingling bells drew the couple's attention away from their snowball fight. Marissa got in one last cheap shot as Jared looked intently down the street. He spun and ran toward her. She dodged his grasp when she ducked behind a snowman holding a pine branch. He lobbed a small snowball over the snowman but missed her.

"You win!" Jared said as he gave up the chase. "Here comes John Gooding and his team. Maybe he'll give us a ride." He walked to the edge of his yard and waved.

The jingling of the bells attached to harnesses slowed as a team of horses trotted to a stop in front of Jared. A bearded man sat on the high seat of the wheeled hay wagon hitched to the Clydesdales. Hay bales on the wagon provided seating for several people who called out their greetings to Jared. The horses snorted and stomped their feet as they stood, making their bells ring.

"Hello, Mr. Sullivan, sir," cried out the red-cheeked gentleman dressed in a red coat holding the reins. "I see you've been working on your neighborhood beautification project." He swept his light whip toward the yard filled with snowmen and snow forts.

"Merry Christmas, Mr. Gooding!" Jared called back. "Merry Christmas, everyone. Giving tours today?"

"That's why I'm here. It's five dollars a person that goes to the library fund. Hop on!"

Marissa didn't need to be asked twice. She ran to the wagon as she dug a twenty-dollar bill out of her secret pocket, gave it to John, and told him to keep the change. Jared helped her on and followed her to an empty bale.

With a click of John's tongue and a light slap of the rein, the horses started off on their trot again.

Jared introduced Marissa to the people on the wagon. She'd never remember their names but she'd never forget the ride. Everyone knew everyone. Scarves and hats and heavy, bulky coats left little but eyes, noses, and mouths showing, but friends recognized friends. They sang carols between the stops at houses around town as people got off and others got on.

Her Texas winter coat wasn't as warm as the Colorado ones. The boisterous activity of snowman-making cooled off in the breeze of riding the wagon, and Marissa started to shiver. Someone noticed and sent a wool blanket over. Jared wrapped it around her and held her close. The friendly faces became more amused, poking each other to notice the grocer and his girl. Eyebrows wiggled, smiles became smug, and whispers were exchanged.

Choosing to ignore it, Marissa studied the town as they drove around. The side streets were narrow, with no sidewalks or curbs marking the edges of the road. Tall wood houses with steep roofs sat along the tree-lined streets. Colorful lights on Christmas trees shone in nearly every front window.

The architecture reflected the history and oldness, accentuating the differences between the modern steel buildings and wide highways where she resided and the quaint simplicity of where she was now. Here, people knew and greeted each other, a stark contrast to the facelessness of her crowded city's population where people seldom spoke and eyed each other with suspicion.

Like the sun breaking through the clouds, it hit Marissa. Jared was a big man in his small pond, and the ripples he made impacted everyone in his corner of the world. He was loved and appreciated for what he contributed.

It was different for her. No matter how high up she got in her big corporation, she'd never be more than a droplet in an ocean of people. Her only impact was closing the stores of small towns and destroying old traditions. She had to make a change in her life. She wanted to be like Jared, making a positive difference in a community.

The wagon pulled up in front of Jared's house, and they rose. She folded the blanket that had warmed her and handed it to a mother with a small child. Jared helped her down, and they gave their thanks to the driver.

The Currier-and-Ives wagon ride had ended, but Marissa knew her life would never be the same. The small-town people had helped her see what she knew but had been denying. She was on the wrong path. Her salary shouldn't be the guiding force in life. Finding her purpose was much more important.

Everything was clear. Her shoulders felt lighter as she and Jared admired their frozen handiwork on his lawn. She'd quit her job when she got back. Her savings would support her until a better opportunity came open or she established her own office.

She turned to look at him. His eyes seemed as happy as she felt inside. "This has been the perfect day! Thank you."

The words were barely spoken when Jared gathered her into his arms and kissed her. No other kiss warmed her the way it did or made her mind as fuzzy as it felt. It was sweet, pure, and sincere. She sensed he was about to pull away but her arms went around him to prevent it. She couldn't get enough.

Her phone rang in her pocket. The muffled sound ended the bliss, ruining the moment.

The sing-song tone kept going as they looked at each other.

His eyebrows went up and he tilted his head a little. "Going to get that?"

Surrendering to the summons, she let him go. "It might be my mom."

"Then you should answer it."

An exhale escaped her as she took off her glove and pulled her phone out of her pocket. Her mother always had the worst timing when it came to phone calls. No use looking at the screen. She knew who it was.

"Hello, Mom." She stuffed her glove in her pocket

"Hi, babe." Tyler's voice dripped with affection. "It's me."

Marissa's blood and steps froze as her hand formed a fist. Her eyes closed as she clenched her teeth to keep anger from spilling from her mouth. Why hadn't she'd looked to see who was calling before she answered it? She'd have declined the call. But here he was. The two-timing jerk was not only ruining her moment with Jared, but also her perfect afternoon.

"What do you want, Tyler?" She hoped her voice was as icy as the snowmen were becoming in the cooling temperatures.

Jared paused as he held the door open for her. Curiosity filled his eyes as he watched her.

"I deserve your anger," Tyler went on. "I did you wrong. But that's just it, babe, I was wrong. I messed up. I'm sorry and want you back, sweetheart. I love you, Marissa. We belong together. You know that's true. C'mon. Let's start over."

Her chest got tight as her mind swirled. She leaned against the door jamb.

"I've missed you," he crooned.

She felt her body sway a little before Jared reached out to steady her.

Her mind and emotions swirled together in a giant blizzard. "I don't know."

The feel of Jared's strong hand on her shoulder helped her to focus. His soft eyes gave her strength.

"I can't talk now. I have to go." Before he could argue with her decision, she pushed the button to end the call.

"Let me guess," Jared began. "It wasn't your mother."

Shaking as she took off her wet boots, she said, "No, it was my ex. He has a lot of gall calling me on Christmas day. His new girlfriend must have dumped him."

She took off her glove, then remembered the other one in her pocket. When she yanked it out, something came with it.

A rectangle spun as it fell, flashing the red-and-blue logo of Food-N-More as it went down. Her ID tag!

In horror, she watched it spin until it hit the ground at Jared's feet. She didn't wait to see which side landed up but dove for it like a falcon on a rabbit. She palmed it and put it back in her pocket.

"Drop something?" he asked.

"It was nothing," she replied as she went into the house.

She spread her new hat and gloves on top of her boots to dry and stuffed the ID tag into the depths of her bag. Her swiftness to preserve her secret had saved her but left her head uncentered from moving too fast.

Jared sat beside her on the sofa. "Hot chocolate? Or something stronger?"

She put her cold hand over his. The temperature difference was harsh.

"We'll start with hot chocolate," he said as he hurried away. Soon the sound of a microwave filled the space.

Without realizing it, she'd chilled more than she thought. Maybe it was from being outside. Or maybe it was from Tyler's call and his smugness at thinking she'd come running back to him. Or maybe it was from nearly revealing her secret with a spinning ID card. All of it was enough to cause shivers.

Her teeth rattled together slightly before a mug of hot chocolate was placed between her hands. The sweet liquid warmed her fingers around the mug and warmed her insides as it went down.

She watched Jared as he lit a match and coaxed a fire into burning in the fireplace. It slowly got bigger and bigger, pushing its heat out across the room until it reached her feet. He took a seat on the other end of the sofa and watched her without speaking. It didn't make her uncomfortable. She now knew he truly cared for her.

"Tell me about him."

While he sipped from his mug, she related the story of her life-long relationship to a man she couldn't help referring to as the worm and loser and all the other bad adjectives she could think of. It was all a waste. She hated her job but had stayed because Tyler wanted her to. He loved her a six-figure salary, not her. She was dumb thinking he cared for her.

Exhaustion spread over her. Whether it was from the storytelling or the active afternoon, she couldn't tell, but suddenly she wanted to be alone in a hot tub of water.

As if reading her mind, Jared set his mug on the table. "I can tell you're tired, but we haven't had dessert yet. Are you ready for it now?"

Surprised at what her stomach said to her, she agreed. While he worked in the kitchen, she watched the fireplace flames flicker and glow. Her feet were slowly beginning to thaw. The new hat and gloves saved her. Her blood was too thin to be comfortable without a warmer coat and thicker boots and socks.

The smell of apple pie drifted in from the kitchen. Memories of her and her grandmother baking pies together took her mind away as she stared at the fire. They'd make several at a time and share them with friends at Christmas.

The sound of forks on plates signaled dessert was coming. Jared entered with a plate holding a pie slice with ice cream on the side.

The bottom of the plate warmed her hand when he gave it to her along with a napkin.

He soon joined her in the living room. He picked up a remote and clicked it. Soft Christmas music played from speakers unseen but nicely placed for the best acoustics. Something modern in this dated setting.

The atmosphere between them was peaceful like they understood each other. Small talk bounced between them, bringing giggles, laughs, and serious uh-humming. He didn't ask her about her job or Tyler, and she didn't ask about his store. There were too many pleasant things to discuss instead.

She didn't notice it was getting dark until he got up to stir the fire. The only light was from the Christmas tree and the fireplace. A cozier holiday ambience she'd never had before.

A yawn came out unbidden as she snuggled deeper into the sofa. Putting the poker back on its stand, he turned. "I've kept you far too long. Linda said you need your rest. I'll take you back to your hotel after you answer one question."

That sounded ominous.

He sat on the other end of the sofa and said, "I'll ask the same one you asked me this morning. Would you be happier doing something else?"

Words are bitter when they're fed back, but she knew what he was saying. She'd let outside influences shape her life much as he had. She had no right to tell him what to do when she wasn't doing what she wanted.

Jared took a deep breath, then said, "Milo Creek could use someone to help people navigate through all the changes that are coming. So many people are selling out and have more money than they know what to do with. They need someone to guide them through unknown territory. Would you consider moving here?"

After the afternoon's revelations, she wanted to say yes but something inside held her back. "I might consider it, but I'm really a big-city girl." She didn't have the heart to tell him it was an impossible dream. He wouldn't want her here if he knew she was going to instigate the changes he dreaded.

CHAPTER 18

The cloudy night sucked all light from the world, leaving it immeasurably dark. Nothing stirred except for the few creatures using the artificial lights on their cars to see their way home. Marissa thanked Jared for the wonderful day and the privilege of building snowmen in his yard. The good feelings sprouting from the fun had dimmed with Tyler's call, tainting the once perfect memory.

They shared another kiss when they reached her door. It wiped away thoughts of Tyler and returned good feelings and goosebumps.

Jared seemed as reluctant to leave as she was to let him go. He told her he'd see her tomorrow and left her standing in her doorway as he drove away.

After a warm shower, Marissa sat alone on her hotel bed, debating on whether to call Tyler back. He'd taken enough of her time and energy. The debate ended when her phone rang, and his number and face appeared on the screen.

For two hours, Tyler confessed his sins and cried and pleaded for forgiveness from her. Nothing was his fault. The woman she caught him with was someone he met at an event at work. She meant nothing to him. Neither did the girl before her. Or the girl before her. All the women he'd gone out with meant nothing compared to what he felt for Marissa. He knew that now.

All the women? Marissa stopped listening after that. Those months she'd been in Dallas pining for her true love had been squandered. Her little gifts, texts, and phone calls expressing her love for him had been dumped into the garbage can of the relationship. When he visited her, it was all an act. Phony in every way. In her starry-eyed state, she hadn't noticed it. She'd been blinded by her feelings and didn't see the lack of his.

His confession drained everything out of her. She lay back on her stacked pillows and let Tyler maunder without interruption. His droning lulled her into dozing until she was awakened by loud shouting calling her name and asking if she was listening. The murmured affirmative was the most she could manage.

"Babe, can you hear me?"

She rubbed her eyes and cleared her froggy throat. "Yes, I'm listening."

"Come to Denver tomorrow," he crooned. "Let me show you how sorry I am. We'll go shopping for rings. I'll buy you the biggest one we can find."

Her breath left her. Had she heard right? Unable to detect whether she was dreaming or hearing correctly, she sat up. In the faint neon glow from the sign out front coming in around the edge of the curtain, she saw herself in the mirror, sitting up in bed, her hair mussed. This was no dream.

She had to hear it again. "What did you say?"

The sound of rustling came through the phone. "Marissa, if you could see me now, you'd see I'm on one knee. My hands are holding the phone tenderly as if I were holding your beautiful face. Will you marry me, my darling? My sunshine. My everything. Please say you'll marry me."

Laughter erupted from Marissa like a geyser. While Tyler yelled, asking whether she was laughing or crying, she buried her head in a pillow to muffle her howling. The man had spent the last hours talking about his indiscretions and now he wanted her to marry him?

His actions made the decision an easy one. His words exorcised the remaining feelings she had for him.

She wiped her eyes and regained control. "Tyler, there's no way I'm going to marry you."

A gasp came before his whine. "But it's what you've wanted since high school. You hinted at it all through college. All those things you said after I moved here. You've wanted to marry me for years. And now that I'm finally ready, you say no?"

The humor in the situation was disappearing, and it sobered Marissa. The man thought he was doing her a favor. He was giving her the one thing he thought she wanted. Himself.

"Tyler, you just got through telling me how unfaithful you've been to me. Not just once, but...well, I didn't count them all. There's nothing left of it. You destroyed it. I don't trust you. We can't have a marriage without trust."

"But I told you I regret them. My wild oats have been sown, and I'm coming back to you. Come on, Marissa, I've finally discovered you're the one for me. Your wish is coming true."

The humor was coming back. Leaning back on her pillows, she responded, "If you'd asked me even a month ago, I probably would have said yes. But when I saw you with that woman, everything changed. In the last few days, my eyes have been opened. I'm not one of your footballs you can toss around and catch whenever you need me. You had your chance with me, and you blew it."

The silence that followed made her wonder if Tyler had hung up on her. She checked the phone to see they were still connected.

"What is it, Marissa? You been stepping out too? Met someone new? At least I admitted my sins. Come on, 'fess up. Let's hear it."

Her finger hovered over the red button that would end this inane conversation. Her battery was almost dead anyway. But she wouldn't leave his accusations unanswered.

"Tyler, you're a big jerk."

"I consider that an admission of guilt."

She drew her arm back, ready to sling that voice against the wall to smash into a thousand pieces.

She paused. She didn't have a car. This phone was one of her lifelines to the outside world. She rethought that impulse and decided against it.

A deep breath restored control. "Think what you will, Tyler. I will not marry you. You're free to do whatever you want."

"Yeah, well, you'll regret it! I'm sorry I even asked now. Your loss, honey. If you ever want to come back, you'll have to come on your knees and—"

Her finger found the red button and pushed it.

CHAPTER 19

Sleep was sweet for Jared that night, his dreams full of Marissa. When his clock radio came on with the local news, he slapped it, hoping to bring the dream back. Snooze time ran out, and the DJ commented how nice the weather would be for those who wanted to go shopping. The hint of potential customers roused him from his soft, warm bed.

Thoughts of Christmas Day kept crowding out what he needed to accomplish at the store. He should sort the holiday items into sale bins...the brown of her eyes...and take down some of the decorations...the sound of her laughter. Her smile.

Without realizing it, he pulled into his parking spot at the store. How he got there, he couldn't remember. He sat in his vehicle, rubbing his face, trying to remove the feelings that were overwhelming him. It reminded him of those chick-flics his sister made him watch when he visited over the holidays. He said they were nothing but fantasy, but here he was living in his own.

Seeing the rows of shelves and merchandise as he switched on the lights restored his focus. Maybe Marissa would come by today.

Slapping his cheek, he cried out, "Wake up, kid! Snap out of it!"

"You say something?" Benny called from the other side of the store.

Unable to run and hide, he walked toward the meat department and saw Benny putting on his apron.

Benny stopped midway and stared at Jared. "You're different. I can already tell."

Not wanting to discuss it, Jared turned to leave and said over his shoulder, "You're seeing things."

Benny laughed loud and long. "You can't hide it, dude. Something happened yesterday. Tell me about it." He patted a stool that stood against the wall.

Pausing, Jared said, "There's so much to do and—"

"Stop!" Benny came around the meat counter display and took Jared's elbow. Leading him to the stool, he made him sit. "There's no one else around. Now spill."

Jared gave his friend a look that he hoped conveyed how much he didn't want to do this. It had no effect. Letting out a big sigh, he issued the only statement he was willing to share. "She said the steak was the best she'd ever eaten."

"What's going on?" Holly walked into the meat section as she took off her coat. "OOOhhhh. You're interrogating about yesterday, huh. I want to hear too." She put her coat over her arm and joined Benny.

The back door open and voices came inside.

Holly yelled out, "Hey you guys, come quick! Jared's about to tell about what he did yesterday!"

Running steps drew nearer and red-cheeked Martha and bundled-up Chad joined the others.

Martha squinted and leaned in a little. "He looks different. Happier. Fewer wrinkles on the forehead. Something good happened." Her smile and nod of approval spread to the others.

There was no escape. He could pull rank and tell them to get to work. He was the boss after all. But nothing would get done at the store until he told what had happened with him and Marissa.

For the sake of productivity, he began. "We had a good time. She said the steaks were better than the ones in Texas. We built some snowmen. John Gooding came by and took us on a ride around town. We had hot chocolate. I took her to her hotel. End of story. Now get to work."

He started to rise, but his audience took a step forward as Benny pushed him back down on the stool.

"Not enough details," Martha said. The others murmured their concurrence. "Let's hear more."

Keeping his eyes focused on a display near the front of the store, he ceded control and began. He told them of talking about the store, of eating their meal, of their frolicking in the snow, the snowball fight, the ride on the wagon, how she wanted to help people with their businesses, how he'd invited her to move to Milo Creek.

His audience drew in a breath.

Martha spoke for all of them. "Wouldn't that be wonderful if she moved here? We could use a lawyer in town. By the way, did she tell you who she works for? She wouldn't tell me."

He shook his head. "Wouldn't tell me either. Just said it was a nationwide company, and she handles sensitive information."

"She's a spy. CIA probably."

They all turned to look at Jason who had come in unseen.

He shrugged and said, "Or she's an undercover operative of the FBI. It's nationwide and has sensitive information." When he took off his stocking hat, his long hair stuck out in every direction.

"She's no spy," Chad said. "What would she be doing here if she was? Nothing happens here."

"I've heard of industrial spies," Holly interjected. "Maybe she's from Food-N-More spying on Jared to see how he runs his store or on how Benny does his meat. She could take that information back to her company so they can copy us."

"No!" Jason spurted out, his eyes wide and filled with excitement. "She's a spy from a drug dealer looking for someplace to set up base. It's a small town. No one would look for a cartel here. I bet she wants to use the store as a front for selling drugs!"

Jared was wondering what was wrong with his employees and their crazy imaginations. "She's not a spy! She's a nice woman who got caught in an avalanche. She couldn't have done that on purpose. She's stuck here by mistake. Who she works for is none of our business." As soon as the words were out, he regretted them. He wanted to know too.

Jason wouldn't let it go. "Did she say anything about moving here? No one would suspect that she was a drug lord so it's the perfect hiding place. I saw this movie once that—"

"This isn't a movie, Jason," Martha snarled as she took off her coat. "I was with her Christmas Eve night, and she's no drug lord. Like Jared said, she's a nice woman, but maybe Holly's onto something. Maybe she's watching our store and looking for ways to horn in on our business. Someday there'll be enough people for two grocery stores. I have a feeling she's a planner who looks for opportunities."

"Enough!' Jared didn't mean to spew the word out. A growing fear he'd tried to hide sprung out of its bonds. "She's no drug lord or CIA operative. I don't know who she works for but again I say, she's here by accident, not by purpose, so her objective, spy or otherwise, is not for us. She's on her way home as soon as her rental car comes. She's a city girl and a Texan, and she's not moving here. Besides, she probably wouldn't last long in our little valley. I know for a fact she can't drive in snow."

He wished his face didn't feel so warm under their stares. He checked his watch and got off the stool. "Doors open in ten minutes. Don't you people have work to do?"

The crowd broke up, commenting amongst themselves about what they'd heard. Escaping to the quiet of his office, Jared shut the door and leaned against it. His and Marissa's story would spread all over town by nightfall, if not by noon. He'd have to endure the looks, the pointing, the winks, but they would pass. Once Marissa left town, things would return to normal.

But he didn't want them to return to normal. He liked having her here. The big expanse between what he wanted and what would actually be was a wide, lonely place. His heart had dared to hope for love but had lost the bet. Again.

CHAPTER 20

The constant influx of customers kept Jared busy and his mind off what it wanted to think about. Time flew by as he hurried from one task to another. His team made sure none of his customers felt unappreciated.

By noon, he had the Christmas candy and decorations in the discount bins. Funny hats, noisemakers, and sparkling cider took their prominent positions on the endcaps. Somewhere in a file drawer in his office was a Happy New Year banner he should put up. He added it to his mental to-do list.

Old Mrs. Butler caught him near the dairy products and told him she was glad he'd found someone to love him. Cutting her off as politely as he could, he got away from her before she could start her oft-told story about how she met her husband back in 1949. The spry lady followed him a few steps before giving up her efforts.

Ducking into his office, he went to his chair to rest and gather himself. The day had started quirky, and the feeling continued. He dug through a drawer and found the banner he needed. Underneath it was an old piece of Halloween candy. He popped it in his mouth before leaving to face the hordes. He couldn't hide forever.

Before leaving, he checked his cell phone half expecting to see something from Marissa. Nothing was there. Maybe she would come in for lunch. He checked his hidden mirror to make sure his hair wasn't tousled before he left his office. Just in case.

He hung the banner, bagged groceries, listened to a customer complain about the lack of selection, and stocked a few shelves, all while keeping one eye on the door. When he returned to bagging groceries, Martha whispered between customers that he should call Marissa. She pointed at the phone on his hip and gestured the urgency with which he should do it.

The next customer in line, one of the new arrivals to Milo Creek, stared at them like they were crazy. He welcomed her to the store and wished her a happy new year. After seeing her off, Jared excused himself and went to the back of the store.

The quiet of his office rejuvenated him. Business was good, but the flurry and ado over the holidays sapped him of holiday cheer. The sooner it was over, the happier he'd be. At least until the next holiday. Glancing at his email, he scanned through them and sent one out. Finishing that, he decided to call Marissa.

His finger shook slightly as he scrolled through the numbers to hers. His stomach tightened when he called and it went straight to voice mail. He tried again with the same results. He called once more and again got voice mail, but this time, he left a short message to call when she was ready for lunch. To be safe, he sent a text with the same message.

The big clock at the front of the store ticked off the seconds like molasses in winter. He began to wonder if he'd said something that made her mad. He replayed the whole day in his mind as he inspected the floors and cleaned a few spots. He hadn't reacted well when she suggested he transform his business into something else. Maybe he'd been too gruff, and it offended her. But if it had, why had she stayed all afternoon? Everything seemed so good after lunch. So natural and comfortable. Where had he gone wrong?

A lull hit the store soon after lunch. Jared checked his phone. Still no response. He hurried to the front of the store to relieve Martha.

"Martha, I—"

"It's about time," she remarked as she checked herself out of the cash register. "I'm getting hungry."

"I have a favor to ask. I still haven't heard from Marissa. Would you mind going to check on her? I mean, maybe something's wrong and she doesn't know who to call or something."

Martha put her hand on her hip. "You should go see about her."

"I can't. She might still be in bed, and I wouldn't want to..." His voice trailed off as his mind filled with images he wished he could stop. He closed his eyes and shook his head slightly, trying to erase what he envisioned. "Tell Holly to make two lunches and put them on my tab. Take one to her. Please."

Martha leaned in close to Jared. "You got it bad, don't you, boss," she whispered. She stepped back. "I may take another long lunch if you don't mind."

Feeling his face blush, Jared took her place behind the counter. "Take as long as you need. And thanks." To his relief, a customer with a full basket came up to the checkout. It was a good way to dismiss Martha and her annoying winks.

Chapter 21

Marissa's dreams seemed real. Eluding a villain who was chasing her through a deserted town left her heart pounding and her mind empty of ways to get out. But what was that loud sound? Was it friend or foe? It was coming from somewhere, but it was out of place in her dream. It grew louder and louder. She felt funny as her mind took her away through a swirling blur of light and dark.

As her mind untangled itself, Marissa found herself lying in bed. When she opened her eyes, she had to blink several times to see. Nothing looked familiar as her brain struggled with figuring out where she was.

The pounding continued, followed by muffled voices saying her name. Throwing the covers back she stumbled to the door and looked out the peephole. There stood Martha with bags from the store and Edith who was fumbling with keys until she found one and reached out for the door.

Not waiting, Marissa unlocked the door and flung it open. The cold air immediately drenched her thin pajamas and chilled her feet. She wiped her eyes. "Good morning," her voice croaked out.

Edith rushed in and looked around. "Dearie, you gave us a scare.

Are you all right?" She peeked in the bathroom before turning back to the others.

Marissa could only imagine what she might be thinking she'd find. Owning a small hotel, the woman had probably seen all kinds of weird things done by guests. She'd find nothing like that here.

"I'm fine. What time...?" A yawn cut her off. Hearing the time sent the morning's adrenaline through her, and she was suddenly awake. "It's afternoon?"

No wonder her guests were acting strange. After assuring Edith, she wouldn't need room service today, the little woman left to go back to her office.

Martha came in, not saying a word. She set her bags on the small table before shutting the door, then flung the curtains open. Sunshine flooded the small room.

"Sleeping until one in the afternoon? I'm pretty sure Jared didn't keep you up all night." Her eyes narrowed. "Or did he?"

"It wasn't Jared. It was Tyler." With a few motions, Marissa made her bed well enough to suffice, then grabbed some clothes and went into the bathroom to change. Still groggy from her dream, she washed her face with cold water to wake her up more fully. When she exited, she was dressed, her morning breath was gone, and her hair was brushed.

"Why didn't someone call me?" A quick glance at her cell phone told her the answer. It was dead. She'd forgotten to plug it in last night. When she did, bells and tones sounded as power resurrected it.

Martha had lunch spread out on the small table and sat in the one chair in the room. She motioned to a sandwich and small bag of chips on the table with its accompanying Diet Dr. Pepper. The aura of unanswered questions hovered above the table, launched by Martha's gaze.

Sitting on the edge of the bed, Marissa's stomach let out a plea for what lay in front of her. She took the sandwich and bit off a big piece, hoping it would keep her from having to say much. Martha was the guest. Let her start the conversation.

She did. "I don't know what you did to Jared yesterday, but I like it. He has a different look about him, like some veil has been lifted and he is seeing clearly. It's the first morning in a long time that his face isn't full of worry. It makes my heart happy to see it. He's too young to develop permanent worry wrinkles. It made him look too much like his dad."

Marissa took another bite of her sandwich. They ate in silence.

"I don't mean to be nosy," Martha said after taking a drink of soda, "but I'd love to know what went on yesterday. All of it, but especially the good parts." This time she ate with vigor, signaling it was Marissa's turn to take over the conversation.

Taking another bite, Marissa thought about how much Jared would want Martha to know. Not much, she assumed. She began with a general description of the inside of his house, the Christmas tree, and the poinsettias around the living room. She talked of his excellent cooking skills and about building snowmen and the fun it brought to her. She ended with the sleigh ride that had truly been the highlight of the day.

When Martha pressed her about what they talked about, Marissa skimmed over it, purposefully leaving out the part about her suggesting he needed to change his business plans. Martha didn't need to hear that.

She wondered how much the stories meshed if they did at all. She'd had a fun day, but maybe she'd misread Jared. Maybe he'd hidden his anger over her suggestion to change his store and was only being polite by acting like he was having fun. But if that were true, he wouldn't have kissed her like he did. Nothing about that was fake. There was no denying he had feelings for her. Martha said his worry lines were gone. That had to be a good sign.

Their lunches consumed and garbage thrown away, Martha sat back in the chair and asked the question Marissa dreaded most. "Now that we've discussed Jared, tell me about Tyler."

The words made her eyes sting. To hide them, she pulled her legs on the bed into a cross-legged position. A loose thread on the bedspread became the focus of her vision. "There's not much to tell. He called and said he wanted me back."

Outside, melting snow dripped in soft splats with the passing seconds as neither woman spoke nor moved. Marissa knew what it meant. Martha wasn't leaving until she knew more. What was it her mother said? Better to get feelings out than hold them inside?

She took a deep breath and told it. All of it. Tyler's late-night phone call. His confessions about his indiscretions. His proposal and snarky response when she said no. The telling of it made it seem not as emotional and stressful as it had felt during the dark of night. The light of day made it all clearer. The woman she'd caught him with had probably dumped him, and he reached out to fill that void. He mistakenly thought he could get her any time with a snap of his fingers.

Marissa unfolded her legs and sat up straight. Her voice grew louder as she worked through how she'd been manipulated all those years. Him making her think she had a chance with him, and her believing that she did. The wasted years she'd spent catering to his every need and command. He didn't love her. He loved all she could do for him. His homework. His errands. And when she got her good job, his tickets to the Dallas Cowboys and Mavericks games.

She'd enabled him to use her. The fault lay with her.

Her insides churned and squeezed like a wet rag being wrung out. It hurt and forced tears out of her eyes. Her hands covered her face as she bent over and buried her face in the bedspread and sobbed over all she'd wasted on the scoundrel.

Martha rubbed her back and told her to let it out. She deserved way better than Tyler. Letting him go meant better days lay ahead.

As her breathing and crying grew slower, she felt tissues being shoved in her hand. She wiped her face as she sat up and blew her nose. Martha stared at her with eyes full of sympathy and handed her more tissues.

"I lay here all night long," Marissa managed to say. She took in a ragged breath. "I couldn't sleep for thinking about all the years waiting on someone I thought could bring me a lot of happiness. What a fool I was! He didn't love me. He loved my credit cards. It felt good to tell him to take a hike, and I didn't even cry. So why am

I crying now?" She blew her nose again. "Because I'm thirty years old, and I have to start over. I have no experience in starting over. How do I do that? Put my profile on some dating website? Hang out in bars? Or maybe be single my whole life?"

"Not at all," Martha said in a voice that reminded her of her mother. She sat on the bed beside Marissa and put her arm around her. "Thirty is young. You're pretty. You're smart. You know what you want and go for it. What man wouldn't love that?" She thought a minute. "Okay, a lot of them, but the good ones will love you more for it. By the way, the good ones aren't found in bars so stay out of there." Her finger traced the outline of a flower printed on the bedspread. "Would you consider Jared? He seems enamored with you."

Marissa glanced at Martha from the corner of her eye as she felt the sides of her mouth go up. "And move here?"

Martha smiled. "I guarantee you won't find a better man or town anywhere else."

Getting up to throw away her used tissues, Marissa had to agree with that. "Did I tell you he agreed to go to the New Year's Eve ball with me?"

Noting Martha's wide-eyed expression, she continued. "Yes, he did. And it didn't take all that much arm twisting to get him to agree. He didn't want to at first, but I told him you knew, and he knew he was no match for you."

Martha stood and danced a jig. "I'm so glad! It will give you time to get closer to him. Find out what kind of man he is inside. You'll find he's pretty awesome. Plus, you'll take more wrinkles off of his face."

Laughter filled the room as the two women made plans for the ball.

CHAPTER 22

M artha's lunchtime stretched into nearly an hour and a half with no indication when it might end. Jared's patience was growing thin. He couldn't nick Martha for staying out too long. She was on his mission by request, and he'd had told her to take as much time as she needed.

Maybe he should have set a time limit.

No. She was responsible enough to know her work awaited her. She'd come when the task was done.

Her return worried him as much as her being gone. Martha's propensity to talk and worm information out of people was well known and that made him nervous. Was Marissa all right or not? What tales might she be telling? Maybe he'd misread her yesterday. Maybe she'd had an awful time or didn't like his house or hated the food he served. Maybe she didn't like how he kissed her. His heart stood still.

Maybe he didn't want Martha to come back and tell him what she'd learned. He might not like it.

Working at the checkout wasn't his favorite spot in the store. Too many customers inquired about the woman he'd been seen with on the wagon ride and whether she was the one he'd rescued from the avalanche. The effort it took to be cordial when he didn't feel like it was getting too hard.

Where was she?

The more people asked about Marissa, the more she took over all his thoughts. He had to be rational. She lived in Texas, and he lived here. She was a big-city woman. He was a small-town man. He'd never leave Milo Creek for love or money. He'd be sorely tempted to for her, but he'd never do it. Any chance of a romance between them was a hopeless cause.

He issued a heavy sigh as fatigue weighed him down. "Are you feeling okay?"

The words pulled him back to his duties. One of the newbies in town stood across the moving belt, looking at him with sympathy and curiosity.

A funny titter came out from him. "I'm fine. Did you find everything you wanted?"

He didn't hear the response because from the back he heard Chad say, "'Bout time you got back."

His heart beat faster, pounding like a jackhammer. The answers to his dilemma were getting closer, but they would have to wait. This was too public a place to discuss such private matters, although by tomorrow, everyone would know anyway.

Getting the groceries bagged and the receipt given as quickly as possible, he logged out as soon as he saw Martha come around the end of an aisle. He didn't say anything to her but searched her face for any sign of what she'd found.

"All is well," Martha said as she took her place. "Nothing to worry about." A customer pushed a cart to the moving belt and started unloading. "I'll talk to you later."

In an instant, she reverted to her checker role. "Hello, Betty! I hope you had a good Christmas."

Leaving her to do what she did best, Jared went to his office. He needed quiet and a chance to get off his feet. Nearly two hours of standing in one place was exhausting. How did Martha do it?

His stomach rumbled. A tuna pouch and a small bag of chips were in his desk for occasions when he wanted to hide. His inbox had new e-mails so he checked them while he ate. The holidays slowed down messages from vendors. Funny how they took the holidays off, but he couldn't. His siblings told him he was crazy for working so hard, but it was people like him who kept America open and moving. He was the kind—

A knock at the door interrupted his back patting. It moved slightly as Chad peeked around the edge of the door. "Got a minute?"

Jared waved him inside as he finished off his lunch. Friends since high school, Chad was the closest thing to a best friend he had even though he was much more laid back than Jared. He skied, he biked, he hiked, and otherwise played outdoors with his wife and kids. Envy sometimes raised its head in Jared, seeing how much more Chad had than him. He'd found a way to stay in Milo Creek and have it all, including a life.

He wished he had one too. "Boss, we've been talking."

"We?"

Chad waved his hand toward the door. "Your employees. And we think you should close early on New Year's Eve."

"No can do. We get a lot of business that night."

Palms open, Chad motioned for him to calm down. "Hear me out. We'll put a big sign on the door. That way, word will spread, and people will come early. You won't lose any business."

Jared sat back in his chair and crossed his arms. His employees wanted the time off but letting them would set a dangerous precedence that would eventually drive him out of business. Yet he understood the request.

"Okay, one hour early. That's all. Have someone make a pretty sign to put on the door." He turned back to his computer. "But tell the troops not to expect it every year. They already have New Year's Day off." He opened another email, expecting Chad to leave with the cheerful news, but he kept sitting in front of Jared's desk.

"Something else on your mind?"

The grin left Chad's face and he studied his hands. "Um, I hate to mention this, but Holly thinks I should." He rubbed his hands across the tops of his thighs. He glanced at Jared; his shoulders slumped more. "It's probably nothing, but she heard on the radio that a woman escaped from jail in Oklahoma, stole a car, and is on the loose. She was in jail for theft and murder. Her description fits Marissa."

Jared understood the words, but comprehension eluded him. All he could manage was "Huh?"

Squirming in his seat, Chad repeated it, "A woman escaped from jail in Oklahoma, stole a car, and is on the loose. The reporter said it was a dark-haired woman, early 30s, southern accent." He stared at Jared. "Sound familiar?"

All Jared could do was laugh. "Chad, she rented the car, not stole it. I saw the rental agreement. She lives in Dallas."

"So she says. But she won't tell us who she works for. Doesn't that strike you as a little suspicious?"

Leaning on his elbows on his desk, Jared rubbed his forehead to smooth away an ache starting to make itself felt. "It's odd, I'll grant you, but she's no escaped criminal. In fact..." he sat back adjusted his shirt collar... "she's invited me to be her escort at Denver's New Year's Eve ball."

Agog, Chad sputtered, "She what?"

"You heard me. I've agreed to escort her to the event. The whole thing is on her. Tux. Room. Tickets. Everything. Would a criminal, or a spy for that matter, invite someone like me to such a high-brow event? I think not."

His eyes wide, Chad sat still for a moment, then burst out in laughter. "You? She asked you?"

Jared frowned. "Why not me?"

"Where do I begin?" Chad wiped his eyes and adjusted himself in the chair. "I mean I'm surprised you'd even consider it. The old home boy decides to dip a toe into high society. Doesn't seem like something you'd do."

The statement was true. It was a giant leap to go from small-town business owner who was barely squeaking by to someone in a tux mingling with high-rise money and power. He'd be completely out of place. What could he talk about with those people? How much groceries were going up? How hard it was to get good fresh produce? Money meant nothing to them. They were the ones who brought in box stores that took away business from home-run stores like his. He had no business going.

He sat back in his chair. What had he been thinking when he said he'd go? He'd made a mistake. "You're right. I don't belong there. I'll tell her she has to take someone else."

Chad got to his feet. "No way! You should go."

Jared rose. "You just said I shouldn't."

A sheepish look covered Chad's face. "I didn't say that. I said I was surprised you would consider it. You should go see what it's like and tell the rest of us who have no hope of ever going. What's it like to be in that kind of company? What do they talk about? What do they do? Is it like in the movies where they talk about how to take over the world?" Chad put his hands in his pockets as he shook his head. "You're so lucky. Man, you have to do it. It's a free glimpse to see what's cooking under the upper crust."

Going around the side of the desk, Jared ran his hand through his hair. "I wouldn't know how to act. What to talk about."

"It's simple. Just stand around and let them do the talking." Chad closed one eye and tilted his head. "You need a haircut and a good shave, but you should look good in a tux. Take a picture so we can all see."

Going to the door, Jared opened it to signal it was time for Chad to get back to work. Lots of customers and chores needed attention before the tuxedo-clad night came. "I'll think about it.

I may have made a big mistake saying I'd go. I don't know what I was thinking."

Chad slapped him on the shoulder. "She got to you, old friend. And it's good to see." With a chuckle, he started to leave.

Jared grabbed his elbow. "No spilling this to the others, okay? There'll be time for that later. This is just between you and me."

Assent came with a wink as Chad left.

He knew that look. Everyone would know about the ball before the close of business.

CHAPTER 23

The next day, Marissa's new rental car was delivered. No longer afoot, she was free to continue her trip as planned although the thought of driving on snow-packed roads made her stomach churn. The roads were still icy in spots, but the lure of her luxurious hotel suite downtown Denver was strong. The Milo Creek Hotel was nice enough, but she was ready for something else.

So why did she feel so reluctant to leave? The people. The peaceful environment. The large sense of family.

In the three days she'd been here, she'd made more new friends than she had the last few years in Dallas. Oh, sure she traveled a lot and met a lot of people, but none of them had come close to doing for her what the citizens of Milo Creek had done. They'd welcomed her like one of their own and made sure she recovered from her snowy trauma. So much gratitude filled her that she wanted to stay among those who truly cared.

But her job....

Once the people found out what she'd come to do, she wouldn't be welcome anymore. The Christmas-movie dream would change into a horror flick with no place for her to hide. Not even in the cemetery. When they broke ground on the new Food-N-More store in the coming spring, they'd come after her with chainsaws.

The previous afternoon was spent online with her office and the developer who was selling the land to the company. The papers for the closing were ready for her signature and the funds were in place.

The plans for the development were finalized and would be sent to the town council for approval which would put the news out to the public. She had to be out of town by then. She couldn't bear seeing Jared's face when he learned of it.

Throwing the last of her clothes in a suitcase, a wave of disgust went through her. Sometimes money wasn't worth what it forced you to do.

Still, it wasn't really her doing it. It was upper management's call. They were the ones who sent her on this mission, and if not her, someone else would have been sent. Potential profits looked too good to walk away from so Food-N-More was determined to establish a store here. And if not them, some other big corporation would come.

The blame wasn't hers. The economic analysis showed Sullivan Food Mart's days were numbered. The growing population was looking for more and were willing to travel to out-of-town stores to get it. Sooner or later, Sullivan's Food Mart would dwindle away.

Her company would provide new opportunities, pay more, and include good benefits. She held enough clout to make sure Martha, Chad, and the others got jobs at Food-N-More if they wanted them. They would be fine.

So why did she feel so guilty? She knew. Jared's view of himself was tied to the store. Whoever hurt his store was hurting him. It was very personal.

The only option to help him was giving advice on developing a new business model, but that would only happen if he'd listen to her. Jared's unyielding clamp on his family's dream would do nothing but hold him back and send him deeper into ruin. If only he could see what opportunities lay ahead of him.

Her phone buzzed. Checkout time was fast approaching. She stuffed the last of her clothes into the bag and took all her bags and her ball gown out to the car. One last look around the small room for anything left behind, and she was on her way.

Unending advice and suggestions flowed from Edith as she checked out. She pasted a smile on her face as Edith fussed over her like her grandmother used to do.

Edith's little motel would be obsolete with the soon-to-be convention center and hotel next to the interstate. Helping Edith would be harder. An old motel was difficult to convert to anything other than what it was. Maybe she could sell the lot for enough to retire on.

With a hug, address exchange, and a final bill, she was done. Just as Marissa stepped outside, the sun came out from behind a cloud, lighting the world with blinding brightness as it reflected off the snow. Squinting, Marissa dug in her bag for her sunglasses so she could see the beauty of her surroundings.

White puffy clouds moved across the deep blue sky. Snowbanks sparkled like they were full of glitter. Up the mountainside, the white of snow and the dark green of pine formed a mosaic that stretched down the valley. The air was crisp and fresher than the air in Dallas. Taking in a deep breath, she stuffed money in her coat pocket and threw her bag into the trunk. With everything safely stowed, she drove down the street of the small town toward her business appointment.

Downtown Milo Creek had a charm that would never be replaced by new construction. Craftmanship skills were still evident in the carefully hewn stones and decorative accent carvings. No one embellished buildings like that anymore. The old buildings would be there for decades if maintained properly. The downtown area would have to transform with the coming changes, but its charm could be preserved if done the right way.

Judging from the cars parked next to it, Sullivan's was doing a good business this morning. Telling her friends there goodbye would be hard. They'd helped her through difficult circumstances, and she was better for having met them. Somehow, she had to find the words to adequately convey her thanks to them.

Several vehicles drove down the street. Two people called out a greeting to each other outside the bank and stood to talk. The library had cars parked in front of it. Two teenaged boys nudged another and laughed at something that made the one guy's face turn red.

Marissa parked on a side street and walked to the door of the real estate office. She quickly looked around to see if anyone was watching before she slipped inside.

"May I help you?" A young woman behind a pair of monitors peered out at her.

"I have an appointment with Robert Langston."

Without a reply, the woman picked up the phone and called someone. "He's on his way up here," she said after hanging up. Whatever she was working on must have been more important because her attention returned to it immediately.

Marissa stood wondering if she was early, but the clock on the wall showed she was right on time.

A man in a suit came rushing out of the back. "Are you Ms. Williams? So nice to meet you in person. I'm Robert Langston." He stuck his hand out.

Taking it, she replied, "Hello. Ready to conclude our business?"

He motioned to the hallway he'd emerged from. "We have things set up in our meeting room."

She started that way but heard whispered arguing behind her. The girl behind the monitors had failed to give her a proper greeting, and Robert wasn't happy about it. A lot of money and commissions were being exchanged, and this woman deserved every courtesy, he told the young receptionist.

Smiling, Marissa made her way down the hallway.

"It's the door on the right," Robert said as he caught up to her.

A man and a woman sat at a long, polished wood table. Marissa's jaw dropped when she saw the third person. It was Benny. A surprised look flashed across his face.

Her cheeks suddenly felt hot as she sat down, trying not to stare at the man who could tell Jared her secret.

Robert sat at the head of the table and made introductions. The other man was Tim Morgan, the bank president and a member of the town council. The woman was Amanda Siefert, the mayor of Milo Creek. He introduced Benny as an interested party with hopes of being associated with the building of Food-N-More.

Interested party? Maybe Jared had sent him to check up on what was going on. A spy sent to see who showed up. Once the meeting was over, she'd get in her car and speed away. So much for the tickets to the ball and her ball gown. So much for saying bye to her friends. The security of a Denver hotel room sounded better and better.

Swallowing the lump forming in her throat, Marissa introduced herself as the representative of Food-N-More Corporation. She glanced at Benny, hoping he wouldn't show hostility toward her.

She made a presentation similar to the one she'd given many times. Having a large Food-N-More store in a community brought jobs, people, and tax revenue that would help fund schools, cities, counties, and all their associated functions.

The well-rehearsed speech fell from her lips while her mind kept wandering back to Benny's presence. It was no surprise, really. Everyone knew he wanted to leave Sullivan's. The only surprise was his look when she walked in.

"Any questions?" she asked as she ended her talk.

Benny's hand went up. "I hear your company buys from local producers. If a meat producer were here in town, would Food-N-More buy our meat for the store?"

So that was why he was here. He wasn't a spy. He was here for his own ambitions.

Her insides relaxed slightly. "Our company always looks for local businesses and producers to buy from. It helps them as well as cuts our freight costs which we pass on to our customers. If there were a reliable meat source nearby, we would certainly want to negotiate a contract with them."

A big smile spread across the banker's face. "This store will do fine things for our local economy."

Unfolding a survey map showing the layout of the new store and parking lot, she finished her spiel and stood back while the Robert, Tim, and Amanda pored over the large drawing. There was no avoiding Benny's stare as he made his way over to her.

"This is awkward," he said in a tone so low only she could hear it.

She backed away from the other attendees. "I'm sorry you had to find out this way, Benny. You can understand why I've been so secretive about it."

"I do, but Jared would be furious if he knew. This is like a knife in his back. He's crazy about you. If he knew, he'd...." He shook his head and let out a low whistle.

Eyes, stinging, she cleared her throat before the lump returned. "I never meant to hurt anyone. I didn't get caught in an avalanche just to increase business. I had no idea who it was that pulled me out...,"

Benny reassured her he understood and would say nothing to Jared.

Amanda asked a question, drawing Marissa back to the business of the meeting. Everyone settled back into their seats as she repeated the offer for the land and conveyed her company's thanks for special considerations on rights-of-way, taxes, and permits. Negotiations went on for over an hour before the mayor stood, shook her hand, and said she was looking forward to shopping at the new store. Signatures went on the documents, and Marissa presented them with the check covering the transaction.

Amid all the congratulations and back-slapping, Benny piped up. "Gentlemen and Madam Mayor, before we adjourn, I have one request."

Silence fell across the table as all eyes went to him.

"This new development will have tremendous impacts on friends and businesses downtown." He looked at his hands and rubbed them together. "I want to keep this news quiet for another day. Give me time to break it to Jared Sullivan who will be hardest hit by this project." He looked around the table. "You all know how much his store means to him and how much it's meant to the town. Give me a chance to soften the blow to him before you start touting how much the new store will do for Milo Creek."

The air left the celebration balloon as somber looks covered everyone's faces.

Tim said, "Benny's right. Jared's a good friend to us all, and his store will receive the brunt of change. No one speak to anyone about this until Benny has a chance to tell him in private. I have a feeling he'll be contacting all of us once he knows."

Marissa added, "I will speak to our PR department and ask them to wait a day before releasing the news to the public."

All mumbled their agreement with the action.

Tim, Amanda, and Robert made their way out, leaving Benny and Marissa behind. The air was heavy with stress as she tried to think of what to say. If he would wait to tell Jared about this until after she left. She'd be out of reach of his anger when he learned the woman he pulled from the snowbank was here to throw his business over the cliff. It was the coward's way out, but for someone she'd never see again, it seemed the simple way to do it.

Benny watched Marissa putting papers back into her computer bag, then said. "We've got a problem."

She zipped the case closed before answering him. "How to tell Jared I'm the spy everyone says I am?"

"Partly. That and I don't want him to know I was here. I've told him I'm thinking of starting my own business but I doubt he knows I've already set up a business plan and bought property for my butcher shop." He paused to look at her hard. "I'll talk to him about this. I'm his friend, and it'll be better coming from me."

"Agreed! I'd rather you tell him everything anyway. I'm headed out for Denver today. I don't expect to be welcomed back." She held her hand out. "It's been nice meeting you, Benny, and thanks for everything. Good luck with your business. I'll put in a good word for you at corporate headquarters."

He stared at her hand but never took it. "I will tell him about me. And I'll tell him about Food-N-More coming to town. I won't tell him about you. You have to tell him. That's your job, not mine. I'm not wading into that swamp." With a nervous laugh, he shook her hand.

He was smart. He wasn't going to do her dirty work. "Fair enough."

"But wait to tell him after New Year's Eve," he said as he picked up his folder and put papers inside. "I'm excited for him to go to that New Year's shindig with you. He needs a night out. Something outside his very small universe. That man is too stuck in his ways. He needs to join the rest of the world occasionally." Going to the door, he paused. "Now to face the dragon. I dread it."

"Me too." Marissa picked up her computer case and bag. He won't be happy with you on either count." She pulled out her business card from a pocket on her computer case. "Here. Call me if you need anything."

"You leaving now?"

She shook her head. "I thought I'd grab a bite at the deli and tell everyone goodbye. Can you hold off your talk with Jared that long?"

"For you? Sure."

CHAPTER 24

Jared watched as Marissa glided in the door and was greeted by Martha and a suspicious-eyed Jason who was sacking for an elderly couple. She was dressed like she'd come from some high-powered business meeting. Odd that she'd dress that way to have lunch before she left for Denver.

He looked down at his apron over his plain shirt. It was one more way their lives differed.

He checked his watch. Knowing Martha would want to have lunch, he went to find Chad to take over at the front. He wanted his time with Marissa too.

He finished what Chad was doing before he headed to the deli. He found the two women ordering lunch from Holly. Marissa smiled when she saw him, making him feel like he was floating.

"Want to join us for lunch?" she asked.

That's what he wanted most, but he didn't want to seem too eager. "If Martha doesn't mind."

Martha waved her arm as she carried her sandwich to the little table in the corner. She arranged three chairs around it before she sat down.

Marissa gathered her vegetable beef soup, roll, and soft drink while Jared ordered his usual coney dog with chili and coffee. He heard the girls start to talk while he waited for Holly to bring his lunch.

The women were talking about ballgowns when he sat down with his meal, not a subject he could talk intelligently about. When they both had their mouths full, he interjected, "Heading back to Denver today?" He quickly filled his mouth with a bite to keep from having to say more.

Marissa nodded.

"We'll miss you," Martha said with a tone of sadness. "You feel like part of the hometown crowd already. You belong here."

Marissa blinked hard several times as she stirred her soup.

Martha was right, Jared thought. She fit in so well and wasn't like the newbies who brought their high-brow ways with them. She blended in like she'd always lived here. She'd be one newbie that he wouldn't mind moving to Milo Creek.

Great time to bring the subject up. "We need a lawyer in town," he said. "Didn't you say you wanted to do estate planning or something like that?"

Marissa stirred her soup as she stared at it as if trying to conjure an answer. "It's a dream of mine, but it's not something I can do right now. I've got too many irons in the fire back home."

"That's always the problem," Martha added flippantly. "Too busy to do what we really want to do. Right, Jared?"

His own face got warm, and he quickly stuffed his mouth with another bite to keep from answering. He knew what she was saying, and Marissa would agree with her. He didn't stand a chance with two-against-one odds.

Marissa took a drink, then said, "The time has to be right for everything. It's like a house of cards. If everything isn't perfectly balanced, it all comes tumbling down. And getting everything to balance takes a lot of work and coordination. Right, Jared?"

That seemed a safe statement to agree to so he nodded. He was ready to get off this log roll. He needed another topic of conversation, but what? The weather? Too bland. They could see it out the window. Wait another few minutes, and it would change. Property taxes were expected to rise but that wouldn't interest Marissa. His mind reached a dead end.

"Have you sent your measurements to the tux rental place yet?" Marissa asked him.

New subject but not a good one. He knew he'd forgotten something. A one-sided smile was all he gave back.

"Don't you worry," Martha said. "I'll measure him myself before he goes home tonight."

"Good," Marissa said. "I'll text you what they need. And don't forget shoe size."

The ladies went back to their talk about the ball, leaving Jared with the remains of his chili dog. Marissa beamed when she was talking about the decorations and the food there. She'd gone once before and been infatuated. Said there was nothing else like that party and was so happy to be going again. She only had to show up, talk to a couple of CEOs if they were there, and the rest of the night was hers.

"And thanks to Jared, I have someone to share it with." She reached over and squeezed his forearm.

Her smile softened his face, and he smiled back. "Shucks, ma'am, I won't be nothing but a country boy in a city slicker suit."

"You'll be a Cinderguy," Martha chimed in. "But beware, Marissa, he may turn into a pumpkin at midnight."

"I hope he waits to transform until at least five after twelve. I'd hate for him to miss all the streamers and confetti they shoot out at midnight."

"I'll do my best," Jared remarked before taking the last bite of his lunch. He wiped his mouth and excused himself from their continuing banter. He was out of his league with these two. He was safer checking out groceries for sweet old ladies who thought he was handsome.

CHAPTER 25

The warm water bubbled and caressed Marissa as she lay in the jacuzzi. Music played through the Bluetooth earbuds in the dim bathroom that was the size of her room at the Milo Creek Motel. A room service tray with empty dishes sat outside her room's door. A gas fireplace gave everything in the other room a soft orange glow. Everything she'd hoped to find when she went on her wild, life-altering trip to the Spruce Canyon Lodge was here in the blissful safety of her Denver hotel room.

She hoped her glowing review of the lodge would run more business their way.

The phone call to her mother about Tyler was over. The expected blowup and threats had come and gone. The offer to come to Denver was turned down. Peace was restored but if her mother ever saw Tyler again, there was no guarantee he'd walk away whole.

She hadn't mentioned the avalanche or Jared. One issue was all she wanted her mother to handle at a time. Depending on how things turned out, news of Jared could wait. Or never be mentioned if it turned out badly.

The past few days were making her rethink the path of her life and reexamine where she was and where she wanted to go. Her high-paying job was nice and afforded her nice things without struggle. Like hotel suites with jacuzzi tubs. But how much was enough? How many shoes did she really need? How many purses would it take to be satisfied? Was having lots of things worth more than doing what you inwardly really wanted to do with your life?

She was lucky. Her large, judiciously invested nest egg and debt-free lifestyle allowed her to choose a different direction. But what direction? Stay on course and enjoy a spoiled lifestyle? Find a different job with another large salary to maintain her standard of living? Strike out on her own to fulfill her dream of helping others like her grandfather and give up her indulgences?

Starting her own practice meant she could get lost in the crowds and buildings of Dallas. Marketing dollars would have to be spent prudently to pull in clients. Office space, furnishing it, and maybe even hiring a secretary would be expensive. The costs of getting started would be enormous, and she'd function in the red for a while. She'd have to start charging her brothers for her services. Wouldn't they love that! They'd probably refuse.

Her phone rang from the other room, pulling her out of her ruminating. Looking at her wrinkled hands and feeling the cool water, it was time to pull the plug on her soak, but not yet. Whoever was calling would have to wait for her call back. Her pampering time wasn't over.

Her post-soak routine took a while, and she wouldn't rush it. Only after she was well moisturized with dry hair and a nightgown on did she look to see who had called.

Jared.

The name made her smile. Maybe he missed her. Maybe he didn't want to lose touch. Maybe he wasn't coming to the ball. Maybe he'd learned her secret. A hundred possibilities bounced in her head.

Leaning back into her nest of mounded pillows, she called him back. When he answered, his voice was strained like someone was choking the life out of him.

"Jared?" Her knees came up to her chest. "Are you okay?"

The depths of his worry lines came through with the sounds of his pacing. He didn't need to say the words. Benny had talked to him. He knew Food-N-More was coming, and Benny was leaving. Sullivan Food Mart wouldn't survive. His purpose in life was coming to an end.

He'd reached out to her. She was flattered but afraid. He didn't know he was talking with the enemy.

She'd seen Benny before she left Sullivan's that day. He'd raised his eyebrows at her, and she knew what it meant. He was reminding her to tell Jared about who she really was.

One shock at a time was enough for Jared. She would tell him after the ball. Until then, she'd remain his friend.

"Tell me about it, Jared," she whispered into the phone.

The man emptied his soul's torment to her. Sometimes with words. Sometimes with silence. Sometimes with choked-back emotions. It all hovered around him not knowing what to do. He would dishonor his father and grandfather by not being able to keep the business open, but how could he compete against a large chain store?

He sniffed and croaked out, "You're a lawyer. Can I sue them for something to keep them out of Milo Creek? Maybe check the zoning laws and sue them over that?"

Her heart sunk a little. He wanted legal advice. This had nothing to do with how he felt about her. It was good and bad all mixed together.

"No, you can't sue them. It's a free country built on free enterprise. There's no basis for a lawsuit."

His voice choked. "There has to be something! I can't let my family business die like this! What am I going to do?"

He was losing control of his emotions.

She took a deep breath and told him to do the same. "First, you need to calm down and stop feeling guilty. You can't face this dilemma when you're panicked and desperate."

Repeating her instructions, she waited until she heard him take a deep breath. "You are not dishonoring your father or your grandfather. If they were here, they would be facing the same issues you are and have the same options you have. These circumstances are not a reflection on your business acumen."

Another big breath was released. "I suppose you're right."

"There's no supposing. I am right, and you know it. None of this is under your control. What is under your control is what are you going to do about it?"

He moaned an I-don't-know, and the phone went silent. Marissa looked her hers and saw they were still connected. Everything in her wanted to reach across the distance and hold him in a tight hug.

Maybe she should have stayed there. She knew this would happen, but she'd fled the scene for fear of seeing him suffer. She was a coward and not much of a friend. His world was crumbling while she was luxuriating in a nice hotel.

He needed counseling. Her mother would know how to do that. Maybe she could channel her.

"Jared, listen to me. Can you hear me?"

Nothing came through but a breath. If that was the best he could do, she'd take it.

"Listen to me. You're going to make a plan. The new store won't open for at least a year—"

"How do you know that?"

Her heart thundered like a stampede. She'd made a slip-up. "Uh... just a guess. It takes a while to build a store that size. In the meantime, Milo Creek needs a source for groceries. The town needs you, Jared. Don't let them down."

He was quiet for a bit, but then agreed.

What would her mother say next? Something simple. "If Benny leaves, he's not taking his people with him, is he?"

"His son will go, but the other two may stay for a while. I could promote one to head butcher." His voice had a tinge of hope in it.

She was making progress. "Good! Work out something with Benny to keep the meat coming. You solved that problem. Other than that one change, everything else should go on normally for a while. It gives you time to develop a new business plan."

"A business plan for what? I don't know anything but running a grocery store."

His hopes had a slippery rope tied to them, she guessed. For a moment, she had a brief glimpse into what her mother had put up with during Marissa's whiny teenaged years. More channeling was needed to find the patience of her mother or Job or whoever had a lot of it.

"Come on, Jared. You're a businessman. You know how supply and demand work. You know how to read customers. You know how money flows in and out, how to figure profit margins, how to problem-solve. You're a boss who deals with personnel issues. You're so much more than a guy who runs a grocery store. You need to look inside yourself. See all the skills you have. Find the determination to succeed."

Silence filled the space between them again, but this time, she could tell he was thinking. A good sign.

She decided to prod him further. "What's the name of your business." She knew the answer but was careful not to reveal she knew it.

"You know that. It's Sullivan's Food Mart."

"Is that the business name or the name of the store?"

"Sullivan Enterprises is the umbrella the store is under."

"Sullivan Enterprises. There's nothing in that name that implies it's only for grocery stores. It can cover businesses of all kinds. If your grandfather wanted the business to succeed, doesn't that mean Sullivan Enterprises must succeed and not merely Sullivan Food Mart? You can keep your grandfather's dream alive and keep your promise to your father by keeping the enterprise alive."

"You make it seem easy."

She let out a short laugh. "It won't be easy at all, but it'll be worth it in the long term. Make a plan and execute it."

He let out his own short laugh. "I don't know where to start."

"You can start here. Let's talk about it."

Over the next two hours, Marissa threw out ideas like a pitcher on a mound. Carpenter. Realtor. Rental management. Car dealer. Mayor. Politician. Coffee shop owner. On and on, she pitched them out, sometimes consulting Google as he argued against the latest pitch. Jared swung at a few ideas but nothing went past the infield. When ideas started running thin, the end of her patience arrived.

"You're looking for an easy solution to a hard problem. There's not one. You're going to have to come out of that comfort zone you've fortified with massive walls. Your castle is crumbling. It's time to rebuild it into something better." She put her hand over her mouth to keep it shut. Any more words might have been hurtful. The ones she'd spoken were bad enough.

"Fine. I'll be an alligator wrestler. Would that make you happy?"

Gritting her teeth, she took a deep breath to calm her rising frustration. "Only if it's really what you want to do." Resorting to one last idea, she added, "How about going to college to become an architect?"

"It's too late for that."

"You're not dead yet." The words slipped out without thinking, but she couldn't suck them back in.

She waved the white flag. "What would make you happy, Jared? And don't say keeping your grocery store. That's not on the table. What business does Milo Creek need? Go visit Dillion or come to Denver and see what's successful. Look for ideas."

He didn't reply but she'd spoken her piece. The rest was up to him. "Maybe you're right. I'll think about it."

"Good. Sitting around won't accomplish anything. Look, I have to go. See you on Friday. Come early and we'll explore a little. Talk about ideas."

He reluctantly agreed and ended their call.

She tossed her phone beside her and leaned back. It didn't lay there long before it dinged, signaling a text. It was probably Jared apologizing for being such a baby. He'd have to wait until she finished her bedtime routine. She took her time brushing her teeth and flossing and putting lotion on her hands. Maybe she'd check her email or watch TV. It would give her time to recover from channeling.

Snuggling back into her nest, she pulled the covers up over her bare legs. There wasn't much to watch on TV that interested her until she found an old movie that held more promise of a plot than all the reality shows combined. Women dressed classy back in the days of black-and-white movies. They knew what they wanted. Men spoke eloquently and were sure of themselves. It was the prescription for what she needed to recover from her inning with Jared.

Her phone dinged again, ruining her attempt to get lost in the 1950s. She growled at her phone when she saw the text was from Tyler. He was still trying to jerk her chain. It would do no good. She was free of the bonds that had held her for so long.

She opened the text and read: *Sweetheart, there are a lot of things I need to tell you. Let's have lunch and talk. Anytime, anywhere. I love you. Devoted to you, T.* The second text message was also from him, begging her to agree to meet.

Resisting the urge to throw the phone against the wall again, she threw it against the bed instead. Men were driving her crazy. They were whiny puppies following her around, making messes, then expecting her to clean it up. One wouldn't go away, and she was afraid the other one would. She was tired of it.

Taking her own advice from what she told Jared, she made a plan. Tyler would get part of his wish. She would meet with him and state unequivocally she was done with him. The sooner he accepted it, the sooner she would be rid of his texts, calls, and emails.

Next, she'd touch base with Jared if she hadn't heard from him by tomorrow. Debating on whether she should apologize to him or not, she settled on waiting until morning to send anything.

Turning her phone off, she nestled against her pillows once again and reentered the simpler times of the 1950s.

CHAPTER 26

A dark cloud hung over Jared's head which shadowed his face. His customers got out of his way rather than speak. His employees seemed subdued, stopping their whispering as he neared. The air was devoid of cheer. Everything was different. He didn't like that.

The cloud got darker. People backed away farther.

Most of the day, he sat in his office staring at the computer screen. An email had come from the high school band teacher asking him to help sponsor their summer band camp. He would, but for the first time since his father started the tradition, he would have to tell them it would be his last year to do so.

His inbox was full of other emails from vendors with requests, bargain prices, and orders, but he wasn't interested in responding. What was the use? It was all coming to an end anyway.

He turned to look at the wall behind his desk. His grandfather and father looked down on him, taunting him with their eyes full of pride and determination. Lining the other walls were certificates of appreciation and achievement with their names displayed in large calligraphy lettering. They all ridiculed him, telling him he had done nothing but rest on the laurels of his forefathers. Anger boiled up inside. Not at them but at himself. He'd been too content to leave things the way they were.

A knock at the door turned the flame of anger up. No intrusion was welcome, and he was ready to bellow it out when he heard Chad's voice.

"Boss, you alright?"

He could say yes just to get rid of him, but it was a lie. If he told the truth, Chad would come in and say all the things a friend should say but none of them would help. The people he wanted to talk to were only pictures on the wall, but they were gone and couldn't provide guidance or advice. He was totally alone.

The chair on the other side of his desk made a sound, signaling that Chad had come in uninvited and was sitting. The unavoidable dropped in his lap. He might as well get it over with. Spinning around, he stared at his friend who stared back. Neither spoke as the seconds ticked past.

Chad blinked. "You're a pathetic heap of self-pity."

Those weren't the words he was expecting to hear. Adjusting his seat, he averted his eyes from the laser gaze. "I've got a lot to think about."

"All you've thought about is how you're a failure. Am I right?" He paused. "Am I?"

The words hit at the core of Jared's feelings. He was a failure but had hoped he could hide it so no one else would know. But some things couldn't be hidden, especially from Chad who knew him so well. His disgrace was out for everyone to see. He was a disappointment to his father and grandfather.

Slapping the desk with his hand, Chad almost yelled, "Get a hold yourself, man. You keep acting like this and you won't fail because Food-N-More is coming in. You'll fail because you ran all your customers off with your surly mood. You've gone from a congenial store owner to a grouch who can't be bothered with anything. No one wants to be around you."

His customers. He hadn't thought much about them. "Why do you say that?" he grumbled.

"Because business is down. It's slow. Even Martha is talking about how our customers are talking about your growling and frowning. I think you've scared off some of them."

Jared rubbed his eyes that burned with self-loathing. Nothing he'd done was right. Marissa said he had to hang on for a while for his customers' sakes. He hated she was right.

"Jared," Chad said in a voice that held respect and friendship, "I know you feel like this is the end, but it's not. If the store closes, then you can turn it into something else. A different kind of store. I'll help you. We'll come up with something."

"Marissa said to make a plan," Jared confessed. "A new business plan."

Chad smiled as he said, "Smart woman. Listen to her. Take a few days off. Get away from it all. Go to Denver and see Marissa. See new things and new people. Maybe something will come to mind. You may be more focused when you get back."

Silence came down between them like a curtain. The tension stole Jared's voice. He couldn't defend himself or offer an excuse.

The idea of running was appealing, but the same problems would be here when he got back.

"Come on, man, get away. Take a vacation."

Looking at Chad, Jared could see the sincerity in his eyes. He could handle the store without any problem, especially if there were fewer customers.

Marissa said she'd pay for everything. The offer made him feel like a leech but facing his business prospects was worse.

Maybe Chad was right. A day or two of rest and new scenery would help bring him out of his funk. He could think better without all the ancestral eyes looking down on him.

"Okay, I'll go."

Chad sat back in the chair, eyes wide and mouth open. "Wow, I can't believe you said that! I haven't used my rehearsed speech to get you to go."

"Want me to listen to it anyway?"

The tension melted away in the warmth of the laughter between the two friends. A sense of normalcy washed over Jared. Not all was lost as long as he had his work family.

CHAPTER 27

S team rose from Marissa's mocha coffee, passing between her and Tyler who stared at her with pleading eyes. The spell he'd cast over her in middle school was broken, and she saw him for what he was. He was pitiful. What had she ever seen in him?

She'd rejected his invitation to dinner, then one for lunch. She settled for a coffee shop, knowing it would limit the time she had to spend with him. Besides, she loved the coffee here. The chairs were comfortable too.

"Marissa, I know I've hurt you, and I'm sorry. Olivia threw herself at me, and I didn't resist like I should have, but please...please give me another chance," he serenaded. He reached out a touched her hand that was wrapped around her cup.

The contact repulsed her, and she quickly raised the cup to her lips. She kept her eyes on him as she took a small sip and tried to think of how best to put what she was feeling.

"Tyler, we had a good time while we were together. When you moved to Denver, it broke my heart. You never called me and—"

"I called you back," he almost shouted. "I always called back."

This was going to be more difficult than she thought and might force her to be more brutal than she wanted to be.

"Yes, you did, but the point is I had to initiate the action, and any response had to be at your convenience. That made me feel like I'd moved a long way down your priority list."

He looked away as if an answer could be found in the ski-themed décor of the coffee shop. "It's not true. You've always been number one."

"Your actions say different."

His face hardened as he looked for a lifeline from the few customers around them. He looked back at her. "We've had lots of good times together. The trips, the Dallas Cowboy games, the Rangers games, the shopping. We could pick up where we left off, and I could make you love me all over again. I know I could." He reached his hands across, palms up, inviting her to join him.

Or was he holding his hands out for her to hand over her credit cards? All the things he'd mentioned were done on her dime. She'd paid for it all because she wanted him to be happy. Tyler didn't miss her as much as he missed the perks that came with her credit cards.

It was all so clear now. All the things he loved to do were fun, but they would be just as fun with friends who paid their own way.

She took a drink of her cooling coffee. "Tyler, your account has been closed. If you want to do those things, put a crowbar in your wallet and pay for them yourself. I'm sure Miss Long-Legs-Blonde-Hair will go with you."

She stood, ready to walk away from her past. "We're done. Goodbye for good, Tyler. Don't call anymore." With a toss of her head, she left him and her coffee there.

CHAPTER 28

J ared's suitcase had so much dust on it, he had to wipe it down. Concerned a mouse might jump out, he unzipped it and lifted the lid with an outstretched arm. Relieved nothing moved, he tried to remember when he used it last. Must have been Christmas three years ago when he went to his brother's house in Pennsylvania. An unforgettable trip after his flight home was delayed two days because of the Denver weather. Being trapped away from home wasn't a feeling he wanted to experience again.

Packing for two days in a fancy hotel left him perplexed. Other than his funeral suit, all he had was casual wear he wore to the store. He picked out the nicest slacks and shirts he owned. Now for shoes. He mostly wore running shoes. From what he'd seen on TV, the executives that inhabited high-class hotels didn't wear them downtown. In the very back of his closet, he found a pair of dress shoes that might suffice once dusted and shined. He wanted to impress Marissa, but he'd take his running shoes in case he didn't care what she thought.

The next morning, he went to work long enough to assure himself everything would run smoothly during his absence.

Everyone at the store seemed happy to bid him good luck in the big city.

Martha gave him a hug and shoved a folder into his hands. "Read it later," she whispered in his ear.

Chad tapped the folder and repeated what Martha had said. Holly came next, wiping her flour-covered hands on her apron before giving him a good slap on the shoulder. "Don't do nothing I wouldn't do."

The implication made his face heat up as Benny and Jason practically pushed him out the back door. They yelled a final goodbye like he was going off on a voyage to discover a new land.

Standing in the snow-packed alley, their enthusiasm at his departure bothered him. They were all in on some secret. He should find out about it before he left, but a click of the lock made it clear he was not going back in. For a minute, he thought of going around to the front. He looked at the folder in his hands and decided it probably held the answer.

He started the walk home, each step becoming quicker and lighter. If left on his own, he'd never gone out of town. Running away wasn't such a bad idea. Funny how he hadn't realized how much he needed a break from his troubles. Having a date to the gala with Marissa gave him a destination without having to find one. The date provided an excuse—or rather, an opportunity for him to know where to go and what to do. He hadn't had much experience with either lately.

What Marissa had in mind for them was a mystery. He normally liked everything planned and scheduled. Going into the unknown was foreign and made him nervous. Anticipation was an emotion he hadn't felt in a long time, and it felt good.

He couldn't stop smiling. The avalanche had brought more than hero status to him. Maybe love.

Out on the interstate, the mountains grew smaller and the plains grew wider. He passed through the last gap and went down onto the eastern slope of the Rockies. The air was browner, and the sky less blue. Gray snow lay on either side of the highway and clung to the sides of unwashed cars. Like ants on a disturbed mound, cars and trucks zoomed and weaved in and out and around him as he drove above the speed limit enough to blend in with traffic.

A visit to a Food-N-More store was his one planned stop. If he knew more about the competition he was up against, he could formulate a better plan to fight them off. He may not be able to contend with a large store based on selection, but he could base his store on service and individual attention. Quality goods at a reasonable price would be all he'd carry.

But he already did that.

Then he'd hire more high-school kids to sack and take groceries to the customers' cars. No big chain did that. Or he could even deliver groceries to those who couldn't get out, especially in winter. There had to be a way to keep his customers.

Ahead a large red and blue sign guided him to his destination. The enormous size of the nearly full parking lot intimidated him enough to almost make him drive away. He parked out on the edge and walked, observing what people had in their carts as they came out of the store.

The doors opened for him, granting admittance to the bright world beyond. The produce section was at least half the size of his entire store, giving a large and varied selection of fresh fruits and vegetables. The wide aisles allowed people with full baskets to pass each other with room to spare. The meat department had everything his offered plus more. A pile of fresh shrimp lay in ice next to a tank of lobsters in water with bound claws awaiting their fate.

He walked down several aisles to see the variety of offerings. A row of potato and corn chips of every kind seemed a hundred feet long. Canned vegetables stretched down both sides of the aisle. A refrigerated row of multiple kinds of milk and juices were against a back wall. The bakery and deli were large enough to provide catering. Then there was the part of the store he had no hope of competing with. Racks of men's, women's, and children's clothes and shoes stretched out before him. Beyond them were the aisles of hardware and home decorating goods.

He stood staring at the far wall that seemed a mile away. His competitive resolution drained out of his chest, down his legs, and through the floor. There was no way he could hold on to his business with this...this warehouse just across the interstate.

"Is there something I can help you find?"

He turned to look at a man in a red Food-N-More apron. Even the employees were helpful. There was no level on which he could win.

The man repeated his question.

"No," Jared said. "I've seen all I wanted." He walked out wishing he'd never gone in.

Back on the interstate, he felt numb as he drove in the increasingly heavy traffic. He had to face the limits of his business and see the ugly truth. Sullivan's Food Mart was at the end of its time.

His grandfather's voice played on a loop in his head, "Don't let my business fail." But Grandfather, how can it survive against that?

Marissa had suggested changing the business. Chad had hinted at it as well. Maybe they were right.

Benny seemed to know what he was going to do and seemed confident that he would succeed. Maybe he could go to work for Benny or lease the store to—

A car cut in front of his vehicle, and he slammed on the brakes to keep from hitting it. A horn sounded. The same car cut in front of someone else in the other lane, then exited like a flash. His heart pounding, Jared realized he needed to concentrate on the traffic. All his worries became moot if he was involved in an accident.

He wanted to go home but he didn't dare. Martha and Chad would be angry. Standing up Marissa wasn't an option. He couldn't do that to her.

In a flurry and a rush and an hour of time, he found himself downtown, listening to his GPS direct him through the concrete canyons. Claustrophobia made him grip the wheel harder as people and cars penned him in at the intersections waiting for the light to change.

He was truly a small-town guy, if for no other reason than bumper-to-bumper traffic was terrifying. Knowing the hotel was close helped him make it through the anxious moment.

A few minutes later, he left the thundering herd and pulled into a circular driveway. A man ran out and offered to help him. Relieved to have his feet on the ground, he got his small bag, then tossed the keys to the man and offered him a ten-dollar bill to park his car. He hoped it was enough.

One adventure ended. Another had begun.

Chapter 29

Sitting in a chair in the hotel lobby, Marissa watched as Jared came in with an old suitcase. His eyes first went up to the tall ceiling with its gold fixtures and chandeliers. Next, he looked around the lobby with its large stone fireplace, a gas flame warming the surrounding chairs and sofas. When his eyes met hers, he smiled.

She closed her book and rose to meet him. "Jared, I'm surprised you're here so early," she said without trying to hide her glee. Martha's text had warned her he was on his way so it wasn't unexpected.

"I got kicked out of my store," he said. Then he laughed a little. He looked around the massive room. "I usually come to grocery warehouses in Denver, never downtown. Wow, Marissa—" he stared at the floor while he rubbed the back of his neck before he looked back at her, "—this is too much. I'm not sure how much this is running you but let me kick in some money for all this."

Grabbing his upper arm and squeezing as tightly as she could, she held his attention. "Those are the very last words you're going to say about it. This is my party. I invited you. Merry Christmas.

The end." She pulled a card key from her pocket. "I've already checked you in. I'll show you to your room."

Like a boy in a toy shop, he looked all around with wide eyes and gaping mouth as they went to the elevators. She'd dressed in slacks and a casual top knowing that he'd probably wear what he usually wore at the store. Her plans for a relaxing afternoon and casual evening were designed to put him at ease before the extravagant night tomorrow. Judging from the way he was acting as they came to the gold-mirrored elevator doors, she'd made a good call.

He seemed fidgety and ran his hand through his hair several times. Whether he was nervous because of her or being out of his element, she couldn't tell. Somehow, she had to reassure him that fun could be had anywhere.

She left him at the door to his room and told him to come downstairs when he was ready to explore downtown. Back in the lobby, she wondered if that was a mistake. He might not want to explore in which case, she was stuck in the lobby awaiting his appearance. Hunger would force him to leave his room eventually. Digging through her bag, she found the paperback she'd been reading earlier and settled in for a long afternoon.

She'd hardly begun when he appeared before her chair. He'd changed his shoes but otherwise looked the same as when he arrived.

"I heard there was an aquarium close by," he said with a sly look. "Being a landlubber, I love seeing exotic fish and other slimy things. Would you mind going with me?"

Slamming her book shut, she stuffed it into her bag and rose to take his arm. "I know where that is," she told him. "Mind walking?"

"Not at all! It's better than driving in this crazy traffic." He thrust out his elbow and she accepted his offer.

The few blocks they had to go provided a chance for them to make small talk. A sadness enveloped him as he mentioned his trip to Food-N-More, then dropped the subject. She didn't question him. It would have only made things worse.

The afternoon went by in a flurry of flippers, fins, scales, spikes, mermaids, and laughter. Watching the colorful fish move through the clear water was hypnotizing. The jellyfish moved in slow motion, their tentacles fluttering like flags in a gentle breeze. Being on eye level with the water life drew them in with the same wonder as the children around them.

An easy friendship between them flowed like the water in the tanks, clean, pure, and sustaining. The common wonder of water life made conversation effortless, sprinkled with silences of appreciation and awe. Tyler, Food-N-More, and Sullivan's Food Mart disappeared in the unseasonably warm afternoon.

Mostly children joined them when they went into the theater to watch a short movie. Jared selected seats against the back wall, but Marissa didn't mind. Sitting in a dark room for a while would let her mind untangle the jumble of feelings that were growing into a tighter knot. She couldn't quite understand why she felt so drawn to the grocery store owner. Could it be rebound feelings, or pity knowing she was going to ruin his business? Could it be friendship growing, or could it be...dare she think it? Could it be real love? Love not one based on her credit card limit, but on affection and respect?

But they could never have a relationship. He'd made it clear he'd never leave Milo Creek, and she wasn't sure she wanted to live in a place where snow tried to kill you by crashing down mountainsides.

The lights went down, and he reached over to take her hand.

The knot in her mind twisted and tightened. Logic told her heartache lay ahead, that all this would collapse when he found out who she worked for. But her heart said they could find a way to overcome whatever obstacle that arose, but there was no crystal ball to show the outcome.

The lights came on, signaling the end of the movie. So soon? Her thoughts had been too deep to let her pay attention to anything other than the colors and images.

Jared looked over at her and said, "Wasn't that interesting?"

Other than water and fish, she had no idea what it had been about. Hoping not to discuss the movie, she threw an idea at him. "I'm hungry."

"Me too." He stood, never letting go of her hand, and waited for the excited children to go first as their mothers and teachers herded them out.

As they made their way outside, the sun was touching the mountains in the west. Hand in hand, they navigated the few blocks to where the nightlife was beginning to come alive. The chill of the evening air started to make itself felt as they made their way down sidewalks and across busy intersections in the rush hour traffic. Cars were lined up behind each other, and the bus stops were crowded with people staring at their phones. Horns sounded when lights changed and the lead car didn't move fast enough for those behind it.

Aromas from different cuisines drifted from the restaurants, beckoning them inside. The smell of olives, sundried tomatoes, and garlic drew them to an Italian restaurant. The smell of fresh bread whet their appetites in the dimly lit booth. After they ordered, Jared spoke more of visiting Food-N-More. The wide aisles, bright lights, and extensive selections had overwhelmed him. His decades-old décor, small building, and limited options couldn't compete against it. His strategy of relying on customer loyalty would never be enough.

As he talked, Marissa felt like disappearing into thin air. The fun of the afternoon and ease of being with him morphed into dread and fear. The truth would come out eventually but by then, she hoped to be far away. He'd never forgive her for deceiving him. If he could read her mind, he'd fling his cold drink into her face and storm off.

She gave him a slight smile as he kept talking. He seemed to be emptying his worries on the table in front of her. Compared to her few other experiences with men, that was unusual. Tyler never discussed his feelings other than what he wanted to do next. Her father always kept his feelings bottled up until they came out in massive explosions. She liked Jared's way better. No shattered dishes or cowering in corners were necessary.

The waiter brought their pollo marsala and valdonstana di pollo. The steaming plates of flavor drew their attention and conversation away from their troubles.

"I've talked your ear off," Jared said without looking at her.

She finished her bite before answering. "I don't mind. You've got a lot going on. Everything is just between us so no worries about me spreading anything around Milo Creek." She gave him a wink as she took another bite.

A smile spread across his face as he nodded. Little passed between them other than comments on the food until Marissa pushed back her plate and declared she had eaten all she could. As Jared continued to eat, it gave her the opportunity to say what was on her mind.

"Jared, I hope you've thought more about a new business plan." Before he could counter that statement, she held her hand up. "Let me finish. I know what your grandfather and father said about keeping the business going. There's no reason you can't do that in a different form. Milo Creek is growing and changing, and your business can grow and change with it."

While he finished his meal, she presented an idea about opening a coffee shop, something the city crowds loved for working remotely. The right décor and a high-speed internet connection would draw people to his charming building downtown. Holly could have a bakery there to offer food with beverages. He could manage it, or let Chad manage it while he lived off the rental fees and maybe a portion of the profits.

He stared at her, his eyes blank. "Sounds like you want me to turn into a lazy slum lord."

The retort stunned her for a second. "That's not it at all, Jared. I want you to succeed. Open a coffee shop and sell premium coffee beans, roasted and ground at your store. You could have a bookstore on the side. Have a small meeting room where clubs in town could meet if they buy drinks and food from you. The list is endless. Your building is amazing in its allure and tie to the past. You could develop that into something people would drive from all over to see and buy from. It's something Food-N-More doesn't have. Your business could even grow into franchising and make your grandfather proud."

She'd thrown in the last thing as a zinger to make him think harder about it. His tight grip on what he'd heard in childhood had throttled him for too long. It was time for him to break free of the haunting memory and become a successful businessman on his own.

If only she could get him over the hump of fettered thinking and put him on the path of ingenuity.

He sat still with an unfocused stare. She'd triggered something but without him saying anything, she couldn't know whether it was good or bad. The most she hoped for was he wouldn't stand and leave her sitting there. That would be humiliating. Plus, the ball was in 24 hours. Surely he could stick around for that long.

"It's something to think about. I appreciate your thoughts." He placed his napkin on the table and said, "It's been a long day. Shall we go?"

Relieved not to be stranded, she paid for the meal, and they left.

The noise of the traffic and revelers overflowing from bars and pubs was too loud to allow conversation. Jared put his arm around her as they jumped out of the way of a scuffle starting over a table and pulled her along. His arm felt strong around her, and she was glad he was there.

One last intersection crossing and they walked across the brilliantly lit hotel driveway. Once inside the lobby, the din died down. A large clock above the gas fireplace showed a quarter to eight. The bar was full of people and a few sat near the fireplace.

"Want to sit for a while?" Marissa asked as they started walking by.

Jared's arm fell away from her. "Not really. Do you mind if I turn in for the night? It was a stressful morning, and I have a lot to think about."

"Not at all," Marissa said.

When they exited the elevator, they stood alone in the hallway. She felt awkward. How did one end a date that wasn't really a date? She hoped for another kiss.

Suddenly, his arm went around her, pulling her up close. Face to face. Her heart started pounding, and her breath was leaving her. When his mouth met hers, stars began to swirl. Everything in her mind fell away. All that remained was the tender strength with which he held her, feeling his hands touching her back and her face, kissing her again and again.

The elevator dinged, signaling visitors were about to disembark.

242

They drew back as two people clinging to each other got off the elevator and walked around them. Jared looked at his feet, then back at her.

"May I walk you to your room?"

Her head still fuzzy, she turned down the wrong way, realized it, and spun back the other way. He trailed behind her, his hand touching the small of her back. The walk down the long hallway to her suite seemed fit for marathon training, but the finish line came too soon. Pulling out her key card, she turned to say something, but no words came. Her body still tingled with the memory of the kiss.

"See you in the morning?" he asked as he took her key card and opened the door.

"Yes. Breakfast at nine?"

"It's a date. I'll be by a few minutes before then to walk you down." He put his hand under her chin and lifted her face to his. He softly kissed her, then murmured good night and left her there.

After watching him go back down the hotel-miles to his room, she went inside and started the jacuzzi filling. Butterflies flitted around her insides. She was falling for him, but she knew she didn't dare. Heartache would be the end result.

She needed to think and there was no better place to do it than in a tub full of lavender bubble bath.

CHAPTER 30

No one would ever know that Jared had given in to temptation and relaxed in the jacuzzi in his hotel room. He always thought hot tubs to be a waste of time, water, and money, and he had no qualms in telling people that. But as the water kneaded away his stress, he changed his mind. It felt amazing.

He might have to get one. His covered patio had enough room. All he had to do was hide the fact he got it. Eating all the words he'd spoken against them would leave a very bitter taste.

The roiling water washed away all his misgivings about Marissa. He hoped she hadn't noticed how his knees shook as he walked away from her after the kiss. If this was love, he was thankful Kayla had walked away from him, freeing his heart for Marissa.

Bearkiller Slide had given him a gift. Never had he felt more at ease with a woman. Her arms felt like home. Thinking about leaving her to go back to Milo Creek was too painful to contemplate. He had one more day with her, and he'd make it a day worth remembering. No talking of the store. No planning for the future. Just living in the moment with her beautiful soul.

Jared slept well, his dreams full of Marissa again. His alarm jolted him awake at six. He lay there deciding whether to go to the gym, especially after last night's meal, or get another hour of sleep. He reset the alarm and turned over.

By eight-thirty, he was showered and dressed as he settled into a comfortable chair next to his room window. Checking his phone, he found an email from Chad with the subject line that read Ideas. Since that didn't hint of troubles at the store, he opened it. Holly, Martha, and Benny had met to toss out brainstorming ideas on what to do with the store after Food-N-More opened. A bulleted list of several options scrolled up from the bottom of the screen. Martha wanted an antique store or gift shop and she was willing to run whichever he liked best. Holly wanted her own bakery. Since that wouldn't take the whole space, she would have a luncheonette with soup and sandwiches. Martha would help her with it, she added. She'd pay rent on the store but needed help in finding suppliers. Benny and Chad wanted a gym where people could work out. As the only one around for miles, they'd have a corner on the local market.

Tossing the phone on the bed, he sat back and leaned his head against the back of the chair. His employees assumed Sullivan's Food Mart was doomed and were eager to move on, but he wasn't ready to pull out the white flag just yet. There had to be some way to save the business his family had worked hard to establish. If he kept thinking, it would come to him.

His phone dinged with a text message from Marissa saying she was ready when he was. The email had soured his bright mood but as soon as he saw her, it returned. She had a way of restoring perspective and pushing aside everything that dealt with the store.

She was stunning even though she wore jeans. He felt like a prince walking past men in their three-piece suits and the expensively dressed skiers waiting to be taken to the slopes. His mail-order khakis fit in with all the high-dollar clothes and monied people when she was around.

With her arm in his, they moved through the bustling crowd and went onto the street.

"I hope you don't mind going to a coffee shop so you can see what I was telling you about," she said as they went out the entrance. "It's close by and one of my favorite places when I come to Denver."

That let some of the air out of his balloon. He couldn't escape the constant barrage of people throwing business ideas at him. As much as he wanted the day to be about her, it seemed the stars were lined up to focus on him instead. Not wanting to disappoint her, he went along without complaint.

Clouds had gathered overnight, and the breeze was icy. Their destination was only two blocks from the hotel. Where the snow had been cleared, it was easy walking, but icy spots couldn't always be avoided. He held her tightly as they skated across.

The aroma of coffee greeted them as they opened the door to the corner shop. People sat on overstuffed sofas and chairs and at tables by the windows. A long counter displaying different varieties of coffee beans was against one side where customers stood in a line to pay five or six dollars for a special cup of coffee. Several pump thermoses along the counter held different types of coffees for sampling.

"What do you think?" Marissa looked up at him, her eyes gleaming. Studying the menu board, Jared was taken aback by the prices of some drinks. "I've never heard of some of these coffees. I'm not sure people in Milo Creek would pay this much for a cup of coffee when they can get a bottomless cup for two bucks at the café."

She took a sample cup and pumped twice to fill it with brown liquid. She waved the steam toward her face. "Mmmmm," she said as she handed it to him. This smells so rich."

With a small sniff, he knew what she meant. The taste of it was amazing. He couldn't say it was the best coffee he'd ever had because it was different than anything he'd tasted previously. He swallowed the rest of it and wanted more.

The wait in line was pleasant. Jared tested several varieties of coffee. By the time they got to order, he didn't know which to select. Deferring to Marissa, she ordered two Hawaiian Kona lattes and two bagels. He normally took his coffee black but he'd try anything she recommended. It had to be good.

They found a love seat in a corner where they could watch the rest of the shop. Most of the coffee drinkers ordered and left, but many stayed. Laptop computers were open as people worked with their half-eaten pastry and coffee cup beside them. Several were gathered around a table, seeming to be in a meeting. A few were curled up on the sofas with books. A man with a sketch pad sat at a table working on something with colored pencils. The tranquility seemed to set the creative juices flowing.

"Well, what do you think?" Marissa asked as she looked around.

He took a sip of coffee and let the liquid trickle past his taste buds and down his throat. "It's really good, but a bit too hot for me."

Marissa giggled. "No, silly, what do you think of this place?"

He looked around again. He really didn't want to admit it even to himself, but he liked it. It was peaceful and calm. Nothing like his store around the holidays. Fewer staff meant lower overhead in salaries. Holly could bake for it. He wondered if she knew how to make bagels. Maybe Martha could learn how to work those coffee-making contraptions. Or Chad. He could stay in the back and grind beans. Sounded almost appealing.

"Yes, it's very nice." He bit into his bagel, thinking back to his resolution not to think about the store today. They could talk about it later, over the phone when she went home. The time belonged to Marissa and enjoying every minute of being with her.

"You really don't want to talk about the store, do you," she said flatly.

He raised his eyes to meet hers and shook his head. "Not really. I want to enjoy the day being with you."

She smiled, making his heart miss a beat. Maybe she felt the same way.

Their conversation moved to the ball that night. Marissa explained she couldn't get an appointment with a hairdresser so she'd do it herself. Jared ran his hand through his hair wishing he'd gotten a trim before coming. They discussed what they could do until returning to get ready for the ball. It started at eight although people would start gathering around seven. That left the rest of the morning and early afternoon to fill.

Finishing their breakfast, they settled on visiting the Denver Art Museum. They could have visited the city dump for all Jared cared. The only thing he was interested in looking at was Marissa, but he'd try to show interest in the artwork to make her feel more comfortable.

The cold wind was whipping along the busy streets so Marissa called for Uber to take them over. They sat in the warmth of the coffee shop until the driver showed up. Once in the car, Jared held Marissa's hand as the driver weaved and turned and sped until a strange building came into view. Jared had seen pictures of the place on TV but seeing it with his own eyes left him disbelieving the building could possibly be sound. The big white building looked like a failed attempt at origami some giant had thrown away.

For him, visiting an art museum was on the same level as going to an opera. It was not something he was interested in doing, but the day went better than he thought. He was fascinated by the architect who designed a unique building to house the art, making it an adventure to find their way around. They ignored the modern art section and spent their time looking at the Western, Asian, and Indigenous art and the photography collections.

The art was interesting, but it was Marissa who captivated him the most. When no one was around, he pulled her in his arms and kissed her. She pushed him away as she whispered there were security cameras everywhere. A quick glance around confirmed her statement. Annoyed, he settled for holding her hand and soaking in every minute she was with him. Her presence left him experiencing new feelings that wanted to explode inside his chest.

As they toured, Marissa spoke of her travels abroad and the art and architecture she'd seen in other countries. Her eyes sparkled when talking about Paris, London, Prague, and Beijing and the history of those places. The woman was a walking, talking PBS station. Her descriptions of far-off places made his brain move into new territory.

He'd been to Branson with his parents a couple of times and to Las Vegas once. Both places left him anxious to get back to the peace and quiet of home. He'd never felt the urge to go anywhere, but hearing Marissa talk about faraway places intrigued him. The talk of grand palaces, stone bridges across rivers, and the beauty of Chinese gardens made his thoughts expand to include the world. His brain felt invigorated by the exercise.

Then the education came to an abrupt end.

Marissa checked her phone. "Look at the time! We need to get back so I can go through my whole beauty routine before the gala." She called for a driver, and they made their way through the corridors and down the stairs to the entrance. The car was waiting for them as they exited the building.

Back at the hotel, they got off the elevator into an empty hallway. Walking her to her room, he put his arm around her waist. "Thank you for a new experience. I'd have never gone to the art museum if you hadn't suggested it."

She unlocked her door and pulled him inside. Throwing herself against him, they shared a long emotional kiss before she let go.

His heart pounded so loudly in his ears, he barely heard her say that she'd be ready by seven. He repeated it to make sure he'd understood correctly. He leaned in and gave her another quick kiss before he left her to get ready for the event.

Back in his room, he started the jet tub filling as he sat on the bed and tried to get his heart to quit racing. He glanced at his phone long enough to see several texts from Chad and emails from various vendors. He didn't open any of them but tossed his phone on the bed, not wanting to be bothered.

The realization hit him like a tsunami of emotion. He couldn't deny it. He'd fallen in love with her. Completely. Wholeheartedly. To the point he didn't want to live without her.

He couldn't leave Milo Creek. He had to find a way to persuade her to come there. If she wanted a coffee shop, he'd build her a coffee shop. If she wanted a law office, he'd build her a law office. He'd do anything to persuade her to move to his town.

His phone dinged with a text message from Martha asking how it was going. He sent a thumbs-up emoticon and turned the phone off. It was time to invent his own beauty routine. The night was coming and what a night it would be!

CHAPTER 31

Marissa stood back from the mirror. She'd swept her long locks to one side and used a curling iron to shape ringlets that hung across the bare shoulder side of her dark red evening gown. Her hair had given her fits but copious amounts of hairspray and a bejeweled hair comb as decoration made it look like she'd sat in the chair all afternoon. The lab-grown diamonds around her neck and dangling from her ear lobes made her feel glamorous. There was no need to buy the real things when the manufactured ones looked as good.

She lifted her skirt when she left the mirror and went to a chair to put on her matching low-heeled shoes. They wouldn't show so no one would know she hadn't opted for fashionable stilettos. The broken foot she'd suffered at cheerleader practice in high school limited her time in high heels. Pain would dim the thrill of the ball.

The night stretched out before her like an unexplored country. Few things had gone as planned, yet they ended up being better than expected. Her veins still tingled with Jared's kisses. He was the kindest, most considerate man she'd ever met and capable of so much. And the most stubborn. His self-imposed exile from the rest of the world limited his potential, but maybe with some prodding, he'd step into it. He'd been like a child at the art museum. It was time he saw the world and the wonders of it.

Checking her phone, she saw she had a little time before Jared would arrive. She took a picture of herself in the mirror and texted it to her mother. They'd talked while she soaked in a bubble bath, but the conversation had morphed into her mother sputtering and ranting about how Tyler was no-good, lousy, worthless, and horrible and how he'd treated her precious daughter like dirt. Marissa told her Tyler wasn't worth the effort and changed the subject to the family. That was a safe and never-ending topic.

Her mother still didn't know about Jared or how they met. Those issues were better handled face to face. Or never. Sometimes ignorance really was bliss, but it would probably come out sometime. Moms could read their daughters' minds, and her mother was no exception.

Another look in the mirror, another light spray on her hair, a dab of perfume behind each ear and on each wrist, and she was ready for the ball.

A knock at the door drew her attention. The night was beginning.

The giant cavern of the grand ballroom was bright and sparkling with gold and red orbs, foil streamers, and sequined ballgowns. Waiters meandered through the crowd with trays of champagne held high until a taker was found. Music filled the air, and people shouted to be heard above each other. The din signaled the start of the festivities.

Jared looked like he'd come off the cover of GQ, handsome and sophisticated, as long as no one saw his trembling hands and damp upper lip. She knew he was entirely out of his element. Most advice books said getting out of your comfort zone would increase your personal growth, but from the looks of it, that might not be the case with Jared.

Her only chore was to introduce herself to a developer in the Milo Creek store. She had to shed Jared long enough to make that meeting. Everything else was about her and her date.

Marissa handed the tickets to the gatekeeper. Given permission to enter, she put her arm through his and pulled him inside the door. Putting her mouth next to his ear, she said, "Relax! This is going to be fun! Let's look around."

He gave her a faint smile and followed wherever she led. He drew up when he saw a dance floor where four couples danced to piped music. He pointed that way, but she shook her head. She hadn't eaten since breakfast. First things first.

The thickest part of the crowd was gathered around the open bar at one end of the ballroom. Marissa signed to him, asking if he'd like to go there. A shake of his head moved her to lead him around small groups of people until they found the buffet in an adjacent room. The sound of the crowd and the music was muffled so conversation was better there.

No open seats were visible. Marissa led them through the line, and by the time they got to the end, she spied two spots against a wall.

"That's lucky," he said as he set his plate of beef tips and rice down. "I wondered if we would have to eat standing up." He held her chair for her, then poured two glasses of water before he sat.

Her plate was laden with two crab legs and shrimp and salad. Jared watched as she cracked the crab legs and pulled out the tender meat. A quick dip into the flavored butter, and the delicious morsel tingled on her tastebuds.

The meat-and-potatoes guy's nose wrinkled slightly as he turned his attention to his plate of beef. His expression eased after he took a bite. He remarked on how good the food was as he ate. At least there was one thing he like about the gala so not all was lost on treating him to the event.

She wanted him to have a good time but felt guilty for using him for appearances. Once it was time to meet the developer near the door, she'd send Jared off to get drinks while she spoke about the new store and gave him the business card tucked inside her bodice. It was a formality, not a business meeting, meant only to put a face on the conglomerate. Her company was using her as much as she was using Jared. All done in the name of good business practices.

She might hate her job, but if it weren't for her position, she wouldn't be here. Some perks were sweet.

Colorful gowns and tuxedos came and went as they enjoyed their meal and spoke of tastes in foods, recipes, and other things. Their empty plates were whisked away by the waiter almost as soon as they'd put the last bite in their mouths. Declining dessert, they rose to rejoin the party.

The crowd had grown. The music was louder so it could be heard above people talking who shouted more as the music got louder. Toward one end of the ballroom where the music was loudest, couples danced. Tugging on his arm, she took him there just as the lively music ended and a slow song came on.

His arms went around her and pulled her close.

She lifted her face so she could speak near his ear. "Tonight, you're my Prince Charming."

His cheek touched hers. "Don't run away and leave me here, Cinderella. Stay with me, and I'll show you how happily ever after feels."

The noise, the people, and the earth evaporated away. Marissa absorbed the beauty of the moment. He might have thought his whispered words of love would be drowned out by the clamor but she heard them. They made their way through her ears and into her heart. She would never unhear them but would store them inside with the rest of her treasured memories.

She clung to him. One of the worst days of her life had given her one of her best nights. It was tonight.

The music changed, and the beat and the people were moving faster around them. Jared started moving with the beat, lifting her arm and giving her a twirl. He gathered her in his arms again, then danced in a small circle.

His strong lead and the fluidity of his moves made it easy for her to follow. Her dress swirled around her legs as they moved together as one. The feeling of flying swept over her, forcing a smile to her face and a light titter from her lips.

He returned both in kind, then swung her down into a dip as the music came to a halt. After a momentary pause, he lifted her up and pulled her into a hug. Applause surrounded them as they stepped apart and bowed to their fans. In prince-like fashion, he lifted her hand to his lips and kissed it.

It was a fairy-tale moment, one that would stay with her forever. The tux had changed Jared into someone as debonair as James Bond. Disguised as a humble country grocery store owner, he only came out of his shell on the dance floor. There was more complexity to him than she'd realized. Discovering the different levels could keep her captivated for years.

He led her toward the bar and asked if she wanted something to drink.

She checked her Fit Bit under her jeweled bracelet. This needed to wait a little longer so she could complete her mission at the event.

"Can we dance more first?" She tugged him back toward the dance floor.

He offered little resistance. Soon they were twirling and moving among the other couples. Their previous performance must have raised the competitive spirit. The space to dance became smaller and smaller as did their moves. The more crowded the floor became, the stiffer Jared's movements became. He'd crossed the threshold and gone back to his area of discomfort.

His smile left and his eyes moved around, observing what was around them. She knew she'd pushed him as far as he cared to be. After one final slow dance, she said she was ready for that drink.

Taking his hand in hers, she led him through the crowd on a circuitous route. The faces were a blur of unfamiliarity so she ignored them and looked at the torsos of people. Some gowns were worth admiring, some were strange, and others seemed too drafty for a winter event. Progress was slow but was halted when a black tuxedo blocked her way. She tried to go around it but it moved to block her again. Looking up, the face she least expected to see stared back at her.

"Hello, babe."

Tyler stood there with a smile like the cat who ate her fish. Next to him was the leggy blonde girl dressed in a gown with more flesh showing than fabric. She moved and coiled around him like a cobra.

Breath left Marissa. The words she wanted to say found no way to get out. What was he doing here? He must have conned somebody to get tickets. Even if he earned enough to afford this, this event wasn't the type of new year's gathering he usually preferred. He should be partying at a bar somewhere.

"Tyler! I'm surprised to see you here."

He threw a thumb at his companion. "Olivia's got connections. Her old man is loaded." He looked Jared up and down. "I knew you were stepping out on me. Who's your new boyfriend? Or is he an escort you hired to dance with you?"

The urge to slap the smirk off his face was too strong to resist. Just as her hand started to cock, Jared took it and held it firmly.

"Someone you know?" he said in a voice clad in steel.

Maybe she could burn Tyler's face off with her laser glare but was frustrated by her lack of success. "This is Tyler, a jerk I used to date," she said, barely unclenching her teeth.

Tyler stuck out his hand. "I'm the hard act to follow," he shouted more loudly than necessary.

Jared didn't move, but his grip on Marissa's hand grew tighter.

This had gone far enough. "Goodbye, Tyler," she said as she started to move past him.

"Did you get all your business done for Food-N-More?" he said as she walked by. "I hear they're building another store around here."

Jared stopped in his tracks, halting her effort to run as the words hit her ears. Invisibility might be impossible, but she sorely wished it wasn't. She pulled Jared away from the sneering man.

Her stomach churned. This wasn't the time or place to break the news to Jared. She had to find a place to talk to him.

They were nearing the door where she was to meet the developer when Jared drew up and stopped her in her flight.

He pulled her close enough to be heard. "What did he mean about getting all your work done for Food-N-More? I mean...that makes it sound something like you work for them."

The pained look on his face hurt her heart. This wasn't how she wanted him to find out. Not on this magical night. Not in a crowd like this.

"Did I hear someone say Food-N-More?" A man walked up to them, a champagne glass in hand. "Would you happen to be Marissa Williams?" His whitened teeth shone out from his tanned face.

"You know her?" Jared asked.

The smile disappeared. "I don't really know her. I have an appointment to meet the Food-N-More's lawyer here tonight to talk about the new store in Milo Creek." His face reddened slightly. "If you're not Marissa—"

Jared gave her a glare. "Yes, she's Marissa, the one you're looking for." He dropped her hand like it was on fire. "I'll leave you to your business."

Marissa tried to hang on to him. He couldn't leave like this. He had to listen to her side of the story. He had to know how much he'd come to mean to her. "Jared, I—" His firm stare shook her like a slap across her face. "Could you get me a ginger ale, please."

He stood like he was petrified, his eyes blank like a statue.

"Please, I'm really thirsty."

With a slight nod, the statue came to life and faded into the crowd. She hoped he'd return, but what could she say to him that would take that look of a wounded animal from his face? Nothing would redeem her in his eyes after this betrayal.

The man watched him go. "Something tells me I caused a problem between you two."

With no reason to conceal her business, she confessed. "That gentleman owns the small grocery store in Milo Creek. The new store will likely put him out of business. He didn't know who I worked for."

"I thought you were here together." The man laughed. "That would be awkward!"

For the second time, Marissa had to fight the impulse to slap someone. Awkward was an understatement. Devastating was more like it. The revelation of her job title had destroyed her happiness. She stood in the ruins of what had been the best night of her life.

Tyler. That no-good, two-timing dog had submarined her on every level. He started this, and her business contact had ended it. Her hope of finding love with Jared was gone. There was nothing left to do other than finish her business and hope Jared came back. If he did, they could talk. If only he'd listen.

She pulled out her business card and told the man to call her next week when she was back in her office. It wasn't the time or setting to talk. Shouting over the din of the music and people wasn't conducive to business discussions. The man got another glass of champagne as the waiter went by and agreed with her. He tucked the card in his pocket and bid her good night.

Her heart raced inside her chest that felt like it had a vice grip on it. Her neatly contrived plan had backfired in her face. She hated her job even more now. Maybe this was the kick that would push her off the ledge of uncertainty.

She spotted Jared's head coming her way. There had to be some string of words that would tell Jared how she felt about him. That she wasn't lying or deceiving him but was only doing her job. That she never meant to hurt him. An Act of God brought them together. They couldn't walk away from something that was meant to be.

Somehow, she had to change his mind.

She could justify her actions but would he understand? Would he even try? Probably not. His ties to his store were rooted too deeply, and she appeared to be the poison that would kill all it touched.

His frown became deeper as he approached.

Her heart stopped, icy with the fear that he would throw the drink in her face and walk away. She would suffer the former if it made him forgive her, but the latter would break her.

"Here's your drink." A growling and snapping pit bull would almost have been less intimidating than the fire in his eyes as he handed her the glass.

As he turned to go, she grabbed his arm with the same ferocity of the pit bull. He might think it easy to walk away, but she was determined to hang on until the end.

"We have to talk."

He looked away, a scowl replacing the frown. "Enough has been said."

Maintaining her vice grip, she told him, "No, not enough has been said. You don't know my side."

His eyes returned to burn their way into her. "I know enough. You lied to me. You really are a spy sent to undermine everything me and my family have worked for."

He tried to pull his arm away, but she wouldn't release him.

"My company sent me to buy a piece of property for expansion into the west Denver market. My mission is always a secret so landowners won't double their prices when they find out who is buying. It's our standard practice. If you want to blame someone, blame the company's economists and strategists that decided Milo Creek was the place to go next. I don't run the company. They run me."

His eyes softened slightly. He looked away at the milling crowd, his eyes moving across them like he was searching for someone who could throw him a lifeline.

She stepped closer to him. "I've hated my job for a long time. I've decided I'm going to quit. I'll do everything I can to help you remodel your family's business so that it lives on." She went in closer, her face in his so that he couldn't look anywhere else. "I'm falling in love with you. Please don't walk away from what we have between us."

The fire in his eyes died down, but something started fanning the embers until they flamed up again. He jerked his arm and snapped it out of her grip. Holding up his index finger in her face, he declared, "I won't desert my family's legacy. Not for love. Not for money. And especially not for you." He spun on his heel and faded into the crowd.

CHAPTER 32

Jared left Denver at three in the morning. He usually didn't leave his home on New Year's Eve because of the risk of so many drunk drivers on the roads, but this was different. He needed to get back to where things were real. Where art museums, opulent ballrooms, and a beautiful woman didn't distract his thinking. Where there were more important things to devote his mind to.

What a fool he'd been! His insides cringed into a knot. He'd let himself be taken in by a vixen who was there to ruin all he loved. Not only was he a poor businessman, but he was also a loser.

The biggest disadvantage of living in a small town was that everyone in town knew what happened to their neighbors. They'd all soon know he'd fallen for a pretty woman's wiles and was robbed of everything. The questions, the pity people would have in their eyes for him, the whispers behind his back. It would go on and on. He'd have to endure the shame of being an idiot who was duped by a total stranger.

The streets of Milo Creek were empty so no one saw him come through town. The less they knew, the better.

He turned into his driveway and into the garage. The snowmen he and Marissa made together were an icy reminder of his idiocy.

His old baseball bat was handy as he climbed out of his vehicle. He took it and pounded them, wielding the bat like a sword as he cut them down. Releasing his rage, he continued until they were nothing but misshapen piles of snow.

Spent and starting to sweat, he hung up his bat, grabbed his bag and slinked into his house. By the light of his phone screen, he made his way past the pictures of his grandfather and father that frowned down at him. Words they'd uttered in the past came out of the darkness to swirl around him, calling him lazy, stupid, and ungrateful.

He pitched his bag on the sofa and plopped in the recliner with his back to their hard stares.

Guilt swaddled him. A beautiful face had blinded him, and he'd let an enemy inside. The damage was done, and there was no undoing it. Like the walls of Jericho, his store would tumble into a cloud of dust, never to rise again. The invaders would be victorious.

"You were right, Dad," he called out into the dark room. "I'm not a businessman. Never have been. Never will be. Your disappointment in me lives on."

He leaned forward, put his elbows on his knees, and cradled his aching head. A sob escaped his mouth but he sucked it back in.

Crying is for the weak, he'd heard his father say when he was young.

But too much was in him to keep it contained. He fought it until the dam broke and weakness flooded out. His sobs echoed off the pictures of his family as he sat alone in the dark.

The pent-up emotion took a while to empty, but the last of it finally rolled away. His hand went to the table beside him and knocked off the remote control. Fumbling around, he felt the tissue box and pulled several out. He wiped his face and blew his nose.

He felt lighter. Empty, but in a good way. Like when his mother would hold him close after a chewing out by his father. She would say it would be all right. If he'd done his best, it was all anyone could expect of him.

He had done his best. He'd given it his all. Fighting to keep the family business alive had taken everything from him. His own plans. Any ambition to achieve anything other than making a living running a store. His chance at love. Twice he'd given his heart and twice it had been shattered. There was nothing left to give.

His vow to never leave for love or money had left him with neither.

When the night sky began to get light, Jared fell asleep in the recliner. His dreams took him back to childhood when his mother would soothe away his pain. Dragged away from her arms, he fought with an invisible enemy who threatened to throw him into a never-ending snowslide that disappeared over a cliff into oblivion. He fought hard against whatever was pushing him but was losing. The edge of the cliff was close. His foot hit it, and he could feel the power of it tugging at him. He struggled to stay on top.

A loud banging and a ringing sound interrupted his struggle. His foot fell off the end of the footrest, shaking him awake as the ringing started again. Sounds and blurry images surrounded him, bringing momentary fear. Several long seconds passed before he realized where he was and what was going on.

He looked at his phone and saw Chad's profile picture smiling out at him. He hit the answer button and morning-voiced a greeting.

Chad's voice held real concern. "Hey, buddy, you all right?"

Jared rubbed his bleary eyes. "I had a late night and was sleeping in. What time is it?"

"Noon."

The word jumpstarted Jared's adrenaline. He sat the chair up. "Where are you?"

"At the door. Haven't you heard me banging? Let me in," Chad shouted and hung up.

Still a little groggy, Jared stumbled to the door and let his friend inside. "Who's minding the store?"

Chad went to the sofa and took his usual game-day position, leaned back with legs across the end of the coffee table. He tossed a folder on it. "It's New Year's Day. We're closed." He looked his friend up and down.

Jared looked down at himself. His clothes were wrinkled and his stubbly face felt rough under his hand as he rubbed it. His jumbled mind needed coffee. Bad.

Putting his hands behind his head, Chad started. "What's up? I thought you weren't coming home until later today?"

Talking about the spy wasn't going to be easy. The pain was too fresh to display without the massive amount of anger swelling inside him. His feelings for her wouldn't die like he wanted them to. A chill went through him as he thought about holding her while they danced, about their time at the art museum, their kisses. He wanted more, but he couldn't relinquish his sense of betrayal.

Chad leaned forward, still eyeing Jared. "We know about Marissa and who she works for."

Chad's words jerked him to his senses. "How—"

"Benny told us after you left, then Marissa called Martha last night and confessed everything. Who she works for, why she was in town." He stared hard at Jared. "And how she feels about you."

Jared didn't want to hear it. That would mess up his attempts to rationalize hating her. She was the enemy. He couldn't love her. He sat in his recliner before his knees weakened to the point of collapsing. He had to stay firm in his resolve. "She betrayed us. Sold us out. Used me for a fool."

Chad's head shook like he was deflecting the arrows Jared was flinging his way. "You got it all wrong. She did her job. The corporation sent her here to sign papers on the land purchase. That's all she did. Her reason for keeping quiet was valid. Did she tell you what that was?"

"Et tu, Chad?"

His friend's mouth opened at the barb, then pressed together in a thin line as he rolled his eyes. "She did her job. And she fell for you. If you want to be mad at someone, be mad at the guy running Food-N-More. He's the one who sent her here."

Anger gave Jared strength, and he rose to pace the well-worn track. Those words. She had said them to him, and those same words had turned his friend against him. "How can you defend her? You know we can't compete with them. We're out of business, pal, and you're out of a job."

Chad looked at his feet for a second, then replied in a calm voice, "She didn't get caught in that avalanche on purpose. It was an accident. Or maybe a twist of fate. Maybe her arrival signals the start of a new era for Sullivan's Enterprises. Me and Martha and Holly been talking. We'd like to be your partners in a new venture."

The house gave way and crumbled around Jared. His best friend, his oldest friend, was turning on him too. Where he expected sympathy and support, he got neither. He was not only losing his store, but also losing his friends. He would never forgive Marissa for that.

"You're talking behind my back now?"

A sound of disgust came from Chad.

Jared stood in front of the wall of family photos. "That's okay." Keeping his back to Chad, he continued. "That store is my family's. My grandfather made my father swear—"

"I know the story." In a voice almost inaudible, Chad mumbled, "All my life I've heard that stupid story."

Anger flared up along with the boom in Jared voice. "Then you ought to understand what that store means to me. I have to continue the business, or I have failed the family. Failed my father and grandfather."

Chad stood up, his face reddening and his eyebrows drawn together. "Listen to what you're saying. You're living your father's life. Problem is, the world has moved on and left you in the past.

Look at this!" He waved his arms. "Nothing has changed since the first time I came over here in second grade. You still sleep in the same bedroom you did as a boy. This isn't your home. It's your parents' home. There's nothing of you anywhere."

Chad's jaw muscles worked like a steam engine before he continued in a softer tone. "You need help, Jared. You've got to leave the past behind and move into the present. Your grandfather and father were great in their time, but society isn't the same as it was then. Your father was wrong to make you vow to keep the store going. You've done all you can do!"

Jared kept pacing.

Chad went on. "You've got a chance to make a new life—your own life—by shedding all the baggage from your family. You can make Sullivan Enterprises into your own vision. Plus, you have a shot to love an amazing woman. Don't walk away from her."

The words shook Jared's core, and the volcano erupted. He grabbed a pillow and threw it at his former friend with all the strength he could muster. His mouth became the steam vent that released the pressure. "Don't tell me how to live. She made a fool out of me!"

"No, she didn't! She did her job the same way you and I do our jobs," Chad shouted. He put his hand on Jared's shoulder. He took a deep breath and spoke in low tones. "I know you love her. The change in you is obvious. Go to her. Tell her how you feel."

Jared felt his body tense up. It was too much. He jerked his shoulder out of Chad's reach. "I thought I could depend on you to have my back. Marissa has taken everything from me, even you.

I won't go after her. I won't give her the satisfaction. I will never leave Milo Creek. Not for—"

"For love or money," Chad shouted back, matching the volume. "I know. I know." He went to the door and opened it. He held up his index finger. "But be careful, Jared. Your pigheaded pride is letting both slip through your fingers, and you may never get them back."

He left, slamming the door so hard it rattled the house. Behind Jared, his father's picture fell off the wall.

Chapter 33

There was a cold spot on Marissa's chest. She moved the half-eaten half-gallon of ice cream to her stomach and continued the slow conveyor belt that spooned the sweet coldness into her mouth. Another hundred-dollar tip to a bellboy would get her an additional half gallon once this one was gone. Maybe she'd try for a gallon next time.

She could see herself in a mirror. Part of her hair was still pinned up in the previous night's updo, but the rest of it stuck out in every direction. Mascara marked where her tears had run. The beautiful ballgown lay in a heap beside the bathroom door. Her Spanx was still where she kicked it after peeling it off. One shoe was under the table and the other was nowhere to be seen.

Her head was still reeling. The magical, Cinderella night had ended abruptly and harshly, leaving her at the ball while her prince fled the scene. Only in this story, she wasn't going searching for him. He left knowing who she was, and if she wasn't good enough for him, then...well, his loss.

A heaping spoon of ice cream went into her mouth to slowly melt and seep down her throat. Calories didn't count when food was used as a depression medication. Nothing comforted her more than cold sweetness. Focusing on how smooth it felt as her tongue rubbed across it, she forgot about what motivated the experience.

Another classic movie started after the other six she'd watched. In the old movies, the people always dressed like Baptists going to church. The characters seemed to have a measure of respect, integrity, and determination. Especially the femme fatale.

That's what she was for Jared. He'd saved her from going over the cliff but alas, she wasn't the woman he thought she was. When he wasn't looking, she crushed him with her signature on the property sale papers. She was riding off into the sunset, leaving chaos and heartache behind.

Another large spoon of ice cream pushed away the self-incriminating thoughts.

What she couldn't figure out was how those movie people traveled with beautiful, well-pressed clothes. If she knew, she'd pack better when she traveled.

As she watched Ilsa Lund walk into Rick's bar in Casablanca, she resolved to get rid of her pair of distressed jeans. Being classy began with dressing well.

She was scraping the bottom of the carton when her phone rang. Unable to pause the movie, she thought about stuffing her phone under the pillow. Curiosity got the best of her and she took a quick glance at the screen.

Martha.

She shouldn't have looked. Knowing it was her made it impossible to ignore the call. She muted the movie she'd seen uncounted times to find out what was playing in Milo Creek.

"Hi, Martha. You're still speaking to me?"

Silence followed her words. It was meant as a rhetorical question, but the silence was real.

Marissa set aside the empty ice cream carton and spoon. She rolled off the bed and headed to the bathroom to wash her sticky hands and lips.

"Why wouldn't I be speaking to you?" A light bulb must have come on because Martha let out an oooooh before she went on. "I have to admit I was a bit miffed after your call last night. Now I'm just a little hurt that you didn't confide in me, but I'm not mad at you. Me, Holly, Chad, and Benny talked it over, and we all agree. You did your job. That's what we all do. But I didn't call about that. I'm calling about Jared."

Hearing his name sent a lightning bolt through her core. A wall came down inside her, blocking off anything to do with him. While they could say she was responsible for driving him over the edge, she wasn't responsible for him being so near it.

"What about him?"

"Well, sweetie..." Several sounds came through, like she was searching through a junk drawer looking for a paperclip. "He's not doing well. He's locked himself in his house and won't answer our calls or knocks on the door. Chad and I think you should come talk to him."

She muffled a laugh. "I'm pretty sure he doesn't want to ever see me again."

"He does but he doesn't know it."

A series of whispers came through. Martha wasn't the only one there. She and others were on the speaker phone.

"Who is there with you?"

The whispering stopped, then started again. Chad's voice came over the speaker. "It's Chad and Holly here. We're eavesdropping in the bakery."

Their voices held no animosity. They weren't upset with what she'd done. At least they didn't sound like it. It might be safe to venture back to Milo Creek for the new Food-N-More's grand opening a year from now, but not before. Even then, she'd wear dark glasses and a hat to hide her identity just in case she saw Jared. His hostility would build in that year, and there would be no holding it back when he saw her.

"Marissa..." Martha's voice was soft and pleading. "Jared hasn't contacted anyone since he got back. He hasn't been to the store either. We're worried about him. What happened in Denver?"

In the background, Holly whispered something and Chad told her to wait a minute.

Snuggling back onto the bed, Marissa began her version of what happened. The aquarium, the museum, the coffee shop, the ball, Tyler and her contact. Beyond the words she spoke were how she felt when he kissed her. She tried to wave the feelings away, but they buzzed around in her head like gnats. Dare she tell them the whole truth? No. Some things were too precious to share.

"Tyler opened his big mouth and that's when it all went south. Jared walked out, leaving me standing in the middle of the ballroom without looking back. It was only ten o'clock. There I stood, abandoned. I thought he'd cool off by morning, but when I went to check on him, he'd left in the middle of the..." her voice wavered so she paused to let it firm up again, "...he left in the middle of the night. No note. No goodbye. Nothing."

She was losing control of her voice with the memory of feeling abandoned. The wound was too fresh to talk about it more with anyone but her mother. Enough had been said for now.

Chad's voice exploded out of the phone's speaker. "That jerk! How dare he do that to you!"

The angry voices were muffled as the argument and shushing continued.

Her gift for stirring the pot emerged again. It always popped up at the most inconvenient times. From what little she could hear, they disagreed over whether Jared was right to leave or a heel for deserting her.

She pushed aside the urge to hang up on the argument but instead, had a better idea.

Shouting into the phone, she said, "Guys. I'll call him." The bickering stopped.

Good. She had their attention. "If he answers, I'll see what he has to say. If he doesn't, it's his choice. After that, it's all up to him."

"Marissa," Holly said, "tell us the truth. How do you feel about him? There seemed to be a lot of chemistry between you. Was it the perfect recipe, or a soufflé that fell flat with the bang of an oven door?"

A smile spread across Marissa's still ice-cream-sticky lips. Leave it to the baker to state things so plainly.

"It's too early to tell. I am...or I was falling in love with him, and I thought he felt the same way about me. But my job with Food-N-More threw him for a loop from which he may never recover. So, it's not up to me. It's all in Jared's court."

No one replied to her, but Marissa could visualize them gathered around one of the little round tables by the bakery, exchanging glances and nods. They couldn't control Jared's reactions any more than she could. There was little any of them could do to pull him out of his misery.

"Could you come see him? Talk to him through the door?" Chad's tone implored her to join them in their rescue mission.

While tempting, Marissa had seen all she wanted of Milo Creek. "No, my flight leaves early tomorrow morning," she told them. "I'm thankful I got to meet all of you, and all that you did for me. You took me in when I needed help and that means the world to me. I'll never be able to repay you."

Martha's voice clouded up as she said, "Please keep in touch. You've been through a lot but keep in mind that we adopted you. You're part of our family. If you ever think about opening your own law office, please come here. We need a good lawyer."

The others agreed with what Martha said and added their own sentiments.

Marissa's heart pounded with appreciation. "I won't promise anything right now but thank you for the invitation. I'm not sure what my plans are going forward. I'll do a lot of thinking and analyzing my options. I'll let you know what I decide. With the way the town is growing, it wouldn't surprise me if you had a glut of lawyers before I make up my mind."

"You're always welcome here, Marissa," Martha said. "Don't forget about us, you hear?"

Holly added, "And don't forget to call Jared!"

After she hung up, Marissa lay on the bed with her elbow across her face. In the longest ten days of her life, she lost the man she thought she would marry, been caught in an avalanche and nearly swept to her death, met a man who attracted her more than Tyler ever had, and been rejected by the same man because of her employer.

Everything was intertwined. If she didn't work for Food-N-More Corporation, she would have never met Jared, and there wouldn't be this tangled web of feelings and misunderstandings. But if she'd never met him, she wouldn't know there was a man like him.

Grabbing a pillow, she covered her face and let out a scream. There was no undoing what had happened. Things were what they were, and that was that. She had to play the hand she'd been dealt even though the deck had too many jokers and everything was wild.

The pillow blocked her oxygen so she flung it aside.

First things first. She found Jared's number and pushed the green button. As it began to ring, she dreaded him answering but feared he wouldn't. Planning what she was going to say before she called would have been a better idea but it was too late now. She'd let her heart speak the words.

She was somewhat relieved when the leave-a-message voice came on. It was too soon to talk to him voice-to-voice.

The beep sounded so she began. "Jared, this is Marissa. I'm sorry about what happened. I'm sorry I didn't tell you who I worked for. Our public relations department is very territorial about when, who, and how the news is announced. I followed company protocols. Did my job. That's the way we do business whether you like it or not."

For an instant, she paused as her mind raced, wondering what she should say next. She gave her heart free rein.

"I didn't appreciate being abandoned at the gala like that. We could have talked everything over like adults. Come to some understanding. Now I hear you've locked yourself inside your house. What's up with that? Come on, Jared, you're a grown man. You've been dealt a blow but don't cut off your friends. We're all here to help you. This can be a new beginning. The start of something bigger and better. Let us help you with this transition. Please. Call Chad or Martha. Holly or me. Reach out. We're here for you. Please. Call someone."

After ending the call, she texted Martha to say she'd done it, adding that if they didn't hear from him, they might have the sheriff do a wellness check. His identity was tied up in the store and if he thought that was over, he could possibly consider doing something drastic to make the point.

Her heart picked up its pace. The thought was too dreadful to dwell on. She picked up the hotel phone and dialed the bell staff number.

"I got a hundred-dollar bill for a half-gallon of chocolate chip ice cream within the hour."

CHAPTER 34

The first rays of the day spilled across Jared's bed and woke him from a sound sleep. He wasn't ready to get up. He pulled the blanket over his head and turned away from the window. A few more hours of sleep were needed.

But his mind wouldn't let him doze off. Like leaves in a dust devil, too many things swirled in it. His life wouldn't be restored by avoiding people. He had to face everything and everyone head on.

He threw the covers back and began the day. A shower and a shave, followed by a search for a bit of breakfast got his blood flowing. His cupboards were bare because he mostly ate at the store. He'd have to rectify that in case he ever wanted another sabbatical at home. Luck favored him when he found a forgotten box of cereal to munch on.

Chad's words had hit home the day before. They echoed through his head until their truth took hold. He had no life of his own. His friends were right. Even Marissa was right. He was living in the past.

Before the sun set yesterday, he decided to change his life and make it his own. He felt like a new man.

Taking a cup of coffee into the living room, he surveyed his progress. The first thing he had done was take the family photos off the wall where they had hung for decades. They went into a box now stashed in the garage and would be replaced by something that wouldn't haunt him.

The curtains were gone, allowing sunlight to pour through the unwashed windows for the first time in years. His schedule of working from sunup to sundown provided little chance to open the drapes. He'd forgotten about how the mountains and sky filled the windows. He would appreciate the view more often after he was through remodeling.

He sat in the recliner as he finished his coffee and went through his text messages. Chad was happy to run the store for a few days. Martha texted her worry about him and asked if she could come over. He knew she was offering her shoulder to lean on, but he didn't need it. He'd never been in control like he was now. All he needed was time to plan out the details.

For the umpteenth time, he listened to Marissa's message. He'd been a jerk to walk out on her like that. He owed her an apology but wasn't ready to give it quite yet. He had to prove to himself he was ready to change. He wouldn't reach out to her without knowing for sure.

A writing pad next to his chair had a long list with only a few items crossed off. A truck from a charity in Dillon would be here later today to take away all the furniture except for the recliner. He'd bought that a few years ago and it was his, along with the flat screen TV hanging on the wall. His sisters wanted the dishes and other things out of the kitchen. They had two weeks, he told them, to box them up and take them away.

Otherwise, the house would be emptied of almost everything that had belonged to his parents and grandparents. He'd lived off them long enough. It was time for him to grow up and live his own life.

As soon as the furniture was gone, he'd rip out the twenty-year-old carpet. Fresh paint on the walls and new flooring would make the place look like new. Then he'd do what was previously unthinkable. He'd move into the master bedroom. This was his house now. He was the master and deserved the biggest bedroom.

He might be crazy spending the money to fix up the house. New furniture, kitchenware, paint, and flooring would cost at least twenty thousand dollars, if not more, but he didn't care. Facing the demise of his business would be easier in a house he claimed as his own than in living in his parents' house where every nook, cranny, and piece of property reminded him of how much he was letting them down.

He'd done all he could do to carry on the family business. His father and grandfather could do no better. A large box store with wide aisles, cheaper prices, and more variety would kill the business even under their leadership.

The guilt of failure had fallen away. He was doing what his mother always said he should do: the best he could. Her words were his new mantra.

In the afternoon, he rolled up the old carpet in the living room and carried it into the garage. He'd haul it to the dump another day. He had just started on the carpet in the bedroom when his phone rang. He wiped the dirt away from his face as he looked to see who was calling. An unbidden smile broke out as he answered. "Hello, Martha."

"Jared, you scamp! We've missed you at the store but I'm delighted you're taking a few days off."

He couldn't help but laugh. "While cat's away, the mice are playing, huh?"

"No, no, no. It's very slow. It's the after-holiday slump. Everyone's on a diet and exercise binge. Come February, it'll pick up again. I'm calling to say I'll be stopping by your house after work. I doubt you have much food in the house. I'll drop off some of Holly's leftovers and tell her to put it on your bill."

She knew him so well.

He had all the flooring out except for the kitchen linoleum by the time she got there. Her mouth gaped as she walked in the door and saw the bareness of everything. She turned a circle looking at the bare walls and floors.

"What have you done?"

"I'm redecorating." He took the bags from her hands as she gawked and went into the kitchen. "You'll stay and eat with me, won't you?"

He waved his hand toward a card table that was set for two. Dishes were available since he hadn't packed them yet. Until he got new ones, he'd use his mother's china.

"I think I better," she replied. "Something's gotten into you, and I need to find out what."

The meal was spent with Jared doing all the talking while Martha ate. He explained what happened in Denver and how he knew he'd fallen in love with Marissa. When he said the words, Martha stopped chewing, her eyes wide. She didn't utter a sound but he waited to let it sink in.

After he made sure she was still breathing, he spoke of his remorse on leaving her there to come home and face the wall of photos. Nothing was held back as he spilled how guilty he'd felt but realized after Chad's visit that he'd done all he could do. The previous day was spent shedding his past like an old coat and discovering the person underneath. Redoing the inside of his house was the first step in reclaiming himself. The future held opportunities he was ready to explore.

Martha wiped her face as she finished. "That's beautiful. You've needed to do this for a very long time." Her voice choked as she said, "Tell you what I'm going to do. I'm going to help you with this house. I've got an eye for decorating, and I can help with the painting."

Jared held up his hand. "I'm not asking for help—"

"You're going to get it anyway. I bet Chad and his wife would pitch in. And Benny and his family. We'll have this place looking like new in no time!"

The control Jared thought he had evaporated. Martha was taking over the project and would have everyone coordinated in no time. He couldn't help but smile. He couldn't control his friends, only appreciate them.

CHAPTER 35

The brutal heat and humidity pounding against Marissa's office window on the tenth floor was repelled by thick glass and heavy-duty air conditioning. She stood in the cool looking down at the innumerable cars vying for position while pedestrians waited for their opportunity to step into the chaos. No one was where they belonged but rushed with the crowd to reach individual destinations.

In the far distance, pavement gave way to trees and hills and small towns where she'd grown up. Life was slower out there. People knew and cared about each other.

The thick carpet silenced her secretary's steps as he set something on her desk. Marissa didn't turn but kept staring at downtown Dallas. Whatever he left could wait until she was done feeling sorry for herself.

She'd spent a lot of time at the window reminiscing and rethinking the path of her life. If all went as planned, in a few more weeks her life would be drastically different.

When she was offered this powerful, six-figure-salaried job, it didn't meet her original plans, but it seemed too good to turn down. The job was supposed to be the pinnacle of happiness and success. Successful people lived to work, and she was determined to be one of them. She changed her goals and worked hard to measure up.

Her earnings allowed her to live in an exclusive condo, have fine clothes from upscale stores that gave her a look that said money, and drive a car that went zero to sixty in under five seconds even though she'd never tested it. It was all she'd ever wanted.

Or so she'd thought. Her job with its perceived success was nothing more than selling her soul to the almighty dollar.

Having all the things she wanted meant she spent twelve to fourteen hours a day, often six days a week in this gilded cage with its private bathroom, plush furniture, and massive executive desk. She spent little time with family other than on the phone and ignored their pleas to visit more often. Her limited social life was spent with a man who loved the perks that came with dating her. Her friends had lives that she didn't have time for so they'd drifted apart. The nights were lonely with nothing but the wall-sized TV to keep her company.

She'd met imagined career goals, but nothing else. Where was the man who loved her for her? Would she ever have a family of her own? How was she giving back to society? Her life was nothing but misdirected time and energy.

She'd watched her father work long hours day after day, year after year, then die a few months after retiring. Most of the people at his funeral were there because they felt obligated to go, not because they knew or cared for him. Few tears were shed for someone many hardly knew. Was that going to be her end too?

After he died, her mother had thrown herself into community service projects. A smile never left her face and everyone around town knew her and greeted her with respect and friendship. She was available to her children and grandchildren whenever they needed her. She brought joy wherever she went.

Marissa wanted to be like her mother.

The yearning for something more and something better had haunted her for several years. She'd caught a glimpse of it in Milo Creek. Friendships seemed to come more naturally there. Her unexpected layover had shown her what she was missing.

Martha's frequent texts and weekly phone calls kept her informed on the latest news of Milo Creek. Hearing about Jared's sudden turn of attitude brought a smile to her face. None of them had ever seen him so happy, and they gave all the credit to her. She didn't deserve it. Her only contribution was being in the wrong place at the wrong time.

Whatever the reason, Jared seemed to have found himself at last which made her happy. He was a great guy who deserved the best.

Her heart twinged a little when she thought of him. Their time together seemed like a dream but one she didn't know how to pursue. She sent him a long text giving an apology and asking for forgiveness. All she got in return was ghosting.

Without a response in the six months that followed, she'd worked to extract herself from her feelings for him. Good thing she hadn't fallen farther or she might not have been able to pull herself out of it. If she kept telling herself that, she might eventually believe it.

More and more the idea of moving to Milo Creek had risen in her mind. It was a small town on its way to bigger things. She had friends there. Two things kept her from it: her mother and the fear of letting go to take that next step. What if she didn't like living in a small town? The opportunities for entertainment and the arts were lacking. What if her big-city ways wouldn't adapt to a small-town environment?

At least one night a week, she worked on her business plans to open a law office, not in Dallas, but in some as yet undetermined small town. The scope of her work would be limited to real estate transactions, trusts, wills, power-of-attorney papers, encroachments, and various other property matters that people needed help with, and maybe expand into elder law.

Her finances were in good shape although her extravagant lifestyle would have to go. She'd wasted enough money on overindulgences to keep up appearances. Her new life would be simpler and cheaper.

Last month she'd had the dreaded talk with her mother to tell her what she was planning because the decision impacted her the most. Had her mother gone into a crying jag, it meant the end of her dream of moving, forcing her to keep working at Food-N-More. But the conversation about moving had taken a surprising twist. Her mother had been thrilled to hear it. She'd been wanting to move to San Antonio to be close to her sisters but had stayed in Dallas for Marissa's sake. She hadn't broached the subject before because she didn't want Marissa to feel abandoned.

The fears that held them back evaporated over the dinner salads and rolls. By sparing each other's feelings, they'd denied themselves things that would have made them both happy. Relief, hearty laughs, eye rolls, and promises to communicate better complemented their T-bone steaks and baked potatoes.

Remembering that night brought a smile to Marissa's face. Everything had fallen into place. She had her plan, and it was a good one. All she needed now was the courage to make the leap. And a destination.

A soft knock at the door was followed by her secretary sticking his head in to remind Marissa she was late for her own meeting. Gathering her reports and stuffing them in her computer bag, she rushed to the conference room only to be greeted with frowning faces as she walked in. Silence escorted her to her seat as she set up her presentation on the big screen for all to see.

"Glad you could finally join us," her boss remarked, his eyes narrowed as he watched Marissa get her computer out. "I hope you have good news for us." He tapped his fingertips together as he continued studying her.

Around the table was everything she hated about her job. Serious, almost scowling, expressions on every face. Older and middle-aged men and women who had spent their lives working and clawing their way to the top. Making decisions that impacted thousands of people without giving them a thought. Only the bottom line mattered.

In the twenty seconds it took for her computer to pull up her presentation, the big boss at the head of the table let out a big sigh and waved his hand in a circle. Several pulled out their phones, moving on to other more important issues waiting for their expertise. No one talked to another. Each was absorbed in their own importance.

Something inside her snapped. These people were in competition with each other, to outdo and impress each other. They were the ones willing to ignore their families and give their time and souls for higher salaries and bigger offices. Behind them were others waiting to fill their slots. Men and women who wanted a place around this table, who desired having the power to control the strings and the money.

She didn't belong here. Too long had she supported and fed their thirst for power. Her soul wasn't for sale. Resolve swept through her like a flash flood. It was time to get out.

She glanced around the long table and smiled her sweetest smile. Meetings rarely had smiles in them. There weren't enough smiles in the board room.

"Gentlemen and gentlewomen..." the words almost choked her, "... I'll make this short and sweet."

None of their expressions changed. The ones on their phones gave her a cursory glance, then went back to their devices.

No matter. They'd hear her one way or another. "Opening another store in Grand Rapids is a bad business move, given the chosen location and logistics for getting our trucks there." She scrolled through her slides until she got to the one with the aerial map. "Road access is a nightmare which would only be compounded by our customers. Some might not shop there because of that. The street out front would need to be redone to remove the barriers for turning left. Since the potential for accidents in turning left out of our parking lot would be high, a light should be installed on the heavily traveled road. The utilities to the site are old and need upgraded. Those options increase construction costs by thirty percent. In conclusion, I advise you either choose another location or another town."

Mouths opened with questions, but she quickly held up her hand and stopped them.

"And the second item I want to present..."

She opened her bag and pulled out a letter. Finding a pen, she quickly put a date on it and signed it. With a flourish of her hand, she sent it sliding across the polished mahogany tabletop toward her boss. "Here is my resignation, effective two weeks from today. I'll take vacation time until then."

Her boss's jaw slackened as one eyebrow went up. His look was accompanied by gasps and the sounds of stuttering as the shock of her move impeded clear speech.

Marissa slammed her laptop shut and put it in her bag, then left the stuffy room. A smile returned to her face as she headed back to her office.

Chapter 36

Jared's heart was pounding. His palms were sweaty. His breathing was shallow. He was a wreck.

Maybe his unannounced trip to see Marissa in Dallas was a bad idea. His brain wanted to leave, but his heart told him to stay.

His morning consisted of going as quickly as possible from one air-conditioned space to another through the hottest, most unbearable air he'd ever experienced. How did people live in this?

The doorman eyed Jared while he called Marissa about allowing him access to the building. His eyes focused on Jared's torso, probably in search of lumps indicating he carried a weapon.

How could he carry a gun under his polo shirt? Maybe he should have worn a button shirt and tie. That would mean a suit coat, and in this heat, no way! The two hours he'd spent packing his carry-on bag left no room for options. He was here, dressed like she'd remember him...if she remembered him.

The doorman hung up the phone and signaled Jared could enter.

Jared's trepidation built as he made his way to the elevators. Seeing where she lived confirmed he had nothing to offer her. The décor was opulent with little in common with a sandstone-store-1960s-house kind of guy.

His finger hovered over the Up button on the elevator panel. He was right the first time. This was a bad idea. He should have never let Martha talk him into surprising her. His flight instinct kicked in as he turned slightly.

But Marissa knew he was here. To leave now was foolish. He had already passed the go-back line. He forced his finger to hit the button. People walked by as he waited. Their tailored, high-end clothes made him feel a little ashamed. Like he didn't belong there. He didn't, but everything he'd waited his whole life for was up on the seventh floor if she'd have him.

The polished doors opened in front of him. Two people stopped their conversation and stared, their eyes going up and down as they surveyed the stranger in their way.

"My suit's at the cleaners." The words came out on their own volition. Feeling his hand start to shake, he quickly stepped aside and let them exit. Hoping no one else would get on with him, he hurriedly pushed the 7 on the panel.

He wiped his brow. What a stupid thing to say! Why his mouth spoke them without permission left him puzzled. Would it do the same thing at Marissa's door?

There was no time to think about it as the floor pushed Jared upward, causing more butterflies to swirl in his gut. With a ding, the elevator door opened, allowing him to step into a carpeted hallway. The thick carpet silenced his steps as he looked for the number Martha had given him. He found it on a corner door.

Holding his fist up to knock, it missed as the door swung open. There Marissa stood, looking more beautiful than he remembered.

Gone were the stylish clothes, the large bag, and expensive shoes. Dressed in leggings and a too-big tee shirt, her mouth hung open as she shook her head. She ran her fingers through her tussled hair.

Feeling more confident since he was the better dressed, he said, "Hello, Marissa. I'm sorry I didn't call but I was in the area..."

"In the area?" She gave a laugh that lit his world. "The man who wouldn't leave Milo Creek for love or money is at my door saying he was in the area. How should I take that?"

His feet suddenly gained his attention as he sifted through how he should respond. She didn't seem happy to see him. His well-rehearsed plan about how this meeting would go jumped out the window and fell seven stories to its death. "Martha sent me. Told me you quit your job." He shrugged his shoulders before looking in her beautiful eyes. "She said you might need a friend."

All he could do was wait for her reaction. Everything depended on that. Otherwise, his apology would be of no use.

"Leave it to Martha," she mumbled. She bit her lip and looked away. "I'm doing fine, just stunned that you're here. Come in." She stepped back and opened the door wider.

The condo looked like something out of a magazine or those home renovation shows his sister watched. It was more of a showroom than a place where anyone lived. Large windows looked out over the city. Nothing blocked the view to the very distant horizon. No wonder there were people who thought the world was flat. As far as this mountain boy could see, it was.

Marissa went past him into the living room and motioned for him to take a seat. She sat in a large chair and curled her legs up under her. Her casualness put him at ease.

"I know I should have called you," Jared said as he sat opposite her. "Martha said you'd be home this weekend so I decided to come while I could."

She tucked her hair behind her ear. "I still can't believe it." She stiffened, then asked, "You want something to drink? I have a pitcher of freshly made iced tea. Or I have a coke."

Grateful for any chance to regather his nerve, he asked if she had a Diet Coke.

She giggled. "I forgot I was talking to a northerner." She made quotation marks in the air with her fingers as she said it. "See, in Texas, all pop is called coke. All the pop I have is Diet Dr. Pepper."

He laughed along with her, not because he thought it was funny but so his nervous energy could be stealthily released.

As she got the drinks, she prattled on about how her mother was moving to San Antonio. Helping her sort through decades of collected stuff and packing what she would keep was almost a full-time job.

Jared really didn't care about her mother. There was so much he wanted to tell her, but fear of rejection kept most of it penned up until he knew how she might feel toward him. Some of it, he would spill at her feet with the hope she wouldn't stomp all over it.

When she settled back in her chair, he took a deep breath. "Please let me say what I've come to say."

With a nod and a sip of Dr. Pepper, she agreed.

He took a deep breath. "Last New Year's Eve, when I found out who you worked for, it was like being hit between the eyes with a sledgehammer."

When Marissa drew in a breath, he held up his hand to stop her from interrupting. "I went home in a rage, feeling betrayed by someone I trusted. I sulked at home alone. I knew I couldn't compete with the new store, especially without Benny. I could feel my father's eyes on me, telling me I was a failure.

"I was in a bad place until Chad came and set me straight. He woke me up to the fact that I was living my father's life and not my own. That sooner or later, the store would die. To go into the future, I had to rethink things. He also said you were the best thing that had ever happened to me, and I was a fool to let you go."

He gave her a quick glance. She sat motionless with her hand on her chin.

Wiping his own chin that was beginning to tremble, he went on. "He was right about that. You are the best thing that's happened to me."

She sniffed but remained silent and unmoving.

His throat tight, Jared took a drink of soda and continued. "After Chad left, I spent a long time thinking about what he said and about what you said. You told me I needed to change my business, but I wouldn't hear it. My own stubbornness kept me blind. I was scared what my father would say about me closing the store, but it finally came to me. My father is gone. The store is mine. I can do with it as I please." He rubbed his hands together.

"Seems like such a simple, obvious thing, but I couldn't see it. I was too caught up in pleasing someone who isn't around anymore."

Pulling up the edge of her sleeve, she dabbed her eyes with it and sniffed again. She never looked at him but he knew she was listening.

Jared took a sip of soda and nearly choked on it when the bubbles tickled his nose. Letting out a soft cough, he tried to regain his poise. "So I came to say I'm sorry and ask for your forgiveness. I acted like a numbskull and I'm ashamed of myself."

There it was. His heart placed in front of her. What would she do with it? He paused to allow her the opportunity to respond.

Her eyes filled with tears as she gave the slightest nod.

Too nervous to wait longer for a response, Jared decided to move on and reveal another purpose of his trip. Jared's insides squirmed as he said the words, "I heard you quit your job. I don't know what your plans are but would you consider moving to Milo Creek? I speak for the town when I say we could sure use a good lawyer. I'm converting the second story of the store into offices—"

"You are?" she cried out in a voice choked with emotion.

Marissa's outburst caught him off guard. All he could think to do for a moment was stare at her widened eyes. "Yes. We, Martha and Holly and I, like your idea of having a coffee shop. We'll divide the store in half. On the front we'll have a nice coffee shop, like the one you showed me in Denver. We'll put tables outside in the summer and have a fireplace in the winter. Martha can put in a gift shop or bookstore or something like that in the other half. Oh, they got big plans for it. With their partnership, they would pay me a little rent and give me free coffee for life. Then, the second story would be rented to whoever wants office space in town which would provide me with income."

Jared sucked in a quick breath. "Not that I want to become an evil landlord. My rates will be reasonable."

Laughing as she stood, she came to him with arms out.

He rose and opened his arms to take her in.

With her arms tight around his neck, she replied, "I accept your apology and your offer. I thought you'd never ask."

CHAPTER 37

The December morning dawned bright and sunny, adding to the already festive atmosphere of Milo Creek. Last night, on her drive into town from Denver, Marissa passed the new Food-N-More store with its enormous parking lot lit enough to provide security for customers, but not enough to block out the stars. Black skies were important to Marissa, and she'd always insisted on downward lights to preserve them. The grand opening was scheduled for later that morning. The success of the soft opening indicated the new store would be an overwhelming success.

More people were downtown than usual, and all the parking places were taken. Christmas decorations were on the light poles and the store windows were decked with multicolored lights, paintings of Santa, and fake snow.

Marissa had been at her mother's new place in San Antonio since Thanksgiving, but today, she had to be in Milo Creek. Today was the last day Sullivan's Food Mart would be open, and she wanted to see Jared, Martha, and Holly at her favorite grocery store. Chad had already left for his new job as foods manager for Food-N-More, Jason was off at college, and Benny was getting his meat market established. Everything looked the same on Main Street, other than big banners over Sullivan's Food Mart announcing going out of business sale and the soon-to-come coffee shop. Together they were sad, but once the business closed, the banner announcing the coffee shop would be a welcome sight. Renovations would start next week.

Entering the nearly empty store, she was greeted with a wave and a shout from Martha as she checked out the lone customer.

"You're back!" Martha yelled. "Come over here and give me a hug." The mighty embrace nearly popped Marissa's neck out of joint, but the emotion was undeniable. The questions came at her like raindrops in a downpour. Seeing the worried look on the customer's face, Martha assured Marissa they'd have time to talk later.

Marissa moved past the mostly empty shelves. Cans of lima beans, pickled okra, and sauerkraut were drastically discounted yet didn't tempt the few shoppers in the store. The aroma from the bakery lured her closer.

As she passed the empty toilet paper aisle, she saw him. Jared stood still with a crooked smile as he ran his fingers through his hair. He looked good. Just like he always did. Just as he did in her dreams. Her heart fluttered like a leaf in the wind. The man who rescued her from the snow had also rescued her from her life of meaningless work. She was eager to find out where else he would take her.

He came to her and took her in his arms to pull her close, then just as quickly pushed her away. His cheeks reddened slightly as he turned to lead her toward his office.

"You should have let us know you were coming. When did you get in?"

"I thought surprise would be more fun. I took an early flight. I wanted to be here for the grand opening and the grand closing."

Jared shut the door behind them. "I've missed you. You're more beautiful than ever. You look...radiant." He opened his arms in invitation.

Marissa dropped her bag and almost jumped into his arms. The kiss they shared made her toes curl.

He held her tight and together they turned circles in the small office. "I'm glad you're here," he whispered into her hair. "Today I turn off Sullivan's Food Mart Open sign for the last time. I need all the strength I can get for it."

A long passionate kiss was her response. Pulling back, Marissa added, "You're strong. Keep your eyes ahead."

He gave her a quick peck and let her go. "I've got contractors coming Monday morning. I'll be too busy to think about it for long."

"I probably won't see you much after that." She picked up her bag. "How about some breakfast? I'm starved."

Leaving the office arm in arm, they walked to the bakery where Holly had two customers. The coffee was fresh, but the pastries were a day old. Jared spoke with customers who wished him well as Marissa settled at a table in the corner where she'd first eaten there.

A year ago, she would have never imagined where she would be and who she'd be with. Her life had been knocked off course and nearly taken from her in the avalanche. When the strong hands of Jared rescued her from the snow, he not only saved her, but saved himself besides. They'd rescued each other from their misdirected lives and had found peace. It was the Christmas gift that kept on giving.